the
MISS
AMERICA
family

a novel

julianna baggott

WASHINGTON SQUARE PRESS

New York   London   Toronto   Sydney   Singapore

A Washington Square Press Publication
1230 Avenue of the Americas, New York, NY 10020

ISBN: 0-7434-2297-X

First Washington Square Press trade paperback printing February 2003

10 9 8 7 6 5 4 3

WASHINGTON SQUARE PRESS and colophon are registered
trademarks of Simon & Schuster, Inc.

For information regarding special discounts for bulk purchases,
please contact Simon & Schuster Special Sales at 1-800-456-6798
or business@simonandschuster.com

Printed in the U.S.A.

this book is dedicated to
my steadfast American family:
Phoebe, Finneas, Theo, and David

Acknowledgments

I would like to thank Nat Sobel and Judith Weber for all of their insights into this novel; my fabulous editor, Greer Kessel Hendricks; my readers Kathy Flann, Bobby Rue, and especially the gorgeous, brainy Elise Zealand; and my writing group, Rachel Pastan, Fleda Brown, Pat Valdata, and Mara Gorman. I'd like to thank Margo Ewing Bane Woodacre for being so gracious and generous and patient with all of my questions. Also, I'd like to thank Mary Lee Kleinschmitt and Carrie Spanburgh, Barbara Pawelski, Ozzie Cuervo, Ronald Lane, Wanda Boyce, and my grandmother Mildred Lane, the ultimate beauty queen. Thanks to Pieter Voorhees for putting me in touch with Richard O'Meara, a wonderful teacher and storyteller.

As always, I wouldn't be able to accomplish anything without my parents, Glenda and Bill Baggott, and my husband, David Scott. They have withstood hearing almost every scene in this novel loudly paraphrased over the background of chaos in my kitchen. And, speaking of chaos, I'd like to thank my kids, who don't make things easier, just better, worthwhile: Phoebe, Finneas, and Theo.

Part One

Ezra, 1987

Greenville, Delaware

Rule #1: Have a set of rules to live by
like a monk or an army general or a
debutante so that you always know just
what to do and say.

'll start just before the beginning, just before the incident with Janie Pinkering and her father's French tickler. I believe you should lead up to sex. And I'll get to death, too— an almost-death, at least, how someone changes when they're about to die. Their mouth and eyes can be wide open like a child's again as if singing the "oh" of one of their favorite songs. That's how Mitzie put it, my little half sister, who's probably a better person than everybody I know put together.

This was just this past summer, six months ago now. Everything started to happen all at once, as if all my life I was waiting for the beginning and finally there it was, like I was leaning against what I thought all along was a wall, and then it gave in, and I realized it was a door, swung wide open to bright, dazzling sun. This was when my mom, for all intents and purposes, left my stepdad, Dilworth Stocker, and Mitzie decided to live with our neighbors, the Worthingtons, a nice, squat but well-postured couple who eat things that Mrs. Worthington has made from scratch, who, you can tell just by looking at them, think all children are precious gifts from God, even though God didn't bless them with any of their own. (The household's fertility seeming to be wasted on the cats, hundreds of them wandering in and out of a kitty door on the side of their house.) All at once, it seemed like people had decided to tell their lousy secrets. My grandmother told hers, things that I've never really understood except that they were dark, too dark to pass on any further than they needed to be, and I guess she decided, in a weakened post-stroke condition, that they needed to be passed on, at least to my mother, who reacted with calm irrationality. And my real dad, too, unburdened himself to me in a convertible a few blocks from a stranger's house, telling me that he's a faggot, after all, not even bisexual, but purely gay, despite the fact that he married my mother and, evidently, had sex with her at some point. Although he pretended that he didn't know I'd been kept in the dark, it was, in fact, a secret and came as a complete shock. Even Mr. Pichard, an old man I met who could sing opera, spilled his guts. And I had to start sorting all this shit out. But I've got to start before everything happened, because you have to know how much bullshit I was dealing with in this intensely dull way. I have to explain what the wall was like before it swung open as a door.

My stepdad was the one who made my short-lived affair with Janie Pinkering possible, and that's really when the wall gave a little under the weight of my shoulder. It wasn't his intention to get me laid—although I think he was kind of proud of me in that tough, boys-will-be-boys way when all of the facts came to light—but I'll give him credit, since there isn't much else that's redeeming about him. Dilworth Stocker turned out to be a sad specimen, after all. I remember him that summer rumpling my hair like he was Santa and I was a five-year-old on his lap, rapping his glass of scotch to get our attention throughout dinner, like a little gavel in between his president jokes, his priests and rabbis, his talking cows, the little gavel always passing judgment. When he introduced me to his friends, he always pulled them slightly aside and whispered hoarsely, "Well, they don't make boys like they used to." Sometimes he'd get on this kick where he'd call me a puny runt, usually when he and my mother had had a fight, when he'd said enough mean things to drive her from a room, with him laughing in that full-bellied way so she couldn't really get upset, or he'd start in on her delicate psyche, and I was the only one left standing there. He's a tan, bullish man with thick forearms and a tight, toothy smile, a jackass.

In any case, he charged into the kitchen one day to inform me and my mom that I was going to stop being sickly and pale like some British kid. He hates the British, mainly, I think, because in his mind they've confused the term *football* for *soccer*, American football being holy, and because they always think they're right. He told me that I was going to work for a living that summer as Bob Pinkering's gardener. Bob Pinkering was my mother's podiatrist, my stepdad's golf buddy, and still is Janie Pinkering's father.

The day my stepdad showed up at the back door of the

kitchen to announce my new-found employment, I was eating French toast that my mom had made for me, and she was flipping through one of her fashion magazines but keeping an eye on me at the same time, filling my juice when it got low, and sometimes reaching over the table to press down a wayward curl in my hair. Mitzie was up in her bedroom, practicing her tap-dance routine. Above the clatter of her tap shoes on the hardwood floors, we could still hear her tinny, sharp voice, narrating the steps, "Shuffle, ball-chain. Shuffle, ball-chain."

This happened after I'd loafed half the summer away. I was home from St. Andrew's, a boarding school smack in the middle of Delaware cornfields and strip malls. The school is only a little less than an hour from our house in Greenville, a couple of towns north. Dilworth insisted I go away to school somewhere. He'd voted for a good, far-off military academy, but my mother would have none of that. So I ended up at St. Andrew's, and my mother consented because it's the best school around, hands down, and I do exceptionally well on standardized tests. Just give me a sharp number two pencil and a piece of paper covered with little bubbles and I can solve just about anything. Unfortunately, Dilworth likes to remind me, life isn't set up that way. I didn't know it at the time, but things would go off-course and I wouldn't be going back to St. Andrew's in the fall.

Of course, I'd set out with good summer goals. I was going to make a list of Rules to Live By, my own set of guidelines that would take me through life. I had a blue spiral pocket-size flip pad to write them down in. But the only rule I'd come up with so far was to have my own set of rules and to stick by them without question, like the only member of my own military or priesthood or something. Instead of coming up with more rules, I'd eaten a lot of fruity cereal and watched reruns of *Gilligan's Island* and stupid stuff like that, and felt all the while really bad about not being a better person with rules. I was down on myself. The morning Dilworth gave us the news about my job, I'd looked in the mirror after splashing my face with cool water. I'd stared at myself, my too-big eyes, and narrow head, my skinny neck, puffy lips, and oversize teeth, my ears sticking out just enough to get sunburned if I don't coat them in lotion. And I was wondering where it all came from and what I could possibly look like to people who met me for the first time.

You see, I come from good-looking genes. My mother was once Pixie Kitchy, Miss New Jersey. But it never did her any good. The pageant stuff happened before she eloped with my father, Russell, a longhaired, door-to-door household cleanser salesman from Wisconsin, and had a sickly four-pound son, me, Ezra, with weak, fluid-filled lungs and webbed toes. They thought that they were naming me after a great literary figure, Ezra Pound. Of course, I've since learned at St. Andrew's, where they had a Pound scholar, that the original Ezra was a huge Fascist with a thing for Mussolini. It's something that probably neither of my parents has ever figured out. I've heard my mother say, "And this is Ezra, named after Pound, the great literary figure." She's never read any of his books, I bet. My mother subsequently left the longhaired, door-to-door household cleanser salesman and gave up on the string of so-called boyfriends who followed the divorce—men she'd bring home where she'd serve them drinks at the green kitchen table and then disappear with them behind her locked bedroom door— before she married a Catholic dentist, Dilworth Stocker, when I was seven, and had a daughter, Mitzie. My mother's talent for the beauty pageants was the accordion. She could play only one song, "Moonlight Serenade," practiced to perfection. She didn't make it all the way to Miss America, not even to the final ten. Some bimbo from Michigan won that year, probably because she let it slip during the interview with Bert Parks that her sister was brain-damaged. Up to that point, Susan Anton, the blond California giant, was the obvious favorite. But my mom was a knockout. And I'd like to say, right here, that it's not easy when your mom's a knockout. I'm not bragging. In fact, if I could unmake my mother Miss New Jersey, I think our lives would be a lot easier. But there are other things that I know about now, or at least have pieced together about my mother's life, darker, meaner things I'd unmake for her first, if I could. It's just that my mother's being Miss New Jersey is an important fact. It's key to understanding my mother, and, if you don't understand her, you'll misunderstand all of this altogether.

I've got to be up front, though, and admit that I don't really understand my mother. People don't *like* her really, but she doesn't seem to want friends. They respect her. She's very frank, and this makes her scary. I've heard her advise Mitzie, who's only nine and has got this high-pitched, screechy voice, "You must *sound* pleasing to be pleasing." But I don't think she believes it. I get the feeling she's handing down a known evil, because, well, at least it's known.

When I think of my mother the first half of that summer, before all of the craziness with Janie Pinkering and my grandmother and then the gun, I think of her as being held together simply out of habit. She was on the verge of something, like at the edge of a cliff, but having a picnic perched right there, a chic little picnic from a Longaberger basket bought at one of those stupid at-home Tupperware-type parties. She knew the edge was there, maybe, but ignored it all the same. I knew that my mother was dangerous despite the fact that she seemed like a normal person, not especially happy but resigned to her life, kind of like a commie who's bought into the whole idea of things being for the common good. But I knew that she had a gun in her bedside table. She got the gun when she left my real dad and decided to use her body to make a political statement, a statement that was never clear to me, but obviously hinged on the practice of having sex with a lot of men. She was armed before she gave up this so-called political life to marry Dilworth Stocker, who charged in to sweep us off our dirty bare feet into the land of upper-middle-class suburbia. I was with her when she bought the gun in a pawn shop in Bayonne. And I always kind of knew that she could pull it out.

That summer it had begun to dawn on me how strange she really was. First of all, she seemed to be two very different people. In the daytime, she was amply gracious, refined, generally connected and straightforward. But she rarely slept—as far back as I remember—because she suffered from terrible nightmares that made her wake up screaming. And so she usually prowled at night. I remember her that summer in beautiful sheer nightgowns with delicate sheer drawstring robes, her

long legs swiftly shifting underneath. I was up, too, sometimes, wandering into the kitchen for a late-night snack and
when I'd find her, she was strange, confused sometimes, distant.

Secondly, I'd just started to notice how bizarre our relationship was, the way she'd never allowed anything to be too
itchy or tight on me, and still snipped the elastic around the
waistband of my underwear and the thick edge around the leg
holes. "It might diminish your circulation," she claimed. I
assumed she meant the circulation to my balls but was never
clear on that. I was once called to the principal's office in sev-
enth grade because she couldn't remember if she'd peeled the
waxy edge off of my bologna sandwich or not, and, afraid that
it might be toxic, she wanted me to check first. The secretary
told this to me, trying desperately to keep a straight face. My
mother had, in fact, peeled off the waxy edge. And she was still
at it, cutting my fruit for me in small pieces to minimize the
risk of choking. I was born sickly and she never got over it, but
it's more than that, too. I mean, when I was Mitzie's age, for
example, I wanted a cat and she wouldn't let me have one, but
she offered to let me pet her slippered feet while she purred.
What was stranger was that I liked petting her fuzzy slippers,
liked listening to her purr. And I still felt this way, drawn to
her, and I hated the feeling. I wouldn't even mention this
embarrassing stuff if I didn't think it was important, somehow, to show how things would eventually play out.

Things are totally different for Mitzie, who was born ten
pounds even, with two budding teeth. She has a whiny voice,
something wrong with her adenoids or something, and she
talks like she's sprung a leak. I remember her complaining that

summer about the pinch of her Mary Janes and my mother flatly responding, "Get used to it. The contraptions they get us women geared up in. Houdini never had to escape from a girdle, a hook-and-eye bra, control tops . . ." She lowered her voice and said to me, "You'll always have to be careful, Ezra. Men are soft creatures, really. Although it isn't presented that way, they are. Trust me." It was a certain tone she took with me sometimes, a way of talking like we went way back, like old friends. It's this "you knew me when" tone, because, supposedly, I remember my real father in his mutton chops, playing guitar, barefoot in our shit-hole apartment, and my mother when she was young, taking bong hits in her Dairy Queen uniform complete with squishy-soled white nursing shoes. And I do recall some of it—my father almost never being home, and how, when he did show up, I'd wrap my arms around his leg and sit on his foot, to keep him right where he was, one foot pinned to our kitchen linoleum. Sure, he read to me, not kid books, but his own textbooks on astronomy and things like that. Mostly, I remember being alone with my mother, sitting behind the counter at Dairy Queen with my coloring book and the skittering roaches, watching her nude stockings swish by. I remember the teenage boys flirting with her. I remember sitting in the shade of our apartment building while she lay out coated in baby oil on a thin faded bath towel, blocks away from the ocean she couldn't stand to be near. There are little clips, not blurry at all, but more like puzzle pieces that are only little bits of some bigger whole that I still haven't figured out. But what I remember best are the men after my father, before Dilworth, a ragtag chorus of them, their faces reflected green from the kitchen table, the overhead light sometimes swinging from its chain's having been pulled too hard, and how the light made the shadows shift on their faces. I remember having bad dreams, hearing my mother cry out in passion, I guess, or fake passion, and how I padded down the hall of the apartment once, my ankles lit by a hall night-light, jiggling the knob only to find the door locked. When she did come into my room late at night, her voice was scratchy, hoarse, and deep; it had a hushed urgency even though she was trying to be calming, a mother trying to whisper her child back to sleep, but it was a voice like two sticks rubbing together, a voice that could spark and catch fire. In fact, I remember her that way, on fire, her robe lit up, a flame all around her, and she is walking toward me as if nothing is wrong, like I was the only one who could see she was burning. That's when I started to hate her, because she wouldn't let me take care of her, protect her. You cannot save my mother. That's one thing I've learned. You can't save anybody really, barely even yourself. My family really is just my mother and me, when you get right down to it. Sure, there have been people subtracted (my real father) and added on (Dilworth and Mitzie), but really it's me and her. And, although she can't say this kind of thing out loud, it's something that we both know. We both just know.

The rest is sketchy, her stories, a ratty photo album kept in the back of her closet with her dusty accordion box. There's a diary up there, too. I've seen it a couple of times, but would never open it. I don't want to know any more than I already do. I know too much about my mother already.

Sometimes I look at my mom when she's not looking at me, like I did that morning before Dilworth marched in to announce my summer plans. She still had that full, teased blond hair. The skin around her blue eyes had gotten softer. She had a few wrinkles, but her makeup was always perfect, her lips always glossy. I'd seen lots of pictures of her when she was younger. I've seen the old reel-to-reel tape of the beauty pageant a bunch of times before. Dilworth liked to pull it out every once in a while when he had a trapped audience, a little dinner party usually made up of his golf friends or dental buddies and their wives, although this type of get-together had eventually stopped happening. He'd let it slip that she was in the pageant ages ago and that they had the old footage in a dusty closet upstairs. Then the guests would say, "Oh, let's see it," the women politely, the men more adamant, "C'mon, Pix, bring it down!" and even though he made fun of it, singing a bad Bert Parks rendition of "There She Goes, Miss America," he'd also say, "Yeah, Pix, let's have a look-see." She'd always protest at first, "No, no, c'mon, now. That's ancient history," but Dilworth liked to keep control, liked to direct the dinner party from the head of the table with his senseless jokes and scotch-glass gavel. Soon enough, feeling good, a little high on scotch, he'd get his way and there she was on the screen. And once she was up there, he'd get all glassy, sit back and smile at himself for having been smart enough to marry her.

I've always wondered what it was like to see her up there onstage for the first time in your life, as if she weren't my mom at all, but some beautiful girl, someone anybody could fall in love with, singing—amid the blinking stage-prop octagons—

the opening number "The Sound of Young" in her short chiffon cocktail dress, her shiny stiff hair piled high on the crown of her head, the ringlets at her cheeks. Her talent isn't on the tape, because she didn't make it to the final ten, but I can imagine her fingers flying over the accordion keys and arm pumping smoothly, her bright, bright smile saying into the microphone how she'd like to help the poor, those in need, especially in war-torn countries; that's what she's told me that she said, meaning, I assume, Vietnam, the war-torn country of the era where her brother was about to get blown up. I was thinking, there in the kitchen, how she was so pretty once, still was, and my real dad had been this lean, handsome, ultra-cool type who sang with his eyes closed and had white, white teeth from having been raised on excessive amounts of Wisconsin dairy products. He was still good-looking, too, always on the verge of closing a big deal and making a million dollars. This was back when I thought he lived this mysterious life in L.A. that I'd always imagined to be filled with beautiful blondes in bikinis, beach parties, and volleyball, like a surfer movie—all this, of course, before I found out he was gay. And so I asked my mom there in the kitchen that morning, right out, "Do you think I'm good-looking? I mean all the genes are there." I didn't look up from my plate.

"Men don't have to be good-looking," my mother said, sniffing a perfume sample in the magazine. "The world is ruled by ugly men married to beautiful women. Beautiful, *young* women, Ezra. Don't forget *young*. My god, once you hit my age, it's suddenly midnight and you're back in your rags with only one glass slipper to show for it all." My mother was on this kick that she was a faded beauty. You could tell by the way she sighed that she'd decided she was old and that her life was what it was always going to be.

Her response didn't help me much. This was my mother being my mother. At St. Andrew's, I never got the girls. I'm still a kind of sickly kid, not as sickly as my mother once thought I'd be or even still imagines I am, but I was always benched on some freshman or JV second-string team because of an earache, allergies, an itchy rash of a sort that the dermatologist had never seen before. I've never known what to say to girls. I ended up telling them about something I've read, or some tiny, useless fact that one of my teachers had thrown into a lecture because he was showing off, like John Gough was a blind botanist from the 1600s who identified plants by touching them to his lips or that a kid in China had grown two small extra tongues in puberty. And I'm pretty useless among most of the cool guys. I flinch when somebody throws a ball to me, and cool guys always seem to be tossing a ball around. At St. Andrew's, I had two good friends. I don't see much of them these days since I'm no longer a part of the student body. One is named Pete Duvet who's been to every psychologist in the world—Rogerians, Adlerians, psychoanalysts, and behaviorists. He's painted pictures, talked to puppets, made little straw hats, and opened up on any desires to fuck his mom—not an attractive woman—and kill his dad, an easier job since the guy's an asshole. He takes imipramine pills every day, but they give him dry mouth and sweaty palms, the pills chafe his throat, so he coats them in Skippy, jars of which he keeps in his closet, and that doesn't help the dry mouth. He's sweaty, always clearing his throat, and he smells like peanut butter. My other friend is Rudy Smithie who's really the one who should be on the couch. He's freaked me out before. He's really not right in the head, but he's brilliant at masking it. Neither Pete nor Rudy is very athletic either. We're all pretty scrawny. Once during a faculty versus students soccer game, the physics teacher missed the ball and accidentally punted Rudy into the back of the net. And for a long time after there was the joke that the physics teacher had scored Rudy Smithie.

I took a sip of juice and asked again, "But am I good-looking?"

It was quiet for a minute, only my mother snapping magazine pages. She'd rubbed a perfume sample on her wrist and the room was now filled with the musky sweetness. Mitzie was still screeching and tapping overhead. My mother let the magazine rest open on her lap. "Honestly," she said, "you remind me of your father, that first time I saw him, selling cleanser door-to-door, a sweet Wisconsin boy. Your father. Well, he is who he is. That much you must remember. You can't change somebody." And this is the way she always talked about him, vaguely, wistfully. But then we both heard the sound of tires over gravel in the driveway, my stepdad home from golf at the club, where he pays over his head for a membership that he tax-deducts as if he's only out there on the links to discuss teeth and woo patients. My mother pointed out the window. "Not that smacked ass."

We watched my stepdad park his car in the driveway, walk to the trunk, take off the sock pom-pom bonnets of a few of his clubs to inspect them for dirt and sand in their ridges—a picky bastard. He nodded, finding enough to possibly throw off his game. He swung the bag up and over his shoulder. I knew he'd wash them in a bucket later that day. Mitzie was still going at it, full-on, overhead.

My mother asked, "Are you having sex at school?" I knew she asked me right then because she wanted a quick answer, that she had a snappy one-liner all warmed up and she didn't really want to get into a big heart-to-heart about it. She isn't mushy. One thing she'll tell you that she learned as Miss New Jersey is that you smile even when things suck and somebody else is wearing your crown. She was still looking out at my stepdad's car although he was strolling up the walkway by then.

"I don't think I have to answer that," I said, swirling a tri-angle of French toast around in syrup, my ears filling with heat.

My mother looked at me. "You should have sex," she said, knowing that my answer meant no, I'd never had sex. For two years, I'd been a virgin at a boarding school where girls were actually lying in their beds just one hallway away, changing their clothes, taking showers. Sometimes it seemed absolutely unbelievable to me that I hadn't ever had sex just once with one of them, even maybe by accident, something slipping into something. I mean, they were so close and fully naked a couple times a day. My grandmother has her own personal theory of evolution, that we come from fish. There's the story of how she came to see me in the hospital only to look at my webbed toes. I've theorized about my webbed toes, too, and that maybe I wasn't meant to be a man but a fish of some sort and that the girls could sense that I wasn't really a man, that they were instinctively predisposed not to have sex with someone with webbed toes—even though I didn't know any St. Andrew's girls who were aware that I have webbed toes; I never went barefoot—but intuitively they sensed that any union with me could lead to an infant fish, with the right mix of recessive genes, not a baby at all. Not that we'd be after a baby, but you see what I mean.

"It's best to have sex when you're young," my mother added, looking out the window again. I probably got my idea to make up my own set of rules from my mother. She likes to make up life rules, things like: *You should always spend money on shoes; you'd be surprised how often you'll be judged on their quality. When you're expecting a day of hard work, like, say, moving day, dress nicely and people won't expect as much from you.* And, *Everyone should always keep their own private bank account, no matter how deeply in love they think they've fallen.* She nodded her head after she'd said this one about young sex, as if she'd just made this rule up and, yes, it was a sturdy rule, one good enough to live by, for whatever reasons.

You can see how I could hate my mom for bringing it up, for saying I'm like my father who only visits once a year, swooping by always in a different convertible borrowed from some "old friend" in NYC, never using the word *lover* or *partner* or *boyfriend,* anything to tip me off, my father, who may as well be a fucking ghost, and for handing me Dilworth Stocker as some sort of manly role model, while even she thinks he's a joke. And my mother was stunning, telling me to go off and have sex, knowing that I couldn't get someone like her, a beauty queen.

That's when my stepdad came in, propping his clubs in the corner of the kitchen so they wouldn't thud and clatter to the floor. "So," he said. "Breakfast at noon. Isn't this living?"

My mother shooed him away with her hand, back to her magazine now.

"Very impressive, son," he said. "You know that no one will really care about that degree you'll have one day from some snooty college if you can't wake up before noon and feed yourself?"

This wasn't really an argument with me. I've learned that much. This type of thing has nothing to do with me. It was an argument by way of me, through me, but not directed at me. Once upon a time, there was something between Dilworth and my mother. He'd pat her hand, almost shyly, when she laid something down on the table for him and she'd smile. He'd brag to his friends in front of her, "My girl's world-class," but that was ages ago. There was no affection left. It evaporated or it got buried. Whatever way affection disappears, theirs was gone.

"Yes, yes," my mother said. "And everyone is just swooning over your degree in dentistry from some institute in Baltimore."

"And what was it that you did back when we met? What was your line of work again?" He was calling my mom a whore, really, because, I guess, she kind of was for a short time in her life. "I suppose you'd like to go back to that or maybe serving ice cream at a Dairy Queen. There's got to be something an old Miss New Jersey is good for." And he laughed. He always laughed at his comments like this, as if it was just a joke not meant to be cruel at all.

"Am I supposed to take you seriously? A man with frogs on his pants?"

"They're turtles," he shouted. Dilworth was always wound up pretty tight.

"Tortoises, I think, technically." I added. "We learned the difference in third-form biology."

"Look," he turned to me. "No one knows what *third-form* means. Enough of this British schoolboy talk. Americans say *freshman, sophomore, junior, senior.* You got me? We're Americans living in America," he said, as if Dilworth Stocker could exist anywhere else on the planet. He turned to my mom. "I'm not paying that kind of money so he can become British. Much less a British *Episcopalian.* At the last function, I met the priest and his *wife.*"

"Technically, he's not a priest." I liked being technical with my stepdad. He had few immunities built up against anything technical that didn't have to do with teeth. It was also a habit from school. In such a tight community, certain catchphrases take over and soon everybody's starting each sentence the same way—from the headmaster to the lowest toad. "Technically," the headmaster would start his sentence, nodding his large headmasterly head. "Technically," your science teacher would say. And soon enough you'd be turning to your buddy, saying, "Technically."

"Of course he's not a priest. He's married! That's my point. Are you all idiots, here? Am I living among idiots or what?" It was little tirades like this that made it almost impossible to take Dilworth Stocker seriously. I looked at him, standing there red-faced, a little blue polo player on the nipple of his pink shirt, and I couldn't hate him. I could only think that he was a boob, a ridiculous boob. I had to remind myself that his mother took off and he was raised by a furnace salesman, a rough guy hard on the belt, stories Dilworth told when he was making the point that I was raised soft and he was raised the right way to become a man. Dilworth took a deep breath, tried to calm down. "I got you a job. You'll be in the great outdoors. You'll get some muscle, a little sun. Maybe you won't look so pale and runty. Congratulations! You're Bob Pinkering's gardener."

It was suddenly quiet. Mitzie had finally worn herself out, flopping down on her canopy bed. My mom and I just stared at my stepdad. I didn't want to be Bob Pinkering's gardener. Of course, I had no idea then how Janie Pinkering would affect me. I pictured Mrs. Pinkering in a sharp pantsuit, a spry woman stepping out for a hair appointment, leaving me with clippers and a mile of uneven hedge.

I'd met Janie only one time at somebody's country club wedding. I remembered her as a twelve-year-old girl with braces, her bangs curled up too tightly with a curling iron. She had a red bubble welt on her forehead where I guessed she'd burned herself wielding the curling iron. She was wearing a taffeta dress that gaped around her shoulders and flapped open at her flat chest. We were introduced and told to talk to each other and even dance, but we ignored each other, eating mints and peanuts off the bar. I might have remembered that she was actually one year older than I was, but she was stuck in my mind as that awkward twelve-year-old, and I figured things had only gotten worse.

I also knew that the Pinkerings had real money. Dr. Pinkering didn't make much more than my stepdad, but both Mr. and Mrs. Pinkering came from a long line of money, unlike Dilworth Stocker, the son of a furnace salesman, and Pixie Kitchy, who was raised on nothing but air, her father a delivery man, her mother a seamstress, her brother a mechanic before he was blown up in Vietnam. I imagined that Janie would be off at horseback-riding camp or sailing school. But I didn't say anything. When Dilworth Stocker made up his mind, he was entrenched—even more like a truck than his usual truck-likeness. I could tell he wanted to say something else, something even more final, a summarizing statement. He liked to sum things up. But there was a pause, my mom and me just staring up into his face, his sunburnt nose, and suddenly he seemed a little wary, shaken, aware that we outnumbered him. He nodded, meaning, *So there, I've spoken.* The truth was that he was already a little afraid of my mother, and he should have been.

He turned quickly and hustled out of the room, whistling as he took the stairs two at a time as usual. We could hear him turn on the upstairs shower to get the hot water going, the jingle of his belt as he undressed.

"I guess I'm the Pinkering's gardener," I said.

"It's good to be something. You'll like it," my mother said. I took this to mean that she'd been Miss New Jersey once and now she was just a dentist's wife. She stood up, straightened, and walked out of the kitchen and upstairs to her bedroom, where, I assumed, she fell asleep on the sofa watching the miniature TV with two white pills dissolving on her tongue, as she often did.

Now that she was through with tapping, Mitzie started

playing with her Barbies. I could hear her talking for them in a singsong. I just sat there with my syrup-smeared plate in front of me. See, I really had nothing better to do. Soon enough my stepdad walked by on his way to the deck, picking up his shoulder-strap golf bag on his way. His wet hair was slicked back with the black fine-toothed comb that came free with every barbershop hair cut. He sat out there in an Adirondack chair, scrubbing the heads of his clubs, shining them up with a white rag, one at a time.

I walked out the back door toward the pool bungalow in the backyard. I'd talked Dilworth and my mother into letting me live out there for the summer. *Pool bungalow* sounds nice, a plush idea for the rich, a term my mom has always liked to throw around. Really it's a one-room shed with wall-to-wall carpeting built on a slab with baseboard heating that doesn't work, a microwave, a mini-fridge, a bathroom and shower stall. There isn't really a pool at all. My mother never liked bodies of water, anything someone could drown in, her father having drowned when she was sixteen. She'd filled the pool with dirt so that it was now just a grassed-over mound.

I passed by Dilworth on the deck. He didn't look up. He said, "Don't model yourself after your mother. You'll end up soft." He laughed. "Do you know how many times she's told me she was going to leave me?" He snorted. "It's only at night when we're in bed and it's dark, and she'll say it real soft when she thinks I'm asleep. But she'd never leave me. I'll let you in on a secret: your mother needs me. See? She needs Dilworth Stocker. That's the bottom line." He laughed some more. "Did you hear that, Pixie?" he yelled up to their closed bedroom window.

I wondered if it was true. I pictured my mother, her head turned in one direction, Dilworth's in the other. *I'm going to leave you one day, Dilworth. One day, I'll be gone, just like that.* I hoped it was true. "She's asleep," I said.

"It's one of the few things she can handle."

I spent the afternoon on the far side of the bungalow where I'd set up an old folding chair. I tilted my face to the sun and closed my eyes and I thought of the dorm master whose apartment had attached to our dorm rooms the year before, a quiet older bachelor who played with homemade rockets, set off in a nearby field. Rudy thought he was an old fag, but Rudy thought everybody was a fag, which probably means that Rudy's a fag. (And there was that one time that was weird with Rudy near his dad's docked boat when we were out in these high weeds spying on some girls, and Rudy kind of came on to me.) And I thought of the minister and his stolid wife who I lived near freshman year, always quiet. When you walked into their place with some sort of question, like the time of the hall meeting, all you could hear was their clock ticking on the mantel. Then I flashed briefly on the breathless Miss Abernathy, a first-year English teacher who'd touted the benefits of perfect pronunciation, projection, posture, and whom Rudy said he heard screaming out, "Fuck me, fuck me," like a porn queen, from her open bedroom window, her fiancé's car parked on the street below. I'd asked how he could know it was Miss Abernathy, and he'd said, "Please! Would she stutter it? Would she mumble or slur? No one can project like she can." I'd have taken living with any of them at the end of the hall over Dilworth and my mother. (Miss Abernathy most of all, for obvious reasons.)

Eventually, Mitzie appeared, still in her tap shoes with their black-ribbon bows, carrying a baton with pink streamers tied to each end. It was so humid that her curly hair was frizzy, a tight puff on top of her head, like a Q-Tip interrupted by a pink headband. She was thick like her father, but with fine little features, our mom's nose and chin and upturned eyes. She presented me with a tin of homemade cookies that Helga had made. Helga is the German maid who's come Tuesdays and Thursdays ever since we moved in, before Mitzie was even born. She's a big woman with such droopy eyelids that she often has one of them sort of taped up with a butterfly Band-Aid so she can see. She likes to dole out advice, a lot of which makes no sense. I've always wondered if she's using cryptic German clichés that have lost everything in translation. She believes everyone should swim, or, so she says, "They will sink in dis life." She once tried to teach me to swim while my parents were on a European vacation, and I nearly drowned. That was all my mother needed to hear. That's when she had the pool filled with dirt, first thing when she got home. I'm still a shabby swimmer.

Mitzie was always a lonely kid. I remembered being like Mitzie, the only kid in a houseful of estranged adults, their world so lofty and strained, a tightrope, and the kid, me or Mitzie, it doesn't matter, having to walk that tightrope in the spotlight just to take everybody's mind off how much they hate everything and each other. There was a time that I knew I was the only thing keeping my mom going. She doesn't remember it that way. Somehow she's idealized that string of men, trudging in and out of our house after she divorced my dad. At night,

I prayed to get sick. In winter, I snuck outside in the evening
with a wet head when my mother was off somewhere picking
up men, and I was with a ditsy teenage babysitter talking all
raspy into the phone with her boyfriend. I'd take off my shoes
and walk around on the freezing pavement. I wanted my lungs
to fill up again, so my mother would have to take care of me.
And during the days I would be her sweetheart, her doll baby,
the perfect child, coloring quietly, singing for her. Once I
pushed my face into a birthday cake just to make her laugh.

It was a lot of pressure, and I could tell Mitzie felt it, too.
Of course, I'd outgrown any cuteness, and I'd never been one
to bring Dilworth and my mother together anyway, always a
sullen obstacle to be shipped off to boarding school. But
Mitzie was in the hot seat. I could tell by the way she'd walk
into a room where my stepdad and my mom were sitting in
their two distant chairs, oceans apart in the same room, the
way she'd try to buoy them up with her cuteness, her curls, her
tap shoes and princess wand—a tightrope walker, really. They
should have just suspended a rope near the ceiling and let her
teeter up there with a tutu and umbrella.

I ate the cookies and watched her twirl her baton just a few
feet away. She'd throw it up and drop it, throw and drop,
throw and drop, while she gave a little monologue of non
sequiturs. Things like: "I wrote a story about a cow who
wouldn't give milk to this angry farmer and a calf named
Jenny who saves the day and won first place in a contest at
school." Then she'd say, "Daddy took the door off Mom's
changing room. Took it off the hinges because he was tired of
hearing her slam it. But she got a new door with a gold handle

that locks. They don't have fights. They have tiffs." A distinction that maybe Dilworth had made for her, to console her, but
it was a little too British a word for Dilworth. I wondered who
else could have taught it to her. It was a little too fancy for my
grandmother. She'd have said spats, but mostly avoided conversations with Mitzie, whose voice grated on her nerves.
Maybe it came from Helga, a translation of hers from something German that she looked up in a dictionary. It certainly
didn't come from my mother. She'd never soften anything.
And then Mitzie'd say, "Don't tell anybody but I like the color
black better than most of the others, because it's like the dark
and because that crayon is always the sharpest." Finally, dig-
ging her baton out of the weeds beside the bungalow, she said,
"When I grow up, I'm going to live out here. I'll probably be
a Miss Somebody, too, like Mom was, but I'm not going to
have tiffs and lock my door. I'll be more like you."

And I wondered what she could possibly see in me that
anyone would want to grow up and be. My ears were probably
getting sunburned, not to mention those webbed toes. Maybe
she didn't know about the webbed toes. There's not even that
much to physically grow up into. Mitzie, for god's sake, will
probably tower over me one day. In any case, it made me feel
old and wise, almost worldly. "Don't grow up," I told her. "It
only gets more confusing."

Pixie

How It Begins:
Moth Wings and Fish Gills

I can't begin with the gun. Nothing starts where you think it does. I was a housewife, and I became dangerous. Sometimes it's the only way possible to regain footing in the world. My mother let her guard down, let her secrets loose, and it changed my life. But by that time, I'd been disappearing into the past for a long while. I can tell you that I remember standing in the frozen foods aisle of the Super Fresh last summer. The outside air smelled like dung from the local mushroom farms, and it was lovely to be in the grocery store, crisp, odorless. I had the glass door propped open, looking for deals on frozen beans or the vegetable medley. The chilled air was rising up, fogging the glass, and suddenly I remembered my mother as she charged down 24th Street in the cold, the big buttons on her coat lined up to her throat, her pocketbook—clicking with nitroglycerin pills for her angina—clenched in the lock of her elbow, and me there at her heels, just sixteen. This is how easily I would slip, and I would disappear, letting one detail illuminate the next and the next until I found myself in a memory so well lit that it was hard to distinguish from the present.

My mother had taken me with her to confession, after which she told me we weren't going back to church, that there was no need. She walked out of the dark confessional, tall, her head upright, stuffing a tissue into her sweater sleeve. She nodded to me to follow her out onto the church steps. It was cold outside but bright.

She said, "Every year, the priest tells the story of how Gabriel appeared to Mary and I've never understood it. I've sat in the pew with all of the heartsick wives, hearing about Gabriel with his sweet talk, no better than a milksop, a drunk in a bar after midnight, no better than any of our husbands, and Gabriel tells her that she's going to conceive the son of God. Who would believe him, Pixie? What woman would believe him? And Mary asks how it can be, her a virgin. Isn't she really asking how the child won't come from rape? I tell you, one day you'll understand how each year just before the priest tells us Mary's answer, always the same answer, why some of us are praying she'll say no, that someone will finally say no. I've learned to say it myself, to push the word up from stomach to mouth and then live with the consequences. I'm not going back. You can't confess a sin you'd commit again if put back in time. I won't repent."

I never interrupted my mother's speeches on God and the church. It never did any good. It only made her raise her voice and repeat everything until you gave in to it all, nodding along. She liked to say, for example, that we evolved from fish, not the lineage of Adam and his rib, and that every once in a while one of us was born with webbed toes, like the old, fat aunt who'd brought her to Bayonne after her parents were both dead. She's since claimed Ezra's toes as proof. She'd learned all about Adam and his rib, yes. And conceded that maybe there were some upstanding citizens who came from Adam's rib, a bit of mud and breath. "The Lazarskis, maybe, are rib people," she'd say. "I hear he's a skin doctor who can remove warts and she teaches piano, has a great big one the size of a pony in her living room. But this family is fish." She thought that if you come from fish, the world is never quite right, all this air, lungs, the way you think you can see what's coming, but you can't really, not even the priests, and here I agreed with her. Could anyone have seen, way back, how my father was going to die? By the time my mother gave up religion, he'd already drowned in the Kill van Kull. He'd jumped in once before, the same way as when he died, with his hands locked behind his back. That time, when he was young and wild, and in love with my mother—he'd described her as a brash-mouthed bony girl swinging her legs off the dock's edge—he came up with two free fists above his head, shaking water from his hair, beads of light spraying from his head. I knew that my mother's leaving the church had to do with my dead father. That much was clear.

That's what I was thinking about when I closed the fogged-up door on the frozen foods and saw myself glass-reflected, holding my plastic bags of vegetables. I remember, early last summer, catching a reflection of myself when I least expected it, my hips widened by the car door, my blank face in the microwave oven's flat shine, and more than anything I had the feeling of barely existing, of being nearly invisible. I plopped the bags down in the cart, one front wheel jostling, bucking on its loose bolt. But the rest of the day would be lost. I was considering religion, that there have been times since my mother's departure from the church when I've missed it, that I've wished she hadn't turned her back but had instead found the struggle worthwhile and had passed along some basic faith. Sometimes there's little I envy more than someone who absolutely, sincerely believes—the type who can hand their worries over to God as if they amount to little more than a pocketful of loose change. Like the check-out woman, maybe, with her chipped front tooth and one slightly dented cheek. I'm sure that I said hello to her, that I asked the bagger, the Gilpin's boy, if he'd like his first year at Clemson, but I didn't listen to their responses. Instead I was remembering my confirmation. I chose the name Christina from a book of saints—Christina the Astonishing. She had some sort of fit and was supposedly dead when she flew out of her coffin at her funeral and soared up to the church rafters. The priest and her sister had to talk her into coming down. She hated the smell of the dirty human body so much that she would clamber up trees, perch on weather vanes, and crawl into ovens to escape it. A crazy woman, really, maybe a crazy saint, I mean supposedly she could fly, but I didn't believe all that rigamarole about saints anyway. I preferred a crazy woman. Sometimes I felt crazy, even then. I didn't say any of this aloud. I pushed my cart with its pitching front wheel into the parking lot.

I'll admit that it's all a bit gauzy to me. There's no chronol-
ogy to memory, and I'm not perfect. My mind still can find a
groove in the record and get stuck in a rut, replaying the same
bit again and again. My mind is still sometimes more like a
damp yard at dusk, fireflies lifting up, lit like a hundred tiny
tinderbox fires. I know it doesn't make sense but I can think of
the word *memory* and see a cloud of moths. And to explain the
moths I must start with the only vacation I ever went on with
my parents. I was, maybe, twelve, my body just hinting at a
figure. It was the last week of the season, and we rented a beach
cottage. To get a deal on the cost, my mother offered to help the
landlady close up all the little cottages for the winter. This was
typical of my mother. She was already nervous about the
expense of the trip, and luxury made her uncomfortable, almost
itchy. She had a habit of scratching the back of her neck each
time she handed over money, as if paying for things could heat
up an allergic reaction, an instant rash. She spent most of the
vacation scrubbing out cabinets, toilets, shower stalls. I
remember watching her make one of the beds in an empty cottage; a moth got sucked up into the billowed sheets. It batted
its wings, tacking against the current of air. But the sheet fell,
and my mother kneeled on the bed, straightening it with her
swift, stiff hands where the moth would stay trapped all winter.
I imagined that we would come back the next summer—
although I also knew we wouldn't—and I imagined that I'd lift
up the sheet and the moth wouldn't be dead, reduced to a fine
dust of its tiny bones, but it would have multiplied into a million moths, the room filling with tiny white beating wings.
Memory can work like that. You can lay something to rest, or

so you think, but it isn't dead. Memory breeds. It swarms. I don't know that I'm making sense. I don't know that I'm being clear. But to understand one dangerous act—and it was dangerous, I was a crazy woman—you have to look backward at a rising white sea of moths. It's not simple. Nothing is, but I'm trying to be as clear as possible.

I remembered confession, being happy that I no longer had to go. I'd never told the truth, not what I thought of as my own dirty sins, not to anyone, least of all some old chain-smoking priest. I'd say, "I took the Lord's name in vain three times," and then I'd fake the Hail Marys. Instead I'd whisper the way I wanted to believe my life would be one day: "Hello, I'm Miss America and this is my perfect family. This is my son, Troy. He plays football. And my daughter, Wendy, who takes piano lessons and tap dancing. And my husband, Stephen. He's the one in the tweed blazer. We're all blond and happy." The way I figured it the world had gone crazy with riots and war. So many of the nice Catholic families at Mt. Carmel Church, good old-fashioned Poles, the ones my mother said came straight from Adam's rib, had these longhaired kids who smoked dope and burned draft cards. The priest had heard enough of it. He wanted to hear some girl say she'd taken the Lord's name in vain three times. He wanted to believe in what he saw, a pure girl, a virgin, and I wanted to be that girl, even though I wasn't. Who would want to be a dirty hippy, listening to Iron Butterfly? I wondered. I'd have done anything to be perfect. The priest probably knew the truth anyway, but together we faked it. Life, as far as I could tell, was as much about faking things as it was anything else.

If I had confessed honestly, I'd have told the old priest that I'd shoved Emily Post's blue book of etiquette under my coat at the Bayonne Public Library. I knew it was wrong and that Emily Post herself would have *tsk-tsked*. I knew that I shouldn't have been cleaning them out of their manners section one Saturday at a time, but I couldn't check the books out. The librarian knew me too well. She knew my mother worked as a seamstress with little Chinese women who smoked like stacks, that my dad died because he was a stupid drunk, diving into the river with his hands locked behind his back. Everybody knew that, for God's sake! She probably even knew that my brother was a shady mechanic, that one day her Buick could have gotten stolen while she shelved books at the Bayonne Public Library, and it might just have wound up with him, so he could make it look completely different to sell it again or sell it for parts, depending on whether she'd taken good care of her precious Buick or not. And even though nobody really knew anything about me—I'd never told anyone about the man, the man who raped me, that I could still see him when I lay down and tried to close my eyes at night, and closing my eyes was like his shadow standing over me, that sometimes even just last summer, almost twenty years later, before the sleeping pills fuzzed over my mind, I could still feel his shadow on me—they could all tell that I was dirty. They knew, I was dead sure, just by looking at me. And I was certain that the librarian would laugh at me, the dirty Kitchy girl, trying to learn her manners! I could see her laughing at me with her coffee-stained teeth and her half-glasses slipping down her nose.

She would have laughed at me for trying to be something I

wasn't, but that's what I'd been doing for years. My mother scrimped and saved to send me to Mt. Carmel High—scrubbing out toilets on her vacation, for example—where, she said, I would finish out the school year, my last, despite her abandonment of the church. "Be dull," she'd advise me before I tromped off to school in the morning. "Blend in." She wanted me to be plain. She said that being pretty was only trouble for me, but there was nothing I could do. The nuns had tried to teach us how to say no. For years they'd only taught us to bend at the waist, to kneel and bow our heads, but after the man— after he came for me—I met Jimmy Vietree and learned to push thoughts of the man out of my head. In retrospect, I assume that's what Jimmy was for, a way to take control, to be the one in power. Last summer I thought often of Jimmy on the damp ground by the tracks, his bony body under mine— always under mine—the train's one eye bearing down, blinding us while it passed and then Jimmy's eyes, his gaze so strong on me, his body touching my body, his skin erasing the man, erasing sometimes even my own skin until I was no longer there, but above, way above, looking down. I'd learned that much, like St. Christina; how to rise up almost out of myself. It was easier to soar to church rafters than to be one of the sorry people kneeling below, even when you saw the top of your own head down there, and your own body waiting for you to reappear inside it. And sometimes, once or twice maybe, I thought that I could love Jimmy Vietree, but I could never slip back into my skin. I could only imagine what it would feel like and I bet it felt good, but it couldn't last. My mother had taught me that much.

You see, she loved her parents. She liked to recall her father washing his coal-blackened face from a bowl, how he'd stick his tongue out at her, his pink tongue, so pink, pinker than bubble gum, and how he came up cleaner and cleaner with each dip, till the bowl was just a dark cloud of water, until his skin shone bright as scales, and her mother, her sweet mother, already dead of consumption, her throat too gummed for air, pink lungs whistling. My mother believed if they could only have put her into water, she would have learned to breathe through gills. My mother thought that for every happiness there was an equal or greater pain. She'd say, "Don't you see how if you really love someone, they're taken away? Just like that. They catch the consumption, a mine collapses, and they're gone. Don't love deeply." She didn't mention my father. Once upon a time, she must have truly loved him, too. Hadn't she fallen for him, a young man who'd jumped into a river to show off for her? She said, "Don't get married. It doesn't help."

Sometimes she scared me when she talked like this, and her eyes took on this strange cast, almost a glow. Like the day she gave up the church when she stopped on the front steps to our apartment building, looking fevered, her cheeks flushed red from having walked so quickly up 24th Street in the cold. She put one foot on a step, her hand on the stone handrail, and she stopped. She said, "One day I'll tell you everything, when you're old enough, and I'll remind you of the Bible passage, how after Mary says yes and accepts that she's the handmaid of the Lord, that she'll bear the son of God, how quickly Gabriel is gone. There was some feathered light, I imagine, a flap of wings, and then nothing, just a girl standing there, all alone, blinded by the bright sun. We're all alone, Pixie. It's how we come into the world, one at a time, from salty water, for us half fish it's our only memory of heaven." I was certain then that I knew everything there was to know. Most of all, I already knew what it was like to be alone. Because even when my mother was saying this, she wasn't looking at me, she wasn't talking to me. I was already flying solo. I was already alone. I preferred it. Now, I can see myself driving home from the grocery store, slowing at yellow lights, coming to a complete stop at each red sign, the windows rolled up tight, the air-conditioning on full blast, its cold air making my stiffly sprayed hair shimmy around my head. Anyone would say that I was a woman in control, solitary, perhaps, but a dignified dentist's wife. I looked the part. I was playing the role, perfectly.

Even at sixteen, I had an air that was unapproachable. I knew that when you look pretty, even if you're not trying to look pretty, men think that you're trying to please them, because they are pleased, like you've designed yourself especially for them. And they think that since you made yourself for them that you're theirs somehow, that they own you just by looking at you. But I wanted to be untouchable. I didn't want anybody to think that they could come too close. I wanted a permanent stage between me and everyone else. That was why I wanted to be Miss Bayonne. And so, as a result, nobody would have ever said to me directly that my brother was some kind of thief and that we were poor when my dad was alive and poorer once he was dead and that I wasn't the pure virgin that I let the priest believe me to be. But I heard it all the time in whispers around me. And it wasn't that they weren't cruel enough. They would have put it right in my face, but they were all a little afraid of me and a little in love with me—even the other girls, lined up in front of the row of bathroom mirrors, staring at me when they thought I was looking at myself—girls like Lizzy Fanowski with her pointy, high nose, and tiny cleft chin, her perfect school sweaters, so new you could smell the wool, and Deb Hastings, too, the kind of girl who did backbends out the windows of boys' fast cars racing down Broadway, her thin shirts riding up and long stringy hair whipping. They both looked at me when they thought I wasn't looking. I'm not being vain. It's just the truth when you've got long blond hair and blue eyes and you develop early. People still stare at me that way, not as often, but I can still feel their eyes on me.

I first noticed it before my father's death. One summer while stepping out of the Bayonne Public Swimming Pool in my pale blue swimsuit, I looked up and everybody was watching me. And it was like I was given a gun, something powerful, and everybody started acting like I had a gun, like I was armed and I could kill them if I wanted. It makes strangers awfully nice to you. It wasn't real power, I would learn, and I'd learn to rely on the gun, too.

Of course it hadn't always been like this. Once, I was just a little girl, and nobody paid much attention to me at all. I was just a kid, kind of straggly, and I had a big brother and a mother and father, a delivery man for bulk food. The apartment was always the same, I guess, small and chopped up into little rooms and a long bent hall to three bedrooms and the bathroom, but once it hadn't seemed so bad. The air hadn't been so stale with smoke and blackened pots, the stir and stir of beans, the way in summer that the exhaust from the street lifted into the unstitched screens, and, in winter, the dust-and-cabbage-stink layer upon layer cooked on the hissing radiator, and always the TV's gray light.

When we were younger, my father was a dreamboat. He'd always wanted to be some sort of magician. He could pull coins out of his nose and scarves from the palm of his hand. He was handsome with a great wide smile and a nose so small you wouldn't guess he could breathe out of it, much less pull a coin from it. He would shout to me when I walked in the room. "Angel!" he'd say. "Come on over here and sit on my lap." And I would balance on his jiggling knee and then hug him around the neck. Some days when he came home from work, he'd knock at the front door, and when you went to open it, he'd pratfall into the house, a straight fall, face-first, and then at the last possible second his hands would flip out, magic, and he'd catch himself. Of course, sometimes my parents fought. My brother, Cliff, would call me to his room and sing in my ear, "Fly Me to the Moon," and he had a pretty voice, too. But sometimes in summer you could see the fresh bruises on my mother's arms in the morning, and once or twice, my father with a puffed eye.

My father wanted to be good. He won the money for that summer cottage vacation off a bartender who worked at the Catholic War Veterans over on 8th Street. The cottage was small but quaint with real shutters on the windows, not the ones you see everywhere nowadays nail-gunned onto

Colonials, my Colonial included. My father fished on a long pier while Cliff and I dug with shovels and buckets in the sand, and my mother sat under a rented umbrella, reading *True Romance* magazine, when she wasn't cleaning. This was around the time they grew colder to each other, and he started drinking too much. My father wore his thin white short-sleeved shirt flapping in the breeze, his Guinea T-shirt, always a solid white, showing through underneath. He had a Hula girl tattooed on his forearm who danced each time he twisted his wrist the right way. He caught a golden, gold-eyed fish and held it up over his head for all of us to see, and that night my mother fried it up. It was the first time we'd ever eaten seafood, because my mother didn't ever cook it. She said she didn't believe in it, because she thought we came from fish. But my father was proud of his catch and she gave in. The rest of us ate it while she stood by the kitchen sink, humming. My father came out after dinner with a present for her. She opened the box filled with tissue, and inside it was a smart hat with pink ribbon, but she wouldn't wear it, even though she thought it was beautiful. She said, "It costs more than a ham." He wanted her to wear it, begged her to put it on, but she got angry. "It's three pairs of school shoes. It's enough bread for a year." After all, it had been her idea to haggle with the landlady, reducing the cost of the cottage by scrubbing things clean for winter, setting mousetraps, too, in each low cabinet.

Finally, he yelled at her. "Where's my girl?" he asked. "Where's the one I married, the one who loved me? Who'd do what I told her to do and was happy to do it?"

She stood up and said, "Marriage is a rotten deal. It's for cheats and fakes. And," she got choked up, "you know I don't believe in eating fish! How could you eat like that in front of me? Picking your teeth with the fine, white bones." And here she'd go on and on, because she'd been standing by that sink, humming, yes, and thinking, too, of exactly what she was going to say sometime when no one expected it. "Like Mary, I've pondered many things in my heart, kept them all locked up there till it feels like it will explode. Angina, my doctor says, but more like the swollen hearts of martyrs pressed to death beneath stones."

"You're crazy," he said. "You're a crazy woman!"

I don't have to tell you that it didn't help her to practice all of her little speeches, because no one understood her. She yelled out, "You could have just eaten a cousin, an aunt, my father!" She ran into their cottage bedroom, slamming the door behind her, and my father left the house, stormed out. They weren't a perfect match. Later that night, I waited up for the sound of him coming in the door. He walked back to the bedroom door and knocked softly, and she said, "Come in." But, I guess, eventually he stopped coming home to knock on locked doors or she stopped saying, "Come in." Things changed.

When I was in the midst of all these memories last summer, I could be stopped at a red light, spraying Pledge onto the mahogany coffee table, painting a fingernail, and there was a sudden flash of my father's face in my mind's eye and tears rose up in my eyes, a sting in my nose and my throat. He got older, tired, and my mother colder, stern. He liked to stay out late drinking, and he gambled all of our money away on the stinking Mets, before they became the Miracle Mets, of course, always hoping for the big payoff. He pissed it away until my mother hated him, but she'd never really admitted it. My brother hated him, too. And I was the only one who loved him, who'd tell him that everything was going to be all right.

The night my father died, he knocked on the door, a faint tap really, and I opened it, and my father fell into our living room, but his hands didn't flip out at the last second. I think that's what he'd meant to do, but he fell down hard on his face. He started to laugh, but this sobbing laugh that turned crazy. I hadn't seen him for more than two weeks. Sometimes he'd do that, disappear on a bender. This time I hadn't seen him since the night the man broke into our house, somehow, and found his way to my bed. Although I didn't remember everything from that night, I knew that it was my father who'd caught the man in my bed and knocked the man over the head with Cliff's bat to save me. I guessed that was what had put my father over the edge this last time, sending him on a two-week drunk.

My father just sat there on the floor, blood from his nose smearing his teeth, and my older brother, Cliff, started yelling at him. He wanted to kill people in Vietnam. He thought it was his war and when he turned eighteen two months later he joined up first thing. Cliff died there. He was tall and skinny with a pretty mouth like a girl's. I remember how he'd always tried to make his mouth small and tight, curling in his lips. He said to my father, "Look at you. You're pathetic."

My mother sat up straight in her chair, her nitroglycerin

tablets for her unruly heart rattling in her pocket. I was wait-ing for her to start in on him, to ask him how much he'd pissed away. But that night was different. She stood up slowly. She said, "What do you want?" She shook the words from her mouth. Her eyes filled up, like she hated him and was sorry, too, like she knew it was the end of something already.

And I just stood there, wanting to clean my father up. He needed a good bath, a shave. I kneeled down to him. There were fine, wiry strands of the green carpet pressed into the wet blood. He looked around at us like he'd never seen us before, his eyes passing from one of us to the next, like he was a stranger who'd wandered into the wrong apartment. He put his hand on the floor, the Hula dancer tense, pulled taut against the muscles and bones of his forearm, and then slack as he pushed himself up, letting one hand drop to his side, and running the other shakily along the wall. He stumbled out the door.

We found out later that he took an old rusty bike lock and key from the shed and went to one of the docks down by the refineries along the Kill van Kull, where he shouted about being Houdini's long-lost son till he had a little crowd of sailors and whores and drunks. He slipped the key into his mouth, locked his hands behind his back, and jumped into the river. We'd heard the story many times over of how he'd done it before, when he was around Cliff's age. He'd handcuffed his wrists behind his back and jumped into the river with a key in his mouth, but that time he'd come up, breathless, smiling. He always grinned at the end of the story, said he did it to impress some girl whom he'd sometimes pretend not to remember. But you could tell by the way he looked at my mother, saying, "Now, what was her name? A real spitfire. Who was she again?" and by the way she looked someplace else real quick, embarrassed, that she'd been the girl and also that she wasn't that girl anymore. My mother was cold, even her hands, almost blue-looking and toughened. I couldn't imagine that she was ever a young girl. The way I figured it my father wanted to be that boy again, that maybe it was some special moment when he'd felt most himself, or the self he wanted to be, and he was trying to return to it. It was the only reason I could think of. It was a beautiful reason, and if my mother had never told me the truth last summer, I could have believed this forever. But it wouldn't have been for the best.

This time my father didn't escape. I've imagined the key settling into the bottom of the lake in all that dust that rises up. I've imagined the key sliding down his throat. I've imagined him writhing, panicked, the water pouring into his mouth, maybe even filling his lungs till they were taut with water. I've thought of the big, dark refineries, smoke spilling from their stacks, and the sailors and whores and drunks leaning over the edge of the dock, watching the rolls of his breath bubble up.

The police told my mother that one of the sailors stripped down and dove in after him, that the eighteen-year-old pulled him up, already dead. I've imagined the eighteen-year-old, not yet sent to Vietnam, but scared already, holding my dead father on the dock. The kid almost naked, just in his wet underwear, maybe crying. The whores and the drunks, the other sailors, too, wandering away, smart enough not to get mixed up with a dead body. Just that kid, a skinny kid, skinny as Jimmy Vietree, skinny as Cliff and Ezra. I see the kid kind of rocking my father until the police showed up.

You see, memory is its own animal. It can hibernate, spawn, and rise up—moths in a well lit room, each thin body lifted by fierce wings. It doesn't make sense, but sometimes the moths are fireflies—their fiery hearts are what light the room. I'm trying to explain memories as things with wings. I'm trying to explain my mind, and it's a faulty, desperate thing. Listen, an ordinary woman, unpacking groceries in a bright kitchen in a cheery Colonial, a mother of two, a dentist's wife, could choke to death on so many white moths and fireflies.

After my father died, my mother stitched my beauty-contest dress on the weekends. I told her it was for a school dance. She could hear me practice the accordion, a good old-fashioned, wholesome instrument that I bought secondhand at a pawn shop. She knew that I was nervous about something, but she didn't know I was set on being Miss Bayonne and then Miss New Jersey and then Miss America. I knew that she'd say that dreaming is dangerous, that this thinking big will only come back to curse me for my swelled head. She'd say, "Who do you think you are, a princess?"

No, I certainly was no princess. I had a lot going against me. I was reading Emily Post like it was the Bible. I memorized this: "Introducing oneself is sometimes the most practical way to begin a conversation with a stranger seated next to you at a party. 'I'm Betsy James. That's my husband sitting opposite you. We live in the country and raise show cattle and dahlias, but we come to town very often in the winter to hear music.' " Well, I couldn't really introduce myself like that. I was only sixteen and I wasn't married. I didn't know there was such a thing as show cattle and I'm still not sure what dahlias look like. I didn't live in the country. I lived in Bayonne, New Jersey. My brother was a thief, my mother worked with Chinese women, and my father was dead. I had trouble paying attention in school—although I worked hard because Miss New Jersey had to go to college, right? I didn't really know how to play the accordion at all even though it came with a Henry Silberhorn instruction book all the way from Chicago, and I didn't really have much help with things like elocution and poise, necessary in a beauty queen. But I had one thing going for me, just one: I was beautiful. People could say what they wanted to, Emily Post included, but I believed that in America beauty could take me anywhere.

Ezra

Rule #2: Always agree with women, no
matter what they're saying, even if you
don't understand them.

When I got to the Pinkerings', Janie was sitting on the hood of a powder blue convertible in the long graveled driveway next to a broad lawn arched with maples and their green leaves. She was wearing a tennis skirt, and her legs were spread just wide enough to reveal the white glow of her underwear, the heels of her sneakers parked on the shiny chrome fender. I was surprised to see she'd changed. Her teeth were big and straight, her nose a little too perky, but she was tan and lean and stacked. Her white polo shirt was so tight that it made a taut ripple from one nipple to the other, and her long legs extended from her little white skirt. She was a good two inches taller than me. She made me nervous.

I was wearing sneakers and beat-up khaki shorts. I felt suddenly very sloppy, poor, like a servant boy. Just because I go to a boarding school doesn't mean we're rich. I'm on almost a full scholarship because of those little bubble tests. Plus, I round out demographics. I'm a way for rich kids to be exposed to the middle class. Dilworth is a dentist with an okay practice, but our house is the smallest on our block, and run-down, the roof streaked with washed-out tar, the gutters rusting through their white paint, the linoleum curling up in the corners of the kitchen. I felt like Janie knew all of this. Just by the way she looked up at me walking across the yard, I decided that her parents had told her that they were doing my folks a favor. I was the hired help, but I even failed at that. I looked nothing like a gardener and felt even less like one. I'd figured little Janie'd have some sort of camp to attend and Mrs. Pinkering would be at that hair appointment that women always seem to have to rush off to, that I'd be alone and that there'd be little to do. The old gardener having just gotten fired, how quick could weeds take over? But now I felt anxious. I walked up to her and said, "I'm Ezra Stocker. The new gardener, I guess." (Yes, I had to take Dilworth's last name, an act of goodwill, my mother the ambassador negotiating between two not-warring but not altogether happy countries: Dilworth and me. I didn't have any choice, really. I was just a snot-nosed kid at the time.)

Janie said, "My Dad fired the last gardener for planting marijuana in the greenhouse," and then she paused to see if I had a reaction. I tried not to. She went on, "He was a hippy freak, with one of those long, gross ZZ Top ponytails and sweaty-pitted tie-dyes, and when you looked at him up close, he was ancient, way over forty years old, like an authentic relic. But I got a bag of weed just by telling him I thought his sandals were cool." That's the way Janie talked, in big gushes of information. I thought of sandals, how I didn't wear them because of my webbed toes and how I was maybe missing out on something. I wanted to know if he wore the sandals with thick wool socks like some of the kids at my school, but I didn't ask. Just then, a small blue butterfly landed on Janie's knee, a peach of a knee with fine golden hairs that she'd missed shaving. We both looked at the butterfly for a moment and then it lifted. Janie slid off the hood of the car to her feet and the butterfly flapped around her head. She closed her eyes and tilted back her head and opened her mouth. The butterfly skittered off on its bumpy path up over the car, up into the trees. Then Janie opened her eyes, put her hand on her throat. "Did I swallow it?" she asked. "Did it go in?"

"No," I said, but immediately I wished I'd said yes. Obviously she hadn't swallowed it and knew she hadn't swallowed it. She was asking me some other question, more personal. I changed my answer. "But maybe," I said, and I thought if only I'd been more diligent in making up my Rules to Live By that there'd have been one to have kept me from making a mistake like that.

"Sure," Janie said matter-of-factly. "It's not a big deal." And she led me across the well-trimmed lawn.

It was about two o'clock. I walked in the front door, the hallway lit up with bright sun. "Nobody's home but me, for like a week, probably more. My parents left for vacation this morning, not together, *separate* vacations." She gave the impression that she thought "separate vacations" were as gross as the hippy gardener's ponytail. She rolled her eyes.

My parents' being divorced and my dad's being absent except for his annual swoops in from California once a summer in somebody else's convertible, I was thinking that she was lucky to know where her father was at all. When I was a kid, my dad drifted in and out of our apartment. I remember hearing a door shut down the hall, thinking that each of our neighbors' shoes on the stairs could be him, waiting for the pause, the jingle of keys or the turn of the corner, feet up another flight. I remember my mother always with me, the nights she spent rocking me on the edge of the tub making me breathe shower steam to cure a croupy cough, but he was always out. Since my mother married Dilworth, I'd ask questions about my real dad every now and then. When I'd ask what he did for a living, people would just kind of shrug. Dilworth, who usually clammed up on the subject of my father, would snort, "He's a dreamer." But my mom would defend him, because, I think, she never stopped loving him. "He was always interested in politics. Maybe he's an activist. I think he wants to have enough money to buy the life he's always wanted to live. He's actually quite shy," as if any of that were a job. To me, he was still a ghost, a growling motor in the driveway. And I said to Janie, "My dad's a ghost." Meaning that my parents divorced when I was five, and I almost never see him, but all that came out was this disconnected statement.

She looked at me, tilted her head, as if what I'd said interested her, made her reconsider me somehow. But she didn't respond to it, and I was too flustered to explain the comment. She said, "I think I've seen your house. I think my dad dropped your dad off once when I was in the backseat."

I wanted to correct her, to make it clear that Dilworth was not my father, but I didn't want to make a stink about it, like people do when their name's mispronounced. "Oh, I don't live at home really. I've got my own place out back. My mother had wanted my grandmother to live there, but my grandmother didn't want to and the nursing home won't take pets. My grandmother has about twenty caged birds, swinging on their little perch swings. So she moved to a condo nearby instead." This was all true, but I wished I hadn't brought up my grandmother at all. I was suddenly imagining her living room, a dark room of old furniture, chirping, feathers, and dust. The mention of my grandmother at all killed the bachelor lure of the place. Sometimes I get nervous and tend to run on. My mother tried to get my grandmother to live in the pool bungalow, which would have meant changing its name to "the mother-in-law's suite," but my grandmother refused. Publicly, she refused on the grounds that she wanted her independence. But privately, she confessed to me that my mother had always been edgy, a fragile child, and my grandmother had learned early enough to lie to her about anything the least bit unhappy. She said, "Not to mention that Mitzie. Your sister's voice reminds me of your mother's god-awful accordion. And that husband of hers." She rolled her eyes. My grandmother hates Dilworth Stocker, which is one of the reasons I like my grandmother even though I don't really understand her. "We might come from fish, Ezra, but he's a sheep, I tell you. He's a descendant of some kind of herd. He's a herded animal, if you know what I mean." I only sort of ever understand her. She's a strange superstitious woman with a lot of theories.

Janie had lost interest. "You can weed the beds out back and at dusk water down the clay tennis court. Oh, and keep the leaves out of the pool. Help yourself to any food." She paused and looked at me, and I guess I was just staring at her. "What?" she said.

"Nothing," I said, glancing around the room. "I'm just taking it all in." There was a lot to take in—a huge shiny kitchen with French doors that opened to a porch banked by windows that overlooked a blue hourglass-shaped pool and a fence-enclosed tennis court. "Is the convertible yours?"

"Yeah," she said. "A gift for my sweet sixteen."

"It's nice."

"Start in the flower beds," she said. "Kermit's coming over to play tennis with Elsie and me. Kermit Willis? Elsie Finner?"

It was kind of a compliment that she thought it remotely possible that I'd know them. But I didn't. I shrugged and she seemed a little relieved. In most places, there'd be more social separation because of wealth, and I was used to picking up on the distinctions of old and new money. I'd studied it in boarding school, had become a pro. But because Greenville is so small, there's some overlapping—tight circles that by social necessity have to overlap, for example, to fill a wedding reception at the country club where Janie and I had met a couple years before.

I just stood there for a minute, hoping the tour wasn't over, hoping she'd tell me which thing was a weed and which was about to bloom into a prize-winning rose.

Janie was pouring juice. She was all business now, no longer the girl with the butterfly in her throat. She turned around. "The tools are out in the garage, hung up." She smiled, but not with her mouth, just squinting her eyes.

Kermit pulled his Saab right up to the court's fence, turfing about ten feet of lawn, which I was pretty indignant about, considering I was the gardener and would probably have to reseed or sod or do whatever gardeners would do in a situation like that and knowing, too, that I'd never do anything about it at all.

But, really, the day would turn out pretty good for me. A few things went my way. Kermit, a real prick actually, had started going with a college girl he'd brought with him to round out the foursome, and Elsie Finner showed up, too, with her mother's cook's son, Manuel. I walked around the yard, watering the grass with my thumb pressed over the opening of a green hose. There was probably an elaborate sprinkler system somewhere, but I had dug up only the hose and only watered as far away from the spigot as it would reach. I watched them from the little row of windows in the garage door, then from the kitchen where I ate a couple bowls of their low-fat cereal. It was obvious that Janie hadn't been expecting the college girl, dressed in ratty jeans and a cut-off shirt. She was beautiful, fresh-faced, like a camp counselor. She seemed to think everything was hilarious and had this loud, kind of throaty laugh. It was obvious, too, that there'd been some sort of relationship between Janie and Kermit that maybe had been a kind of touchy-feely thing but unspoken, just my guess, and that it had abruptly dissolved, because of this college girl, which was the first news flash that Janie had gotten about it.

He and the college girl swapped a flask back and forth and played doubles drunk. Elsie was there with Manuel, who wasn't wearing a shirt. She kissed him open-mouthed in front of everyone. She was being bold, breaking boundaries. She was slumming, and Manuel didn't seem the least bit unhappy about it. I don't know if Manuel spoke English. I never heard him say anything, and he smiled like a foreigner all the time, especially if anyone gestured his way or said his name. He didn't play but sat along the fence and became, as a matter of course, the ball boy, which he seemed okay about. Janie was the only one playing to win and she did win, each match, each point, a little grunt with her backhand. And then everyone went home. Elsie let Manuel drive her Volvo, and they spun out of the driveway, Manuel waving happily out the sunroof, followed by Kermit and his college girl, who beeped twice.

I think it was the following combination of things that made Janie interested in me: 1) Elsie Finner introducing the concept of slumming. I was, after all, the help, the gardener, a servant, really, just like Manuel's mother and Manuel, the ball boy; 2) Kermit Willis being out of the picture, all caught up in his newfound interest in older women. I'm not stupid. I don't think Janie Pinkering was ever really in love with me, but somehow the idea of me wasn't so bad or was suddenly convenient. In any case, she came up to me while I was struggling to get the hose to the clay courts to water them down for the night. It was dusk, and bats had begun to circle high above us.

She said, "You seem like a tireless virgin. Are you like fanatical about it? Or just by chance and sticking with it, doggedly."

I froze, bent over the hose like something not fully evolved. "What?" I understood what each word meant; they were the kinds of words she'd probably recently picked up studying SAT vocabulary. But I thought maybe I'd misunderstood her completely. It had happened to me before. My grandmother said she'd bought my stepdad rubbers for Christmas and I kind of freaked, staring at her like she was crazy, and then she said, "Galoshes, to wear over his shoes and keep them dry in the rain." Or I thought maybe she'd said something wrong. I once told Rudy that one of the senior guys had gotten an IUD over Christmas and I'd meant to say DUI. So I've learned to just be calm, like everything's normal, and to make people repeat themselves.

But Janie didn't repeat herself. She said, "You heard me." She touched my arm, first the part covered by my shirtsleeve and then the bare arm itself. "C'mon. I'll show you how to lure a bat."

"I've got to water the courts," I said, as if I suddenly cared. "Bring the hose."

She stepped to the middle of the court and swung her racket back and then hit a ball up into the sky, her skirt swishing around her taut thighs. The bats dipped and swooped, diving for what they thought were fat juicy moths. I stood there spraying water as evenly as I could across the court. I had no idea what I was doing, how much water courts needed to be healthy. I watched Janie in the dim light, her white skirt swishing, the swing of her arm, her hair, too, swaying on her back, and all the time the smell of wet clay rising up around me. Each time she shot the ball just a bit lower until the bats were flapping around our heads. One came so close that she screamed and grabbed me around the chest, laughing, breathless. She jerked my arm in a way that made the water shoot up over our heads for a second, like a quick rain. I took my thumb off the hose and let the water pour out around our feet.

Janie giggled, holding her hand to her throat, as if the butterfly were there tickling her. And then she looked at me. "We've got to do something about you, Ezra Stocker. You need serious work."

I agreed.

By now it was dark, and I followed Janie through the house blindly. She held my hand but walked quickly, almost jogging up the turned staircase to her bedroom. Her hand was smallish and a bit damp. I thought about Pete Duvet and I felt lucky that I didn't have his sweaty palms, dry cough, and that lingering scent of peanut butter. I said to myself, *Well, if nothing else, you've got that going for you.*

In her bedroom, she turned on one lamp in the corner and closed the curtains. She rummaged through a little top drawer of her dresser, underwear, I imagined, little flimsy things by the way she flicked through them. She pulled out a plastic baggy of pot, a box of wrappers, and, from the side of a fat candle on her dresser, a matchbox. Her room was big with a high ceiling and a window seat. She kneeled on her bed and began rolling a joint. I'd smoked once before on Rudy's dad's boat the previous summer. It was actually Rudy's dad's weed that we'd stolen from some little almost-hidden hatch belowdecks. It was just the two of us. We smoked just one joint while his dad was onshore. Rudy got so hysterical that he said he thought his ribs were going to puncture some major organ. I didn't think that I felt much of anything at first, a little scratch in my throat, but that's about it. I was a little freaked out by how much Rudy looked like a donkey, his horsey teeth, all that braying, a donkey with braces and miniature rubber bands. Then, out in these high weeds where Rudy took me to spy on some girls who were supposedly naked, he kind of lost his mind. Smoking pot makes me a little nervous. I've seen it affect people, you see.

Janie said, "Sit down, Stocker. You're so, you know, stiff."

I sat down, but gently, like an alarm might go off if I applied too much weight to the bedsprings.

"Can you believe that girl Kermit brought? Did you see her? What an idiot. She can't return a serve to save her ass. Did you see her ass? College girls gain fifteen pounds, I hear, as soon as they unpack. I won't because I'm aware of it." She was spreading the dry green leaves, trying to work out a few clumps. She licked the rolling paper with the tip of her tongue, just the tip, just wet enough. "I'm going to go to Brown. It's the only school that's laid back, but still respectable."

I was thinking about my dad, that he'd have had a guitar with him. He'd have been barefoot, showing off his webless toes. He'd have started strumming and singing with his eyes closed. I worried suddenly about the scissor cuts that my mother had made in my underwear. I wondered if we'd get that far. I thought, too, of my stepdad. He'd scored my mom, so he must have done something right. I tried to puff up my chest a little to give the appearance of being bigger, broader, but Janie picked up the matches and looked over at me.

"Are you holding your breath?"

"No," I said, letting the air slide out of me.

She lit the joint and took a drag, her lips a little loose around its tip. I could hear a small crackle. She held it all in, swallowing now and then, and passed it to me. I did my best, took a drag, my throat burning.

Janie said, "My mom's in Santa Cruz and my dad's speaking about feet at some convention in New Orleans, but how many conventions about feet can you have in New Orleans in one year? My mom knows, of course, that there's someone in New Orleans, but she looks the other way. It's such bullshit. Adults are cowards."

I passed the joint back and nodded, trying to hold the smoke in.

"My mom told me that when they were young, they were crazy about each other. That once she asked my dad this question: 'Would you have an affair with me if I was the other woman?' What do you think the answer to that should be?"

"No," I said. "He should say no because, you know, he's loyal."

"Yes," she said. "That's how my dad answered. 'No.' But my mom told me that she started to cry, that they were on a beach vacation on Martha's Vineyard. It had rained for three days straight, and she locked herself in her bedroom. Do you know why?"

I had no idea.

"She said that he didn't think she was sexy enough, you know, to take him away from his wife. As if his wife were just a ball and chain all of a sudden and not her at all. And so what did he do?"

"He changed his answer?" I was guessing.

"Sure. He said that of course she was beautiful and sexy

enough to tempt him away, and, although this was really the answer she wanted, she never really trusted him after that."

"That's crazy!" I said.

"Sure," Janie said. "That's the point of the story. How crazy people are. Totally fucked up."

And I thought of Dilworth Stocker, how if he didn't have so much to prove, he could be an okay guy. I pictured the way he seemed to love shaking hands, gruffly pulling the person toward him, always clenching too hard. Why does he have to go around shaking every guy's hand so rough like he's trying to nail everybody down to earth? I thought if only there weren't all this handshaking bullshit, each man tethering himself to the next, each handshake saying, *Still one of us, right?* If we'd just let ourselves go, without all this bullshit handshaking and nodding, and then I imagined Dilworth Stocker dropping his nail clippers to the tiled floor, rising up, right out of the steamy bathroom, out the open window, up into the sky. I imagined all the men on our block at their lawn mowers and mailboxes, waxing their cars, suddenly lifting off the ground, swimming through the air. My stepdad's towel now flying over his head like a flag, all of them rising and rising and singing, in unison, like choirboys.

Janie went on, "And if they are happy, just happen to be by dumb luck, they will fuck it up on purpose. That's what I'm trying to say. My mother says that a woman is never just one woman, but she's sometimes all the women she's ever known or thought about or heard of. That's the only intelligent thing my mother's ever said to me. I don't really understand it, but I do at the same time."

By this point, I was stoned. I thought of my mother, how she was night and day, two women, at the very least, but also she'd been my dad's wife, and then the opposite, Dilworth's wife and in between the two, this woman dragging man after man into her bed, and Miss New Jersey, too, that she'd once been my age, her dad just newly dead. And I believed that Janie Pinkering was not only the most beautiful girl in the world but also the wisest, and I said that part out loud, stupidly. "You're so wise," I said.

In any case, no matter how stupid it sounded, something about it was right and Janie said, "Let's fuck in my parents' bed. It's way bigger."

Pixie

Dreaming of Underwater Keys

I wasn't sleeping much. I could take pills and drift off, but then I would have the dream about my father and the keys, and I would wake up. When Dilworth and I were first married and I couldn't go back to sleep after this dream, I would wake him, and he would drag himself up from sleep and say, "What is it, kitten? What's got you so upset?" But he caught on soon enough that there was nothing that he could do to help and so he became a heavy sleeper, he learned to roll to his left side with his deaf ear up—the one blown out as a kid when he exploded a bike tire by over pumping it. I couldn't lie in bed, listening to Dilworth snore, the deep rattle of his body. I got up and walked through the dark house.

Last summer it was at its worst. I walked from room to room. I watched Mitzie sleep, knowing that if I woke her she'd put her chubby arm around my neck and stroke my hair, that she wouldn't fall asleep until I had drifted off first. She has that kind of conscientiousness. Mitzie is the type of child who looks at your face wanting only to please. And if she makes you happy, she smiles so brightly you'd think there was a light glowing up from her stomach. It's a dangerous need in her, but who knows how to stop it? I never woke her. Sometimes I caught Ezra in the kitchen, filling up his growing body. I thought that perhaps the past was coming back to me so strongly because Ezra was almost the age I was then, that he was reminding me of what it was like to be young, everything stretching out in front of me, and that may have been part of it. Ezra has known me forever, or so it seems, because I reinvented myself when he was born, became someone else in motherhood. When I was first pregnant, I couldn't imagine a child inside me. I envisioned a landscape, an ocean turning in on itself, a moving mountain, a field that could fold and unfold, my body overtaken by a living map. I didn't have the knowledge that life was simply passing through me, that the child wouldn't be born as much as he would be taken from me, if you know what I mean. And maybe giving up Ezra, handing him over again to the world, this time as a man, I was losing a piece of my self-invention. I was becoming less of a mother and since there was no new role to slip into, I began to look backward for old ones. It isn't a good idea to escape to a place you've escaped from. Like trying to dig your way out of a prison only to wind up having tunneled into the solitary confinement cell; it makes things twice as difficult.

I watched Ezra hunched over a cereal bowl, his almost man-size hands dwarfing the spoon, and I imagine telling him things about my life. Every once in a while my mouth would open, but I didn't know where to start. Sometimes I thought he already knew. I have always had the feeling that we are wound by the same infinite string, a cord that keeps us attached, that is always just taut enough for us to tell if the other is trembling. His relationship with the troublemaking Pinkering girl, for example, was obvious enough to me, even though I was barely holding on myself. We were both aware of a change in the other. Ezra knew that I was feverish. I think that he could see me trying to tip myself forward into my life. It's hard to explain. I could be there with Ezra, and I would feel like if I could only take a deep breath, fill my chest with air, I could catch up with myself, my own existence, which seemed to sit just three inches in front of me. Sometimes I would clean in the middle of the night. I would scrub down the floors with a bristle brush on my hands and knees, because it was physical. It was real. No one could deny that I was a woman scrubbing a floor, and that afterward the floors were shining. Ezra would see the shining floors, the look of my eyes, a glaze, maybe, and he knew something. He could tell.

The dream kept me up, made me sleepless, a creature pacing the house. I'd had the same dream ever since my father died. It was about my father and the man. These are not things you talk about, dreams of little bike-lock keys pouring out of my father's mouth, my father underwater, his thin hair haloing out of his head, a fan of hair waving back and forth like seaweed. I'd never told anyone about them, especially not when I was young. I'd memorized a quote from Emily Post: "Don't dilate on your own problems. Your audience has them, too, and won't be entertained by yours." But I don't think that I've ever known anyone who dreamed about their dead father's mouth spilling over with keys for nearly twenty years.

In the dream, I was there with him, always trying to catch one key, just one, but there were so many he was coughing them up, and I was caught in a storm of them like in a game show, one of those windowed closets with all the money swirling around the contestant, who was always some panicked housewife. And the man was always coming toward us, swimming but with his arms to his side, like an eel, his hair perfectly in place except for that one greasy lock that fell on his forehead, even though he was swimming toward me and all his hair should have been back.

Walking the house at night after these dreams, I missed Cliff singing to me when I was scared as a little kid. Often, in the quiet darkness, I took out a box of his letters and organized the envelopes, spread the pages out on the dining-room table. The paper was thin, their folds as comfortable and worn as a map's. I'd try to hum the way Cliff hummed, but I couldn't get it right. I've never gotten it right. Sometimes I can almost hear his voice, I can almost replay it in my head, but then just as quickly as it shows up, it's gone.

Cliff claimed as soon as he was on the plane he'd forget all about Bayonne, which he called "the shit-hole," that he'd forget about my mother and me and my father, too. But in the first letter, he said that he saw us in his head even more than he had when we were all living together and Dad was there, too. He was feeling the same way I was last summer, divided between past and present. This was my favorite letter. "I can see us all together in the kitchen, shuffling around each other, sometimes talking, sometimes not. And it's clear as a bell, as a drain at the bottom of a tub of water." I read it again and again, and I could see us in the kitchen, just as he'd said it, shuffling, mumbling, a chorus of bodies that made up a family. The image of the tub stuck with me.

I read all the letters, although I didn't want to, although I wanted to stop right there, before they became ugly. I read about the wetness, that they could hardly ever get dry over there what with the constant rain. He was in places I didn't remember ever hearing of: Laik He and Phu Cong and then Highway 15; I imagined the American slice of highway running through jungles and old-world villages. He slept in rice paddies and pea fields that seemed to have rising tides. He talked about the leeches that they had to burn off with cigarettes or, sometimes, lighter fluid. There were rats, too, that would run right over his face while he was lying down at night. And when they did get dry, they'd do anything to stay dry. That was how they lost a soldier named Briggs. Cliff didn't know Briggs very well. But when my brother got there, everybody was dry. The rain had stopped for a couple days. They'd moved camp uphill; that's where he joined up. He became good friends with this black guy named Jamison from New York City, and all Jamison could talk about was how fucking glad he was to have dry socks. They'd hung them on tree limbs to dry out with what little sun made it down through the wide leaves. But it didn't last long and soon they were sent down toward the swamps, and that night there was gunfire and a few of them were on patrol, Jamison and Briggs and Cliff. And an older soldier told them to jump in the swamp, for cover, and my brother did and Jamison, too. But Briggs didn't. He couldn't get wet again. He stood there with his gun just loose at his side. Cliff turned around to yell at him. And Jamison's face was a dark purple, the cords of his neck standing out, he was screaming at Briggs so hard. But Briggs didn't move, just shook his head, and the bullets kicked into him, his stomach first. He folded to his knees, and then his shoulder, his legs out straight, and he was dead, that's how Cliff put it. Just writhing with all that bullet fire and then nothing. I thought about these things last summer more than I did when I first read about them. I went over them in my mind. I was stuck, the way I get sometimes, like a needle in a record groove, a hitch in the song played over and over. I imagined Cliff replaying our lives, too, as he tried to sleep. He was just a kid for Chrissakes! Not much older than Ezra.

In an early letter Cliff wrote that he hadn't killed anybody yet, which had been a surprise to me. I'd thought that he'd open fire the minute they let him down off the plane he'd been so angry. But he told me he was ready. He said it was his job, his duty. He said he was an American more than anything else. More than he was a Kitchy. He said that anyone could tell he wasn't much of a Kitchy, nothing like our father. But that wasn't true. Everyone always said that he looked like our father, aside from Cliff's girlish mouth. He said he was an American, first and foremost.

And I remembered this letter better than the rest, because it made me sad, much sadder than when he'd left that afternoon with his suitcase for basic training, because, I guess, I'd felt like he was really gone and that maybe he hadn't ever really been there anyway. I knew that Cliff was doing the only thing he could do, and even though I hated people killing each other, I hoped he did get to kill someone and that he could come back home to us having done what he needed to do, still alive.

Meanwhile I was living with my mother, the two of us alone. After my father died, my mother drank coffee, smoked cigarettes every night, and then she went to work with the Chinese women who chattered like a horde of mice when she walked into the room. My mother rarely spoke, and I never saw her cry. We were quiet, not even polite. Once I remember she told me to get out of the bathroom and stop staring at myself.

She was standing outside the bathroom door and she said, "You'll cross your eyes, staring at yourself that way, and they'll stick. A curse!" The truth was that my mother could stop going to Mass if she wanted, but she couldn't stop being superstitious. It's how she was raised. It's the way thoughts occur to her in her brain.

And I started to cry because I hated her and I believed she was never a beauty. I hated her bent shoulders and the way she wiped her nose with the back of her hand. The only person who ever looked at her was the butcher, Mr. Graziano, with his belly as round as a rump roast. After my father died, I was the one who went to the butcher, and he looked at me like I was the saddest thing he'd ever seen. He gave me an extra side of beef for free. He said, "How's ya motha doing? She needs her strength." He was married to a pug-faced woman and had three kids, older than me and Cliff, daughters that he couldn't marry off. But aside from him, no one even glanced at her. I always knew that there was something about the butcher, but what exactly I couldn't say. My mother grew up in the mountains of West Virginia, dirty and barefoot. She wasn't a beauty, but she had some other kind of power that I've never been able to put a name to. But I knew that she didn't understand what it was like to be beautiful, to be me, and I thought of Christina the Astonishing in a tree, in an oven, soaring to church rafters like an angel—anything to escape these awful dirty, heavy bodies. Twenty years now and sometimes I can still smell the man on me.

I opened the door and said, "I'm not staring into the mirror," even though I had been. I said, "I was in here crying because Daddy's dead. Why don't you cry? How come you've never once cried?"

She stared at me, shocked, the color drained from her cheeks. Her eyes looked like they might cry. They were suddenly wet and shimmery. And then she narrowed her eyes and she spoke in this deep, low voice that I'd never heard before. "Women can't chain their hands behind their backs and jump into a river. We can never give in. One day you'll know that I never once gave in, not even in the smallest way."

I have held on to this all my life. That's what I do. I remember all the things that I don't understand. I remember them vividly, hoping that one day they'll become clear.

I didn't talk to anybody about these things, not even Jimmy Vietree, who talked all the time when we met by the train tracks. He talked about geometry class, his dog's gimp leg, his brother's sleeper hold. And he told me to say something, to tell him anything, but I didn't. I wanted to tell him that my family—what was left of it—had given up on religion, that my body wasn't meant to genuflect like the nuns taught us. My head wasn't meant to be bowed, that my body arched naturally like all those blades of wet grass blown back by the passing trains. My knees were naturally weak and my head got heavy with something just as simple as wanting, and mostly that I wasn't anything like my mother: afraid of pleasure, afraid to be happy because she couldn't stand the loss of it. I could have told him about our vacation at the Jersey Shore, how my father caught a golden, gold-eyed fish and held it up over his head, its scales shiny, polished-looking in the sun, that my mother cooked the fish in our cottage, but how she couldn't wear the hat, couldn't just make him happy and put it on her head. I should have said all these things and more. I needed to, but couldn't.

With Jimmy I didn't have to say anything. I just looked at him, his freckled face, his rumpled hair. He was plain and dull. I didn't think anyone would believe him even if he told people about us. We stretched against each other, almost like two pale cats. At school, the nuns kept it up, filmstrips of dirty loveless girls, lessons in how to say *no*, because everyone should say *no*, but all I could think about was how I tried to shake my head when Jimmy pressed against me. I mouthed *no*, until it became a breath, a whisper, until it felt like my hips rang with it, *no, no, no*, as mechanical as the train's churn and above it, I could always hear its whistled moan rising.

Cliff's letters spread out on the dining-room table, its dim chandelier overhead, I remembered lying on top of Jimmy Vietree, almost hearing myself say that I wanted to live some-place else, anywhere else than with my mother, the smell of her cabbage, limp from being cooked and cooked, meat boiled till it had no taste and how, if I walked into the room she pretended

not to see me, that it would be easier for her if I was gone like
my father and Cliff and even God, too, since she'd kicked Him
out. I'd been the only one left to remind her of what used to be
true. She said things like, "Do you have to walk so loud, like a
horse clomping in a stall?" and "Don't slurp your broth." She
said, "Why do you practice accordion? It's too hard for you. It
just comes out squeaks." I knew what she really wanted. She
wanted me to disappear, to no longer exist, to drown, to fall to
consumption, to go to war. She would turn the television up,
and the house filled with the beeping sounds of a game show, of
happy, happy people cheering. I remembered her saying once
that she couldn't love me, that it was for my own good, because
I'd just be taken away, that life was a giant scale of good and
bad, and that if she loved me too much, the scale would have to
tip. I remembered her words, the idea of her words pouring
through me, maybe even the sound of water rushing in from
somewhere, but I couldn't remember where we were or when.
And despite herself, despite all her efforts to keep that scale balanced, I thought she did love me, in some way that she couldn't
help. But what I didn't realize, in my thin nightgown on those
sleepless summer nights, was that I finally was giving in to her.
After all these years I was finally disappearing.

There's one other thing about the dream and this you have
to keep in mind. I knew that if I could get one key, just one
key, I could unlock the bike lock, and my father could save me.
He could fight off the man, and I could climb on my father's
back, like when I was little in the Bayonne Public Pool and my
father would take me for rides, my arms hugging his neck. But
I could never get a key, and the man never stopped coming.

Ezra

Rule #3: If you can't play guitar, or
if you do but don't have a guitar handy,
the next-best thing with women is
to do what you're told, to follow
directions.

M r. and Mrs. Pinkering's bedroom was enormous with a
king-size bed. Evidently, Mrs. Pinkering had complete
control over the decor, because there wasn't the slightest trace
of manliness, no dark colors, no stripes, only white and lace,
pillows and perfume bottles. There was a giant fan in one corner as if at some time during the day Mrs. Pinkering lay in bed
and had a servant fan her, maybe two servants, the second just
to feed her grapes. I was feeling more relaxed—not relaxed
enough to expect servants to come in with fans and grapes, but
relaxed enough to sprawl out a little in the Pinkerings' bed,
almost like a king myself. Janie flipped off her tennis shoes
and peeled off her socks. Her feet were pale and petite.

She said, "Well, get naked." And she opened a double
closet door and stepped inside where I saw her rummaging
again in a chest of drawers. She pulled a chain in the closet

ceiling, and a bulb switched on. I could see her father's suits on hangers, sweaters folded in cubby shelves.

I took off my shirt. It smelled like grass and clay. I remembered Rudy telling me that you can't come too quickly or the girls will be pissed. Rudy thinks he's a real stud because he did it with his cousin's friend's sister in somebody's basement remodeled to look like a billiards room, somebody's dad's smoking lounge. Rudy is a pervert and sometimes he goes too far. He told me to think of something else, something boring, like Mr. Quitter's geometry class, but Arlene Mercer sat next to me at the round table in Mr. Quitter's geometry class, so close I could hear her breathe. I could smell her bubble gum. We aren't allowed to chew gum, which made her all the more rebellious and tantalizing.

I thought instead of Dilworth Stocker. What could be more dull? My stepdad, the finicky fuck, with a towel around his waist, parting and combing his black shiny hair, shaving with his electric razor, clipping his toenails with one foot on the toilet seat.

Janie unbuttoned and unzipped her tennis skirt, let it parachute to her feet. Her panties were indeed white, as glowingly white as I'd glimpsed them when she was sitting on the hood of the powder blue convertible earlier that day. She was still looking through her father's socks. I unbuckled my belt and stepped out of my khaki shorts and my underwear in one swift motion so the underwear would be hidden in the shorts. I quickly pulled off my sneakers, my socks, and slipped under the Pinkerings' flower-printed sheets before she could see my webbed toes. I realized that this might really be it, sex, the real thing. I thought about what I'd imagined it to be like, the way I'd first struggled to put pictures to the sounds from behind my mother's bedroom door where she took the men from the green kitchen table, and Dilworth's awkward, racy jokes, and Rudy's stories from the basement/smoking lounge, plus *Blue Lagoon*-type movies and books by Henry Miller. I hoped that I'd figure it out, but I was nervous—despite the pot or maybe more aware because of it—rattled, especially in comparison to Janie, who was calm, self-assured. I wondered how many guys had been here before me, imagined them lined up, in order of ability. I wondered where she'd shuffle me in, if I'd get to scoot up past Kermit, and how I'd leer at him as I passed by. But of course I wasn't so sure I'd get to pass Kermit at all. I decided that I'd be led to the end of the line, the usual spot I had on every team I'd ever been on.

Janie Pinkering shimmied out of her shirt. She had something in her hand and flipped it at me while she unhooked her bra, tiptoed out of her panties. "It's a French tickler. Like my dad couldn't just have a normal condom."

I opened the package and saw a condom with a plastic flower on its tip. I looked at Janie, standing by the bed, naked, her breasts full and round, her stomach tan, little bikini lines running up her hips.

"Scoot over," she said. And I rolled to my back to wrestle the condom on. Janie kicked back the sheets, and I felt like a god, not a great god, but a small, lucky god, my dick a giant flower on the flower-printed sheets. She straddled me, bending down to kiss me. Her mouth warm on my mouth, her tongue soft and wet. She writhed around and then slipped me inside her, and my mind shot past Rudy, Mr. Quitter's calculus, Arlene Mercer's sweet bubble-gum breath. It flew past Dilworth Stocker flying naked with all the men in our neighborhood lifted up from their sod, their lawn chairs. It landed on my mother smiling at me from the stage, her hand cupped in that Miss New Jersey wave. She's proud of me. I can tell by the way she kind of tucks her chin to her chest and then I look up at Janie Pinkering—the heave and sway of her breasts, her soft hair, the soft puffs of her breath, and, although I know it's wrong and I hate it, I see my mother, too. And that's the end of it.

Janie wasn't mad at how quickly I came, the way Rudy claimed all women would be, an opinion he probably formed on the basis of having once disappointed his cousin's sister's friend in that remodeled basement/smoking lounge where he probably remembers himself wearing a velvet smoking jacket. Janie didn't seem to think anything of it at all. She just lay on her back a little breathless. Not smiling, intense, her eyebrows knitted as if she were thinking hard, and I figured that the line of guys who'd gotten this far—Kermit Willis plus whoever else—they had come quickly, too, and that there wasn't so much a line ordered on ability but just a shaggy crowd, a gang of us all wondering what might happen next.

She pulled the covers up under her chin and stared at the ceiling. "I hate my dad."

I'd really only just started recently to hate all the people around me—Mitzie was okay, in her own high-strung, sad little way, and my grandmother was weird with all the superstitious stuff but quiet and disinterested in me enough to be sincere, just fine with me. But I hated my stepdad for walking around all forearms and beefy shoulders, as if he were the quin-tessential man, and my real father for getting away with call-ing himself a father at all, and my mom, too, but for her it was the kind of sick hate that can only come from loving someone too much.

I didn't want to offer too much. "I hate my stepdad," I said. "He likes to suck his teeth, little channels of cold air. He likes to sit in his leather chair, tugging at the crotch of his snug golf pants, flipping from one sports channel to the other. He'll watch anything supposedly athletic, even those so-called sports shows where fat guys haul refrigerators around on their backs." But I knew that this wasn't what Janie was getting at.

She looked over at me and smiled, a kind of "that's sweet" type of smile. Then she got up and walked to her bedroom naked. A minute later she came back into her parents' bed-room wrapped in a towel.

"I'm taking a shower," she said. "I'll see you tomorrow."

"Will you?" I asked, because I wasn't so sure she'd really be here. It sounded like a brush-off.

"Yes, Stocker," she said. "You're the gardener, right? You've got a job to do." She walked over to me and kissed me lightly on the mouth. "I'll see you tomorrow."

I got dressed to the sound of Janie's shower. I imagined how the water was spraying her back, her chest, pouring down her yellow hair. I found my way out of the Pinkerings' dark house by sliding my hand against the walls. I walked home, not on the sidewalk, but almost in the middle of the street, which was empty. It was late, nearly midnight, and I felt like I was seeing things new, for the first time, maybe not the way they actually were, particularly, but as they could be. The sky was jammed with stars, and I walked slowly, watching my shadow grow tall and shrink and grow tall again as I passed under each streetlight. It was quiet, but everything seemed loud, each streetlight buzzing. The moon, a perfect bright circle, like a spotlight shining down on my life. I imagined it shining down on me and Janie, our bodies writhing on her parents' wide bed.

I didn't go straight to the pool bungalow. I was starving. I walked around the house to the back door into the kitchen. That's where my mother found me, staring into the fridge.

"The turkey doesn't jump into a sandwich and smear itself with mayonnaise." She shoved me out of the way and pulled out the fixings for a sandwich, her hip holding open the fridge door. She was wearing a short, thin bathrobe, tied to a tight knot at the waist as if put on angry, and I knew she was angry. I thought maybe it was just that it was so late and I hadn't called. But maybe she knew about Janie already, that one of the Pinkerings had come home early and had found out and called my mother, or that she could just tell, she just knew, because mothers can know these things. "So, you do a lot of gardening in the dark?"

"No," I said, laughing. I sat down at the breakfast table and looked out the window to the pool bungalow. I'd left a lamp on all day. There was light streaming out of the windows.

"I hear the Pinkerings are out of town. Dilworth was worried if you'd know what to do without at least one of them there to help you through it." I didn't say anything. She paused. "Are you going to answer me?" she asked, her knife clinking around in the near-empty jar of mayo and then spreading the little white clumps on the bread, a little too hard, with her elbow cocked.

"You didn't ask a question," I said.

"I take it you met Janie." But then she rephrased it, like a contestant on *Jeopardy!* who's just remembered to phrase the answer in the form of a question. "I mean, did you meet Janie?"

"Yes, I did, in fact," I said, extra-politely, a reward for her having followed my rules.

"And?"

"And what?"

She cut the sandwich into four triangles, the way I'd always requested it as a little kid. "Why are you being so coy? All I'm asking is if that's the reason you're so late? Did you two hit it off?"

I took a bite and talked with my mouth full. "Janie's okay. Didn't I meet her at somebody's wedding? At the country club a couple years ago?"

"I'm not so sure she's right for you, Ezra. I know Janie Pinkering. I know how much trouble she can get into." She was standing over me, the light at her back, her face was all shadows. I couldn't tell if she was really angry now or if it was just the shadows. But she seemed to be pressing down on me, like she really knew everything, like she'd been in the audience for the spotlight performance.

I panicked. "Didn't you tell me just yesterday to get laid?"

"Ezra! My god, did you sleep with her?"

I repeated my question, "Didn't you tell me *just yesterday* to get laid? To have sex while I was still young?"

"What kind of a mother do you think I am?" she asked in all seriousness. "What kind of a mother would *say* something like that?" Suddenly, she looked a little wild to me, her hands thrown off her hips, palms open at her sides. Her eyes darted back and forth, searching mine.

"A very strange mother," I said. "Very, very strange." And I picked up my plate and walked out the back door. I strode to the sunken spot in the yard where the pool once was and I sat there, ate my sandwich, and then lay back, looking up at the sky, knowing that my mother, from one of the dark windows of the house, was watching me.

Pixie

Practical Tips from Miss Bayonne,
Runner-up

Ezra believed that I only had him to concentrate on. He'd gotten it in his head that all of my thoughts swirled around him. And I was doing my best to keep him on a good, straight path. I was trying to keep our lives as close to normal as possible. I knew that things were teetering around me, the entire house precarious—Dilworth, Mitzie, Ezra, and me— the four of us like little glass figurines. I didn't know it then, but looking back I know that there was a lot of static, that sometimes I could barely hear people above the noise in my head, like the loud hum of an air conditioner. And when I think of it, didn't Mitzie's voice get louder, more shrill, so loud, in fact, that someone could hear her across a great divide? Sometimes I wasn't sure if I was talking too loudly as well, if I hadn't started to sound like Mitzie with her adenoidally shrill voice. But it wasn't Ezra that I was thinking about, although I should have been—he was becoming a man, wasn't he, moment to moment, taking on some new shape. Sometimes I swore that I could see his bones stretching, his boy's bones hardening, thickening until his jaw was really almost tough, his Adam's apple sharp in his throat. And I wasn't thinking about Mitzie, who needed to be allowed to be a little girl, not weighed down by the responsibilities of making her mother happy and contented with her life. I tried, I did, to look at the two of them, to focus on Ezra and Mitzie, to remain present. I could almost hear them calling to me from the other side of the loud hum. And the hum was the past, the train barreling down those tracks, the rushing air, and the quiet scraping of my mother's spoon against the bottom of a pot. The hum reminded me of the time my first husband, Russell, took me and Ezra to a college buddy's garage where he wheeled out a huge electric telescope so that we could see Saturn, what turned out not to be a fiery, burning planet but a disappointment: a ball, its simple hoop as ordinary as a fourth-grader's paper cutout for the science fair. But I remembered the thick black cord, the instant rattle of the machinery when it was plugged in, how when I looked through the eyepiece, my cheek quivered, the buzzing was so loud. My tongue vibrated. That's what it was like, the way I saw everything in those days, through the humming, buzzing electric past.

Like the night Ezra told me he'd slept with Janie Pinkering, probably losing his virginity with her, I looked out my window to the pool bungalow and the indentation where the dirt-filled pool was. I could see Ezra sitting on the grass. I tried to imagine Ezra and Janie Pinkering; Ezra something of a delicate flower, just a boy, really, and I circled back to the image of Jimmy Vietree, words forever pouring out of his crooked teeth, nervously talking to fill up silence, and Janie, a teenage girl, headstrong, just learning that she's powerful. I remembered how it felt, the new power of it, what it was like carrying that gun, and I imagined her firing the gun all around, not Ezra's head but Jimmy Vietree's. See how it's all confused.

The past, its hum swelled, and although I was standing there looking at my son in the middle of the night, one thought collided into the next, and suddenly I was thinking about Wanda Sorenski. You see, I gave up on reading everything in the Bayonne Library on the subject of manners after I met Wanda and she took me under her wing. To be Miss Bayonne, to pull it off successfully, I needed more practical tips than show cattle and dahlias. She lived in the neighborhood, and I knew her from when we'd been regular churchgoers. Wanda had been runner-up Miss Bayonne four years earlier. She'd since married and had two kids and a husband who was never at home. He was in the Coast Guard and stationed somewhere not too far away, but still he didn't come home even when he could. She'd spread out a little since her pictures of the pageant. Her face was wider, her legs thicker. There was the beginning of a sag under her chin. And she was always a little tired, always sipping tea and eating only toast. She was almost always feeling just a little sick. But still when you came into her house, even though it was small and dark, all the furniture matched, the curtains and the rug, too, and it didn't smell like cabbage and cigarette smoke like our dingy, mismatched apartment. Her kids rolled around on the floor, a girl and a boy, fighting most

of the time, so you had to talk real loud, but she said that was
good for me, to have to talk with confidence, loudly. She got me
on a schedule. She wanted me to win. She really did. She said
that the first time she saw me at a church-basement social she
thought that I was special. She said that sometimes she wanted
me to win so badly she could almost cry, and once she almost
did. But then she shaped up and said that runner-up Miss
Bayonne didn't ever cry. You could cry like crazy if you won,
but you couldn't even get glassy-eyed when you'd lost. She said,
"You really should never cry. It's never appropriate."

She gave me a list of tips. For shiny hair, I got some hair
serum and put a quarter-cup of vodka in my shampoo. I set my
hair with stale beer to help it hold, and put peroxide on strips
of it and wrapped them in tinfoil to make it lighter here and
there. Lemon helped with shine and blondness. I coated my
hands and feet in Vaseline and slept in gloves and socks to make
my skin softer. I put Ajax on my toothpaste after I'd brushed
my teeth normally and then brushed them again. It sometimes
made me gag a little, the sharp bite of it, but it made my teeth
white, even whiter with some whore-red lipstick for contrast.
That's what she called it, whore-red. She taught me to dab a bit
of clear nail polish on my cheekbones to paste my tendrils to
my face so they would stay put and not grow slack. I got flip-
proof adhesive for the soles of my shoes, and every day I practiced dancing with a short pencil sideways in my mouth that I
bit down on, so I got used to smiling for long periods of time.
Wanda had Super-Glued her ears back, but I didn't have to
because mine were flat enough to my head, and she used
Preparation H to make her eyes less puffy, but mine, she said,

were just fine. I was really and truly becoming someone else.

She knew all about my family. And she said that she didn't want to know anything about boys. She said, "Falling in love should be a secret. A woman should never reveal her secrets." I thought Wanda Sorenski had fallen in love a time or two. And I knew that I wasn't in love with Jimmy Vietree, that I didn't want to be, even though it was plain that he loved me. If I had told him one thing, one true thing about me, I think I might have been able to fall in love with him. It would have been that easy, because I needed love so much and an outlet for it. But I wasn't going to see him anymore by the tracks.

I told Wanda that I got letters from Cliff and I tried not to read them. I did read them, but only once, and then I stuffed them away, to be pored over nearly twenty years later, each one spread out, arranged, and refolded back inside its envelope. In one he said he'd become good friends with this black guy, Jamison, and that he'd never really been friends with a black guy before, not really, even though he'd worked with them and gone to school with them. Now they sat together on patrol. Jamison wasn't letting him know him all at once, the way another white guy would. He kept some things to himself. He did tell him one story, though, about when Jamison was a kid getting money out of the bank for a summer camp, and he ran back to the car where his daddy was waiting for him. When he got there, his daddy slapped his face and told him that a black man never runs down the street with money in his hands. Cliff said that Jamison thought that his daddy was right, and that he'd do the same to his boy if he had one, "because some shit never changes." Jamison had a kid brother who was autistic. He told Cliff that he missed hearing the boy sing, not word-songs, just all of these long beautiful sounds, pure and whole. Jamison said it was the closest thing to hearing God talk right to you.

Cliff said that he'd told Jamison everything about me and our mother and father, and how our father died. He said, "And, Pixie, you won't believe it because you don't understand everything, you don't know what all was going on, but I told Jamison I was glad he was dead. I told Jamison that I'd have killed him if I'd gotten the chance." Cliff said that maybe I'd understand him one day. Maybe not. And that he hoped that I never understood him, and I didn't think I would, not really. Even though we never spoke of it in my family, I knew that he knew about the man, the one who came into my room that night, maybe, I thought, looking for Cliff or looking to steal something, and that my father came in and took care of him. It was dark, but I knew that I'd felt the man on top of me, and I'd seen my father, back-lit by the hall light, his arms over his head, bringing a bat down hard on the man's head. I didn't remember anything else, only the taste of blood because I'd bitten my tongue, warm blood and nothing else. I'd been over it and over it in my head so many times that there was nothing I didn't understand, there was nothing I couldn't see in all of its details. Nothing. Cliff was my big brother and I figured he was being like my mother, who pretended there was some knowledge out in the world that only *she* could give me, and that when she did I'd suddenly be a grown woman. But I was becoming a woman without them. (The same way, I guess, Ezra was becoming a man without me, and certainly without his own father, who'd never really played much of a role.

Dilworth was there, of course, but I wasn't so sure that I wanted Dilworth to be passing on too much to Ezra anyway. He believed in raising boys with a certain amount of roughness and so I never encouraged him to think of himself as Ezra's father.) I wondered how Cliff could hate my father; even with all the lousy things he did—that he was weak for drink and he spent all of our money until there was nothing—he was still our father. I decided that there was something almost evil in Cliff. Really, sometimes I thought that about Cliff, and I hated him. Once I wrote Cliff a letter and told him not to write me and that I hated him, but I couldn't send it.

Wanda told me that she could see another person just under my skin, coming out. And it was like she was my new mother, like my old mother was fading each time I came home, fading into the upholstery of the chair by the window. One day, I figured she wouldn't be there at all. Wanda told me to look in the mirror, and I did, the wood mirror painted to look like gold in her hallway, and I stared and stared. She said, "Do you see her?" And I stared until I saw a pure girl, glowing almost. "I do," I told Wanda. "I really do."

But last summer when I looked into the mirror, I saw only what was behind me: the living room, a floral sofa, big windows with white sheers, the furniture polished to a wet shine. I looked at myself. I tried to make out my face, but there was nothing that I could really latch onto, nothing that seemed like it was really me at all. And if I looked hard enough, I saw the fake-gold-framed mirror, Wanda over my shoulder, her nose and cheeks pink with rouge, and my clean young face, me as the girl I once was, wanting to be pure.

Ezra

Rule #4: Eventually, things
come undone.

All that week, Janie and I lay out in deck chairs by the
pool. I never took a dip. I didn't want to embarrass
myself, having to hold my nose when I jumped in. I'd tell her
it was too cold or I was too tired. But I watched her do laps,
strokes that she made look exotic, backstroke and butterfly.
We ate like grown-ups on an airplane—honey-roasted peanuts
and convoluted mixed drinks that Janie invented at her dad's
bar. We played tennis, and she taught me how to serve, reliev-
ing me of my broad, arching backswing that she said
reminded her of her mother on their vacation to St. John last
spring, teetering on a footstool trying to kill mosquitoes.
Sometimes we'd take the powder blue convertible out on back
roads, where Janie hugged curves and gunned it on straight-
aways. We had sex in the afternoons in her parents' bed. We
rinsed off in her parents' shower, together, lathering up with

her mom's sweet foaming lotions, apricot extracts, and stuff like that. We dried off with her parents' monogrammed towels. It was all perfect. I never weeded or watered the clay courts or cut the grass. Each time Janie jumped into the greenish pool, leaves stirred up and swirled and floated like in a lake you'd find just off a nature trail. I never did actually set foot in the Pinkerings' greenhouse. Every night, it rained, a quick, sometimes thundering rain that had built up all day in the thick humidity causing tight ringlets of the hair not swooped up in Janie's ponytail. The grass grew so heavy and full that it curled over on top of itself. The flower beds were thick and green with weeds that choked the prissier blooms, flowers I couldn't name if my life depended on it. And I dreamed of living there, even when the Pinkerings returned from their separate vacations, and that Dr. Pinkering would see my webbed toes, by accident, one day poolside, and he'd take me into his office and zap the webs right off. I dreamed of becoming part of the family, Ezra Pinkering, although that didn't really make much sense since I supposed I'd have to marry into the family through Janie, but that's what I wanted, not only the steady sex life, although I marveled at that, but to be a Pinkering, from my head to my toes.

I filled out time sheets, ones that Dr. Pinkering had left for me that were normally used by the part-time help at his podiatry office, ones you'd usually punch into a clock. But I filled mine out by hand. I was afraid of getting caught, and suggested every once in a while that I take a crack at mowing the lawn. But Janie would say, "Don't be ridiculous!" Once I took the mower out while I thought she was sleeping, but after the first two or three

ragged pulls on the mower's cord, she appeared at an open
upstairs window, topless, calling me inside. She encouraged me
to count every minute on the time sheet that I was on the
premises. But, in good conscience, I couldn't include the hours I
spent having sex with their daughter and lounging in their bed.
I did, however, put down time spent in their pool, on their clay
tennis court, whenever I was outdoors and generally getting sun
or developing muscle. Those were Dilworth's chief goals, in any
case. But Janie was always at me to put down more hours.
"Look," she said, "my parents wouldn't notice if I shaved my head
bald and burned the house to the ground. It doesn't matter!"

My mother, on the other hand, had decided to create a
diversion. After our late-night conversation about me and
Janie having had sex, my mother hovered around me whenever
she got the chance, dusting under my elbows, sweeping up
under my feet, all of it already cleaned and polished by Helga.
She would say things like, "This really is a nice thing we've
got here." And "You know, your stepfather works very hard.
He provides for us." I was pretty sure that she felt like our life
had a hairline fracture because of my lost virginity, that she felt
like she was losing control and was trying to convince me, and
herself, that our suburban life was like Eden and that I was
eyeing the apple tree, or maybe I'd already taken a bite, but a
small bite that could maybe get Super-Glued back. In any
case, one day she caught me walking out the front door, head-
ing for Janie's. I walked down the stone steps into the yard and
she followed me. She was wearing pink Bermuda shorts and a
pink short-sleeved sweater, her toenails painted to match. She
said, "Ezra, I've made a decision."

"About what?"

"About you. I think that you should spend as much of this summer as possible getting to know your grandmother. She's finally living so very close and she's old, Ezra. An old woman."

"Why don't you get to know her?" I asked.

"She's a link to your past, Ezra."

"She's a link to your past," I said.

"The past is overrated," my mother said. "Just do what I tell you, okay?"

My grandmother had been over a few times for quick dinners with the family, ones she cut short by saying things like, "The bird cages need to be covered," or "I'm missing my program." She was a regular *Columbo* devotee. She never seemed to care in the least that I'd only stopped by once to drop off a stick of butter. She was a no-nonsense type.

My mother said, "She's expecting you to come by today. *Before* the Pinkerings."

I imagined my mother presenting the idea to my grandmother and the old woman saying, "What are we going to talk about, for God's sake? What do I have in common with a sixteen-year-old boy?"

"I don't have much time, you know. I'll go, but I can't stay forever." I walked back up the driveway to get my bike from the garage.

"Apartment 2B," my mother called out.

The hallway of my grandmother's apartment building smelled like dog piss and Chinese food refrying in a wok. It was dark, especially after I'd been outside in the bright sun, and I felt almost blind.

"Who's there?" my grandmother said.

"Ezra."

My grandmother unlocked bolt after bolt to let me in. She never spoke much, but when she did, it was something that you could tell she'd edited down to some essential point. She never wore makeup, never filed her nails, but cut them bluntly across. Her hair was always pulled back in a low clip at the base of her neck, tightly, no tendrils. She was not the type for tendrils. Maybe she'd been beautiful once. There wasn't any technical flaw in her face. In fact, you could trace some of my mother's fine features back to her, but she was missing beauty. She was a big-boned woman, and I'm not trying to say nicely that she was fat. She wasn't ever fat. Her bones were actually big. She was sturdy and had that look that some people have of not just being people but having been put together. She was well constructed. "Cheep-Cheep died in the night," she said. "You'll bury him for me in your parents' yard. I'd do it myself, but I don't have a yard."

All the curtains were drawn, and there were just a few slices of light that fell on the floor through the curtain's edges. Every once in a while, you could hear a feathery rustle from the cages hung on hooks around the living room, wings brushing the cage bars.

She walked into the kitchen, a catch in one hip making her limp, but not really slowing her down. The kitchen light overhead was a weak fluorescent tube that flickered. There was a dead green bird on the counter, limp, its head tilted back, beak shut, eyes open. Its claws were sharp and splayed, rigid. My grandmother pulled a Nescafé jar from the cupboard, twisted its lid, and dumped the grounds into a bowl. Then she stuffed the bird into the jar. It was a tight squeeze, and I could see the bird's one eye pressed to the glass. Its claws folded up under its body. She screwed on the lid.

"Take it," she said.

But I couldn't.

"Here," she said. "What's wrong with you?"

"It looks so dead," I said.

"Think of it as sleeping," she said. "It looks like it's sleeping."

"No," I said. "It looks really dead. Technically, it's dead."

She lifted my hand for me and put the jar in it. "It's just a bird," she said.

"Okay," I said.

And then we fell quiet. "You want juice? I've got juice for you, if you want it."

"No, thanks."

She walked into the living room and cooed with a roll of her tongue. She pulled peanuts from her apron pockets and fed them to the birds. "Are you doing good in school?"

I nodded.

"Your mother wants us to get to know each other. I don't believe in that kind of thing."

"Me neither."

"But lately I haven't been myself. When you get old, I suppose you can sometimes feel the breaking, like the walls of my mind had once been so strong, but now they're cracking here and there. I think of things that I haven't thought of in years! Imagine, suddenly, they're here and each memory real."

She smiled. "I remember a kindly butcher," she said. "A sweet-heart of mine." And then she straightened. "It's not the kind of thing you can explain, Ezra."

"Oh," I said.

"You should go. You're a busy man. I can tell. You proba-bly have a sweetheart of your own."

My cheeks felt hot. I nodded.

"I don't believe in falling in love, either. It seems like a bad investment. I don't recommend it." My mother had mentioned my grandmother's mistrust of marriage and love. I'd heard vague stories about my grandparents' fights. My mother said that they had brawls, really, like two kids. I didn't know much about my grandfather except that he drowned trying to show off, that it was late at night and he was drunk. She walked me to the door. "Poor Cheep-Cheep," she said. "But it's just death, Ezra. It's the way we are punished, the ones taken, but even more, the ones left behind. You ought to get used to it."

I didn't know what to say, although I guess I kind of agreed. I mean I'd never really known anyone who'd died, but my father had gone on to a different life, and I always felt that I was the one who'd been left behind, my same old life minus him. "I'll try," I offered and this seemed to please her.

She nodded. "And say a prayer, too."

"What?"

"Over the bird when you bury it. I would, but I'm not a believer."

"Okay," I said and I walked out the door. I carried the dead bird under one arm, riding my bike one-handed straight to Janie's. I wasn't going to bury the bird and I had no intentions of saying any kind of prayer on behalf of my grandmother for her Cheep-Cheep. I didn't know any prayers anyway. My mother had never taught me to pray. By the time I'd pedaled to Janie's, I decided that I'd toss the jar in the garbage out back, but when I rode up, I saw Janie first thing. I quickly parked my bike by a tree surrounded by pachysandra and I hid the jar behind the tree in the short dark leaves around it.

Janie stepped out on the porch with its white wood furniture and floral cushions. "Where have you been?" she asked.

"My grandmother's place," I said. "I'm supposed to get to know her."

"Oh, I thought maybe you weren't going to show, but here you are."

"Yeah, I'm here."

"Let's forget the swim," she said. "I don't feel like tennis."

She walked upstairs to the bedroom and I followed, trying to shake the images of my grandmother, her dead bird, and all of the strange things she'd said about death. I could still feel the dust in my nose.

Janie and I talked a lot. Not usually during the day, really. Not outside during my tennis lesson or lying out by the pool, but after we'd gotten stoned and had sex, mostly while we ate chocolate chip cookies and her dad's Slim Jims in her parents' bed. Every night when I got home, I went over all the bits of conversation that I could remember, writing some of it down in my pocket-size notepad, things Janie had confided and things that I'd said, and I rated the things I'd said on a five-star point system as to how well they'd gone over. As far as I could tell, Janie liked personal stuff. I was thinking of making it one of my Rules to Live By, to be personal to get women to like you. But it wasn't a rule really. It didn't have that tone. It was more like good advice. She liked when I revealed how much I hated my life. It spurred her on to tell me more, and mostly Janie liked to talk. Janie liked to entertain me, which was fine by me. She didn't want to hear long monologues about my life. She wanted me to be amazed by her and yet a little mysterious myself. Most of the time I wasn't pulling it off. But that afternoon, after sex, lazing in her parents' bed, right toward the end of the week, I thought she might have been falling for me.

We were talking about my mother, that she was Miss New Jersey a long time ago, 1970. I told her it was only the second-ever Miss America pageant to be protested, women walking up and down the Atlantic City boardwalk, chanting, "Ain't she sweet? Makin' profit off her meat." I told her how my mom remembers the marching crowd, the signs like WELCOME TO THE MISS AMERICA CATTLE AUCTION. She remembers the sheep they hauled out in a crown and sash.

Janie said, "I think the Miss America pageant is gross. It's demoralizing to women."

"This is what my mother would say to that: that she's been judged her whole life by everybody, hateful women and sick men. That's the world. The Miss America Pageant is just a civilized version of our disgusting world. At least it's honest about it." I'd heard it a million times. My mother has spent much of her life arguing with the protesting women, people she doesn't know, never met, people she's never spoken a word to in reality, but still she seems to collide with them everywhere all the time: on the news, on talk shows, on NPR, which she hates. She sees them as they step into VW wagons from the co-op health-food store next to her hair salon, women in wool sweaters with no makeup and bumper stickers about animal rights. And since she's never gotten out of the car and argued with them through their nonautomatic windows, she's presented her argument to me, over and over. I've got the speech memorized.

There was a long pause. Janie put her head on my chest. "I don't know, Ezra," she said, "your mom might be smart. I mean, she might understand, you know, things about being a woman."

"Well, she *is* one. She's got a lifetime of experience," I said, which suddenly seemed like an unfair advantage.

"I want to meet her," she said.

"I don't know." The thought made me feel a little queasy. "I'm not so sure."

"Yes," she said, sitting up in bed. "Definitely. I want to meet her. Tomorrow morning." And now suddenly I saw how it would be if Janie Pinkering were my wife, how she would decorate our bedroom so that there wasn't one single trace of me and how I'd want to have a little chickie down in New Orleans who thought I was smart, who followed all of my advice, who might have a little crying jag about my wife back home from time to time, but who'd be easily sedated if I told her I loved her best and patted her hair and started arranging my calendar for my next so-called foot conference.

"Call her up!" she said. "Call her to make sure she doesn't have plans."

"I'll tell her tonight. Later on," I said, knowing that my mother would be prowling the house until I came home, knowing that she'd be waiting for me to saunter in the back door or for the light to flick on in the pool bungalow, waiting, too, for it to eventually flick off.

"Just call her," Janie said. "Just call her now!"

But just then Janie and I heard the sound of tires in the driveway. I pulled the sheets up to cover my chest like a granny. "Are you expecting somebody?"

"What's today?"

"Friday."

"Oh, yeah," she said, getting out of bed and walking to the front window. "My dad's supposed to be coming home." She paused, squinted. "But, actually, it's my mom."

I jumped out of the bed and picked up my elastic-snipped underwear, stuffed them into my pocket, and started pulling on my shorts.

"It's not a big deal," she said. "She won't even notice."

I found that hard to believe. I pulled on a T-shirt. The front door was opening.

"Seriously, Ezra, I thought you were making progress." Janie was casually stepping, toes-pointed in such a way that made me think she'd taken her share of ballet lessons, into her panties, front-hooking her bra. She stood there with both hands on her hips. "But this is a major step backward. Your reaction is totally wrong."

I was thinking how being with Janie was like taking a giant social exam. I'd thought I'd been hanging on to a modest C-, what with all the personal stuff, but now I wasn't so sure that I was passing at all, and at the moment, didn't care. I whispered sharply, "She'll kill me! I think I'm being very calm, considering!"

Mrs. Pinkering must have sensed something right away. We hadn't cleaned up after ourselves all week. The house was pretty disastrous, wet towels hanging everywhere, the empty bar glasses. I could only imagine what it looked like to her. She was calling nervously for Janie as she scurried up the stairs. "Janie! Janie!" There was already a sharp edge to her voice.

"Just stand there, Stocker. Everything'll be fine," Janie said. She called to her mother, "In here." Janie was still only wearing her bra and panties.

I tried to look casual, my hands on my hips, then crossing my chest. I smiled for a second, pretty generously and then quit, stuffing my hands in my pockets.

Her mother opened the door and held on to the knob unsteadily. "What in God's name," she said, breathless. She was, in fact, much the way I'd pictured her before I'd ever stepped foot in the Pinkerings' home, except not hopping out for a hair appointment, obviously.

"You remember Ezra Stocker. The gardener."

"What in God's name!"

And then Janie snapped. "Oh, don't be so surprised. Where have you been for the last week! What have you been doing! You make me sick."

Her mother was pale, looked like she might throw up. In fact, she lurched forward and I thought she might throw up *on me*. I pressed my back up against the bureau. She glared at me.

"Your father can't even fill a filling," she said. "He can't even fit a bridge."

"That's my stepdad, actually. My real father's a politician."

"Get out! Get out!" she screamed.

And Janie was screaming, too, at her mother. "You never change. You've always been selfish. You've lost your mind completely! Listen to you!"

I slipped past Mrs. Pinkering and ran down the hallway, the stairs, out the door. I left it wide open behind me, the hall light bleeding out onto the overgrown lawn. I jumped on my bike, forgetting the jar with my grandmother's dead bird, and pedaled home as fast as I could, the breeze kicking my sweaty hair off my forehead. I was saying to myself again and again that it would blow over, that Janie would win, that we'd be back at it soon enough because Janie needed me for whatever reasons. I'd become indispensable, plus the way she'd pegged my mother as so wise, a source of knowledge she'd be needing. By the time I got home, I'd convinced myself that not only would it blow over, but that Janie could very well show up sometime to meet my mother the next morning. I decided that we didn't need the Pinkerings' house and its amenities at all. We had the pool bungalow, no actual pool, but the bungalow, a love nest, until the Pinkerings cooled off and took me in as one of their own, and Dr. Pinkering would zap the webs from my toes. And what could anyone say about it? I decided that no one would say anything.

I knew that my mother would be up. The kitchen light was on. I stood there catching my breath. I didn't want to talk to her, wouldn't tell her anything about Mrs. Pinkering walking in on her daughter and me—realistically I knew she'd find out soon enough—but I decided to just stick with the plan, to tell her that Janie wanted to meet her the next morning. I wanted to prove how normal everything was.

When I walked in the kitchen door, my mother was standing there, hunched over an ironing board. She hadn't turned the lights on and so there was only a little light seeping in from a lamp still on in the living room. She never ironed, not the type to starch the collars of her hubby's work shirts. She has all of her clothes dry-cleaned or pressed by Helga in the basement. And although she didn't look authentic, bedraggled, eyes dark-circled, the way a wife who irons in the dark should look in a cloud of spray starch and steam, the iron's red light zipping back and forth in the dim kitchen, she was sweating, a thin sheen to her bare arms, and I'd only seen my mother sweat when she was riding the exercise bike in her changing room. She looked up and nodded at me. She was still dressed for the day, in her pink outfit. I was nervous that she really knew this time, that Mrs. Pinkering had, in fact, already gotten word to her. I was almost certain of it.

I sat down on a cushioned kitchen chair. "What are you doing?"

"Ironing," she said. "A few of your things. Just a woman ironing her son's clothes. If you're to be a man, you need to look a little sharper, don't you think?" She was chipper. "This is the beginning."

"Of what?"

"This is the reason I saved you, I guess."

"Saved me from what?"

"Your lungs filling up like water through a wicker basket. I dressed you in doll diapers you were so small."

And I could see now that she was spray-starching a T-shirt of mine, just a ratty one that I only used for sleeping in. My mother is always having some other conversation with me, one that I'm supposed to understand even better than if she were actually saying what was on her mind.

"Janie wants to meet you tomorrow."

"Oh! Your girlfriend. Bringing her home to meet the folks. Isn't that a big step for a young bachelor? Well, you should invite her out to your place," she said.

"The bungalow?"

"Of course! It would be strange if we met here. And I'll pop by, announced, of course. I wouldn't want to cramp your style." She tilted her head and smiled, a fake smile.

"Lovely," I said. And I knew that my mother was losing it. I thought that it had to do with me primarily, with me and Janie Pinkering. She wasn't freaking out really. She still looked almost perfect, but she'd come just a little undone, just a little. In someone else, you might not even really notice the change. But in my mother, who always *appeared*, at least, completely put together, this one hook-and-eye unclasped was glaring. I've seen my mom really lose it. Once when I was just a little kid, she lay on the sofa for weeks, wearing the same old white slip until it looked oily. That was when I was five, just after she left my dad, heartbroken. And we moved back to Bayonne, a little apartment where I rubbed lotion into her legs, combed tangles from her hair, made peanut butter sandwiches that she barely picked at. I remember once brushing her teeth, one cup for rinsing, one cup for spitting. This is before she bought the gun, passing it back and forth in her hands like it was a small wounded animal, something she'd found on the sidewalk, almost dead, until the pawn shop owner said, "It's a gun, you know. Not a Hummel for your mantelpiece." This wasn't like that time, but still there was something familiar about it.

I was about to stand up and walk out the back door. I must have sighed and half-hoisted myself up with my hands on the kitchen table, but then she said, "Your grandmother had a stroke while you were out." Like it was my fault for having been out of the house, like if I'd been in the pool bungalow tucked in, it wouldn't have happened. And although it didn't make sense and wasn't fair, I felt guilty, and disoriented. I remembered what she'd said about feeling different, about the walls in her head crumbling. I guessed that I should have known there was something wrong, that at least I should have stayed with her a bit longer and done what I'd promised to do for her dead bird. I could feel the bulge of my underwear balled up in my pocket. I could still smell Janie on me, the sweet pot smoke mixed with her mint lotion.

I'd heard my mother, but I said, "What?" It was dark; the red light on the iron was still streaking back and forth. My mother's arms were slick, shiny in the dull light, like chrome, something you could look into and maybe see your own reflection but warped, too long or too wide.

"A mild stroke. A neighbor found her. She'd struggled to the front door and collapsed in the hall. There was a bird, the neighbor told me, eating peanuts from her pocket, nesting in the middle of her chest. The nurse at the hospital told me not to come out, that she's sleeping, to come in the morning. But it may be the beginning, they told me."

"The beginning of what?"

"The end," she said, finally looking up at me. "The beginning of the end. Haven't you been listening to me?"

Pixie

Remember: Miss America Never Cries

Mothers get old and sick. Husbands are difficult; marriages complicated. And your children can look at you sometimes like they are pleading for something, but you don't know what to give them. They grow up. They leave you. The picture of me last summer should be pretty clear: my eyebrows were neatly plucked. My toilets were freshly scrubbed. The potpourri was apricot-scented. And I was consumed by the past, caught up in a cloud of it. I spent any number of days, for example, trying to remember what it was like to be with Jimmy Vietree and what it was like to break his heart. I don't know why I was thinking about this, but my mind was fixated. There were more pressing issues, of course, and I was painfully, but also only remotely, aware of them, because I was remote myself, distant. I was walking on the edge of it all, in an apricot-scented, freshly scrubbed, eyebrow-plucked kind of way, and there was Jimmy Vietree out by the tracks, just a normal cold day, his hands already warming under my coat and sweater, on my stomach. I tried to remember his hands, small and hot. Wanda had told me about falling in love being a secret, and at sixteen I already had too many secrets. I decided to get rid of Jimmy. Honestly, if Wanda hadn't fallen in love with her husband, who was never around anyway, then maybe she'd have tried again for Miss Bayonne, maybe she'd have gone all the way.

I said, "Jimmy, I can't be with you anymore."

He pulled his hands off me and balled them up in his pants pockets. "What? Why?"

"Because I have to decide between you and my future. And my future is very important to me. I am going to become someone."

"But you are someone," he said. "You're my girl, first of all."

I thought for a minute how it might be to be his girl forever and ever. I thought of my mother and father as kids, him jumping into the Kill van Kull, and what that river was like now, freezing over, the cold stiffening around my father's body, even though my father had been pulled out by the soldier; what it would be like if he was still there locked in a new skin of ice; how my mother looked like she'd frozen too. "I can't be your girl," I said, but I thought I might love him and how much I'd miss him loving me; that's what I'd miss most of all.

His face crumpled up, and I thought he was going to cry, which I thought might have made me cry. But he didn't. He said, "It doesn't matter. No one thinks you're normal, you know. Not at all."

And I was relieved that he was mean, so that I could leave him behind easier. I said, "That's not news to me." And it wasn't.

Wanda had been sick. She could barely keep anything down. She was pregnant with her third, but she made me swear not to tell anybody. She was worn out. She looked like a rag. She kept all the dishes out of the sink so she could throw up there and just wash it down the drain. She said she couldn't go through labor again. With her last one they'd given her Twilight sleep, a form of truth serum, a drug to dull her memory but not the pain. But she did remember the dark ward of moaning women, how the nurse told her to quiet down because the girl one room over was having her first and scared enough already, and that the nurse rolled her to her side and handcuffed her to her hospital bed rails, standard procedure. Her last memory was of trying to fold the bones of her hands and slip free. She didn't remember the baby coming out of her, nothing, until later, a tight girdle of pain and bleeding. My mother had told me that when she was in labor with me, they'd closed her legs when she started to push, because the doctor wasn't there yet. It made me sick to think of it. I told her that I planned to have a boy and a girl, but not until they got labor down a little bit better. (Of course, they didn't get labor to be any easier. It won't ever be *easy* to have a baby come out of your body. It would be misleading if it were.)

One day when I stopped by, Wanda was lying down on the sofa, and the kids were tearing around the yard. It was cold and they were underdressed in unzipped coats, sneakers without socks, no hats, scarves, mittens. One of the neighbors had already strung Christmas lights; her husband was on the roof wrestling a plastic reindeer.

Wanda had eaten a green apple earlier and had to go to the bathroom. I could hear her moaning, and when she called to me for a cool washrag, I found her on the bathroom floor, just lying there, and she said, "It's not his."

And I didn't know what she meant. "His what?" I asked.

"Baby," she said. "He's on Governor's Island, putting out barge fires. How could it be his?"

"Who then?" I asked.

She shook her head. "Nobody you know." She looked up at me, and I sat down on the floor next to her. "Will you help me?"

"How could I help you?"

And then she said, "Of course not. I must be crazy sick. No. No. Forget that I told you anything. Forget all of this." She coughed a little and the cough made her gag. "Just watch the kids fifteen minutes, will you? Just ten. So I can rest my eyes."

I watched the kids for an hour or so, but it was getting dark. The kids' cheeks were bright red. I had to wake her up to tell her that I had to go home and sort out my homework. She propped herself up on the sofa and said, "Forget what I told you. Okay? I'll be fine."

But I thought about it all the way home. I wondered who the father could be and thought how awful it was to be a woman. I remembered the first time I bled and I didn't know much of anything. I told my mother that I was really sick, that there was blood down there. She took me to the bathroom and fixed me up with a thin elastic belt and a pad. She said, "You'll get used to it." But it turned such a bright red on the white, white pad, sometimes still it shocks me, the red, and I'm amazed that no one knows that there's blood coming out of me, and not just me, but all of us women, at some time or the other, and how it is that we keep all of this red blood a secret, and not just that but there are so many secrets, each woman a storehouse of them.

When I got home, Billy Trexler and his cousin were sitting in a car, waiting for me in front of my building. I walked up in the glare of their headlights, and they each hung out an open window, their breaths like ghosts above their heads. They said, "Pixie, come on for a ride, won't you?"

I said, "No, thanks. I've got things to do. Don't you boys have to study?"

And Billy said that he'd rather study me.

I said, "No," again.

His cousin said, "She's ice cold, man. I told you Vietree was a liar. Let's go."

And I knew that Jimmy had started talking since I told him that I couldn't see him anymore. Then Billy asked me again to go for a ride. He said it was his uncle's car and he wouldn't have it for long.

Finally, I said, "Jesus! No. Haven't I said it enough?" I stepped inside the door to the long hall of doors and started to cry. My chest was suddenly heavy, welling up. I shut the door and I couldn't stop it. I walked down the hall and behind the stairs, hid there, sobbing, because I didn't know why those boys always had to think I was going to go off with them. It was proof to me that everybody knew, they could tell that I wasn't really pure, and then they hated me when I refused them. I was thinking about Wanda, too. I was scared for her, because I knew what she was asking me to do, how I was going to help her get rid of it somehow, the way I'd heard about. And once I started crying, I couldn't stop. I was crying about my dead daddy and Cliff, and my mother, too, how I was going to have to go into that apartment and find her smoking by the window, how we were going to have to eat across from each other at the dinner table, and we wouldn't even say a word. Most of all, I cried because I didn't want to cry. How was I ever going to be Miss America if I went around crying?

I wiped the tears from my face, took some deep breaths, fished the key from the pocket of my coat, and walked inside. My mother was eating a corned beef sandwich over the kitchen sink, the way people who live alone do.

I said, "I'm going to be Miss Bayonne and then Miss New Jersey and then probably Miss America and there's nothing you can do about it."

"What?"

"I'm going to be Miss America."

"And this is supposed to help things? To make things better?"

"Could things be much worse?"

"You'll make a fool of yourself. They'll ask you questions. Do you want to answer all of their questions?"

"Like what?"

"You know nothing. Go ahead. Do what you want." She took another bite of her sandwich.

And so I decided that I would. I would do what I wanted, always. If she could make me disappear, then I could make her disappear. I watched her for a moment, the knot of her jaw tensing on the meat of her sandwich, clenching and unclenching, and then I looked past her, to the spice shelf, the cabinets loose in their hinges. I looked and looked—the same way I stared at myself in Wanda's fake-gold mirror—until I saw through her. You see, last summer when my mother was in the hospital, she was gone. I'd already let her go.

Ezra

Rule #5: When things come undone,
try to have your pants on.

As you might imagine, Bob Pinkering wasn't happy
with my gardening skills and even less happy with the
fact that I'd spent my time at his house screwing his daughter. He called while my family was getting ready to head out
to the hospital to see my grandmother—me and Mitzie eating Pop-Tarts, my mother upstairs dressing, Dilworth hidden behind the morning paper. When the phone rang,
Mitzie hopped up. "I've got it! I've got it! Hello, this is
Mitzie Stocker." (*pause*) "Yes, he's here. One moment,
please."

She wrinkled her nose like the person on the other end was
a stinker and handed the phone to Dilworth, who folded the
newspaper on his lap. He said, "Hello," and "Hey, Bob," and
then "Whoa, wait a minute. Slow down." He glanced at me,
confused. I glanced at him but without really moving my

head. I was as still as possible, the theory, I guess, being to blend in, like a fern, an extra chair.

Dilworth stood up and walked out of the room as far as the phone's long cord would allow him. I could hear him saying, "Well, now." And "Honestly, that surprises me. I mean, not the part about your lawn, Bob. But, ah . . ."

Mitzie whispered, "What did you do?"

I shrugged and shook my head, "I think I've disrupted some order, but I think that's what I'm supposed to do. Don't you?"

"Sure," she said. "Especially if you think it's what you're supposed to do. Then how could you be wrong?"

"Exactly, Mitzie! Absolutely!"

By the time Dilworth hung up the phone, rubbing the bridge of his nose where his reading glasses had made little red indents, my mother was standing in the kitchen, picking a piece of lint off her skirt, putting on her sunglasses. There wasn't a hint of the undone quality I'd seen the night before.

Dilworth cleared his throat and lowered his voice. "Did you know that Ezra has been"—he paused as if coming up with some code that Mitzie wouldn't understand—"*umphing* the Pinkering girl? That he hasn't done one single thing to actually garden anything?"

"Yes," my mother said. "Oh, well, yes to the *umphing*. No to the gardening."

"And can you believe he expects to get paid for this? That he had the audacity to"—and here he lowered his voice again as if this were the dirtiest part—"fill out a time sheet?"

"Well, *there* he's got the right idea," my mother said. "We are a world of whores and pimps and johns. That's how everything divides." This was part of her grand speech, the one she always seemed to give to me, but that was directed at the old pageant protesters, the no-makeup, wool-wearing women she saw everywhere. "I always thought he'd be a pimp, what with all of this education, but I might prefer him as a whore, as long as he keeps his center, a pimpless whore is best."

"Does *umphing* mean what I think it means?" Mitzie asked.

Dilworth was startled. "Mitzie, go to your room!" he shouted. He turned to my mother. "Jesus! What are you teaching her, for Chrissakes."

Mitzie stood up.

"I'm ready to go see my mother. I'm perfectly prepared," my mother said. "Mitzie, get in the car."

Mitzie looked at the back door and then back at her father. I was motionless. My mother unsnapped her pocketbook, checked the contents, snapped it shut, and walked out the door to the car. Mitzie followed, leaving me alone with Dilworth, who was just standing there.

"I didn't know you had it in you." He shook his head with his chin to his chest, the way my mother had looked at me in that flashing image I had of her while having sex with Janie Pinkering for the first time, and I thought he was smiling. It was hard to tell, because the chins of skin looked like smiles piled on top of each other. But then he looked up and his eyes were squinting, proud almost. I was uncomfortable. It was a new twist to our relationship. I wasn't sure what to do with his admiration. I wasn't sure if it made me indebted to him somehow.

"What do you mean you didn't know I had it in me?" I asked, because that sounded like an insult wrapped up in a compliment and I didn't trust him.

He shook his head again and sighed, "Deflowering the Pinkering girl."

"I don't think I deflowered her," I said.

"Oh, no," Dilworth said. "That would be too much like gardening. God forbid you actually work."

"Janie Pinkering *is* work," I said, wondering when I'd get to see her again, if ever. It was clear to me now that she wouldn't be coming over to meet my mother.

And with that Dilworth got very serious. "All women are work." And I agreed with him. He smiled at me, sadly, and I smiled too, and I felt, for just that second, that we were both men, which meant we both knew some secret. It was just a flicker of emotion, as if we suddenly existed inside of a brief, flimsy bubble of solidarity that popped as quickly as it had come to surround us.

The nurse was young and nice, and despite the hospital's overwhelming smell of Lysol and, beneath that, urine, she smelled lilac-sweet and reminded me for a second of Janie Pinkering's mother's basket of bath products. I'd spent the ride to the hospital devising a plan to get Janie to the bungalow. I thought maybe I'd call, and if her mother or father answered, I'd pretend to be Kermit Willis, but then I didn't want to hear any disappointment in her voice when she answered the phone and found out it was me. I thought about pretending to speak in a Spanish accent, to be Manuel looking for Elsie Finner or something like that. Down the tiled hall, a man's voice was calling out in pain, but most of the doors were closed, and those that were open blocked my view with white screens on rollers. The halls were white and the music that was pumped from some unseen place over our heads was sickeningly sweet, heavy on the harp, like they were trying to tap into heaven's radio station.

Before ushering us into my grandmother's private room, the nurse warned us about the partial paralysis of one side of her face and told us that it was very likely she'd regain total use. She spoke quietly. "I think you'll find that she's not really been herself. Most families do, and that's normal. Strokes are very strange and affect people in very different ways. She'll probably be back to her old self soon." And then, with her eyebrows pinched in sympathy, she added, "She'll confuse words and things and she may not recognize you."

My mother touched her sleeve and said, "That could only work in my favor."

When we saw my grandmother propped up in the bed, she looked very small, like a doll version of herself. One side of her cheek sagged just slightly and one of the nurses, probably the lilac-sweet one, had put rouge on her cheeks and a smudge of pink lipstick on her lips, which were in constant motion, a little whisper, like she was chewing words. Her hair was down, flat, but neatly combed away from her face. The ceiling-mounted TV was blaring. She didn't look like she was at the beginning of the end as my mother had been told or made up in her own mind. But she certainly seemed all wrong.

She looked around the room at the four of us, Mitzie in her

bow, Dilworth in a loud yellow shirt and tie, my mother perfectly groomed, and me, shuffling in last. She was startled, as if she thought for a moment that the television characters had stepped out of the television for a visit, or, by the suspicious look on her face, to sell her something.

"Yes?" she said, expectantly. "Are you all more churches? I don't need another." But the sentence didn't end there. Words continued on. I could make out only a few—*teaspoon, zigzag, soup bone.*

We looked around at each other. "No," my mother said. "Family. We're family. We are *your* family." She spread her arms around the room, showing her all of us. Dilworth popped a Tic Tac and waved. Mitzie curtsied. I nodded, stepped forward, said, "Hi." I was still trying to be as inconspicuous as possible, hoping the Janie announcement this morning wasn't going to bring on more heat for me.

"I think you look pretty," Mitzie said.

"Oh, you. I know you," my grandmother said, a little horrified, responding to Mitzie's voice, I figured. "Fever," she said, "croaking, wheezing box."

"You don't look like you're going to die," Mitzie said.

"Die?" my grandmother whispered. "Is that what they say? Chirping all around me. White like moving buildings in and out all day and night."

"No," my mother said. "Of course you're not going to die!" She glared at Mitzie.

But my grandmother was already agitated. "It was a white burn," she said, "and half my body drawn up to it, like too much sun and then dark, dark, words filling it like white splotches, the memory of sun, like snow, but wet, words like water, like drowning." There was pain etched deeply into the lines of her face where the makeup seemed to cake, making her wrinkles stand out pink so that her face almost looked striped.

"You'll be fine," my mother said. "The nurse told us on our way in."

Dilworth, the only Catholic in the group, said, "Well, you're lucky to have done so well with this. God must really be watching over you."

"Who? Who?" she said. "There's nobody there for me, except some jealous God, spiteful," my grandmother said. "We're all evil, created like they say, from wet muck and we learned to breathe." And then she stared at my mother and pounded her fist into the bed. "The tile here's too white, like the butcher's shop. Remember the butcher with his blood-stiffened apron? Did he ask about me?" My grandmother's face opened for a second. I remember that my grandmother had mentioned a butcher, a sweetheart. I wondered if I'd remember Janie when I got old and addled.

"Who?" my mother asked. "Mr. Graziano's been dead for years."

With that, my grandmother's face shrank back to its tight knots. "The lights here are too bright. I close my eyes and the bright bulbs seem like they're on the underside of earth, the lamp on my father's mining hat, like a swung lantern going down, or like looking up from underwater to the surface. My eyes opened, it's an explosion, too bright." She looked around the room, her face suddenly vacant. "Where's my Clifford?"

"He's no longer with us. You know that," my mother said.

"Go away," she said. "What's done is done." My grandmother's words kept coming. "*Hemline, parsnip, hive.* Can you hear them, humming, *fedora, Formica, whipstitch.* Like those Chinese women, their teeth, clattering. My birds. Where are my birds?"

"Helga is taking care of them," my mother said. "They're fine." I couldn't imagine Helga taking care of birds. She hated birds, called them "flyink rats."

"Let's go," Dilworth said. "C'mon. We're just upsetting her." But it was clear that Dilworth wasn't really being considerate, just uncomfortable, antsy, and I felt guilty because I wanted to go too. I couldn't stand to see the old woman this way.

My mother stood there for a minute, locking eyes with her mother.

"Can't you hear?" my grandmother asked.

"No," my mother said, "Hear what?"

"Go away," my grandmother said. "Go."

Dilworth took my mother's elbow, carefully, like a stranger helping an old lady across a street, Mitzie and I close behind, and we walked out the door, which swung closed behind us.

No one spoke until we were at the car.

Then Mitzie said, "I think she looked pretty. I thought that she was going to be ugly because she's going to die. But she doesn't look like she's going to die ever."

"No," my mother said. "I don't think she's ever going to die." And I wondered if someday I'd feel that way about my mother, if there'd ever be a time when she would seem unstoppable, and I imagined the hearts of my grandmother, my mother, even Mitzie's, beating on and on, like the old Baptist buses you see on the highway with engines that keep at it forever.

There's no phone in the pool bungalow, so I was forced to call Janie from the kitchen. With the long cord, I could make it into the study and shut the door, just barely. From there, I was on a very short leash, my face six inches from the door. I'd decided to go with being Manuel. Something about the accent, which I'd practiced a good bit in my bedroom mirror, gave me confidence.

The phone rang three times and then a woman's voice said, "Yes?"

But I couldn't make out whether it was Janie or her mother. I decided to be safe, "Is dis Chanie Pinkering?"

"Yes," she said. "Who's this?"

"Oh," I said, dropping the accent. "It's me. Ezra."

"What's with that voice?"

"Joking," I said. "I was joking. It was a joke."

"Oh," she said and there was a pause. "Well, at least you got your sense of humor back."

"I was wondering if everything's, you know, blown over."

"God! I mean do they *hate* you!"

"Really?" It sounded like a compliment.

"And I don't know what your father's done to their teeth over the years, but he's no favorite anymore either. They're switching practices."

I wanted to say *step*-father, but kids with their original parents still together had trouble catching on to this kind of distinction. I just said, "Oh." I felt bad about Dilworth's losing his dental patients.

"I've got to do a lot of quality-time stuff with my mom everyday. And my dad is taking me fishing. We've got to *bond.*" She said it like she hated the idea, but at the same time she wasn't convincing.

"And so when am I going to see you again?"

There was a pause. "Bonding takes up a lot of time," she said. "And, well, can I be frank, Ezra? You didn't *transform* the way I thought you might."

"Oh," I said. I realized that I was a failed project, a botched experiment, but that maybe a botched experiment was what Janie had wanted, one that would really singe her parents' eyebrows and burn the lab to the ground. "Is Elsie still dating Manuel?" I asked.

"God, no! That was a fling!"

"And Kermit. Is he still with the college girl?"

"Yes," she said. "But I'm almost a college girl myself, you know. Seniors have to think that way. Look, I've got to go. Maybe we'll go for a swim sometime before summer's over. The water's perfectly warm now."

Pixie

How It Ends: One Day You Stop Telling
the Story of Your Life to Yourself

This was the end of the story. It's where I decided to stop.

I got a letter from Cliff, his last. His battalion had moved down to secure a village called Phu Hoa Dong. There was a firefight, VC somewhere. It was after curfew, and there were gunshots in the forest just outside of the village and everyone started firing. Then right behind him he heard noises. He turned and shot off his M16, but it wasn't VC. It was a kid in his backyard, trying to pull a dog into his hut. The boy fell, his thin brown arm pinned under him, the dog skidding out and running away. Another hut caught fire, and later after the firefight, after some VC were shot dead, Jamison went in to see who'd been burned. He pulled out a woman and her baby and an old man, their charred bodies lined up in front of the smoldering house. That night Cliff could smell death, felt like he was eating it with his rations, bite after bite until he threw up. He said that Jamison had climbed a tree and sat there not coming down, just humming in this tree, like his little brother, the autistic kid who could sing like an angel, songs nobody's ever heard before, songs without words, just long beautiful o's and e's. The dog came back, Cliff said, a skinny stray, and his buddies were feeding it rocks, tossing them up and watching it snap. One guy told Cliff that the kid he shot was probably going to eat the dog, put it in a pot. Cliff found the dog later, a bitch on her back, her stomach filled with stones. She was moaning, and he shot her in the head. His hands were bloody, he told me, and that blood wouldn't ever come off.

Two days after I got Cliff's letter, Wanda called. She sounded agitated. She wanted me to come over as soon as I could. I hadn't been to her house in weeks because she'd been too tired and busy. I thought it'd be good to see her, because I didn't want to think about Cliff, and I knew that Wanda wouldn't let me talk about him anyway. It made me sick to think of him, because I knew I would always hate him as much as I loved him.

When I got to Wanda's house, I knocked and nobody answered. I walked in, because the door wasn't locked and I found Wanda on the sofa, the middle cushion blood-soaked, her dress and blanket, too. I found her holding a small blue thing, wet and limp in her hands. It was the baby, half hidden in the blanket, but it didn't look like a baby, it was so small and blue, its head smaller than a plum, a girl. Wanda was shaking, her whole body, and the baby's chest was rising and falling, alive.

She said, "Call this doctor. Only this one. Don't talk to anybody but him." She recited the number and I dialed it. I said I needed to talk to the doctor. It was an emergency. A man's voice came on, Dr. Roberts. I told him that I was with Wanda Sorenski and there was something very wrong. He had to come over alone. I sat with Wanda and waited. Her hair was soaked, her body shaking hard. She told me to get a towel, and when I got back, she handed the baby to me. I held it in my hands and kind of propped it on my chest. Wanda closed her eyes, but I could see her chest still breathing. The baby, though, died. Finally, its little ragged breaths quit, and I thought of my daddy when his breathing quit—and how it must have been for the soldier, the stranger on the dock, rocking his dead body. I put the baby down and pushed on its tiny ribs, but they were so small, I stopped. I thought of putting my mouth over its mouth, but I didn't. Its arms and legs were limp. I felt sick, stunned, breathless, and hot. I was shaking. There was nothing I could do. I picked the baby back up and held its sticky body to the front of my dress. It was puny and wrinkled, and I felt helpless and small. I patted its back like it was still alive, only asleep, maybe. I told myself that it wasn't dead, and I hummed a lullaby.

When the doctor came, he called from the open door and then walked in. I stood up. He could see what was in my arms. He didn't look surprised, though, only matter-of-fact.

He said, "Okay, let me have a look."

I handed him the baby although I didn't want to. He checked it quickly and wrapped the baby in a towel, covering its face, the small hole of its mouth, and placed the baby

wrapped in the towel on the kitchen counter. He was very professional, checking Wanda's pulse, again and again. He barely
spoke to me except orders, to get him things from his bag, to
wipe down the blood on Wanda's legs, to get her clean underwear and a pad, more towels. There was so much blood, the
room smelled like metal, the rusted iron of an old gate. I did
everything he said to do. Wanda's eyes would flit open, but she
was too weak to stay awake.

"Should we get her upstairs in her bed?" I asked.

"No," he said. "Here on the sofa's fine."

I looked up into his face; I saw there were tears inching
down his cheeks. He said to me, "What did she do? I have to
know."

I told him I'd found her there, the baby still breathing, but
then not.

"But she did something," he said. "Did she put something
inside of herself?"

"I don't know," I said, tears coming down my face now too.
But I thought I did know how she did it. I'd found something
between the sofa cushions. A knitting needle, but I couldn't
say it.

"Tell her that I couldn't stay. I can't, you know, stay with
her. I have to keep going. When she wakes up, tell her that."

And I knew then that he was apologizing for something
else, not just the way a doctor apologizes, but a man. I looked
up at him sharply then, wide-eyed.

He said, "You didn't know?"

I shook my head.

"There's nothing to know," he said. He packed up his

things, but it was clear to me he was the father and that the tiny body wrapped in the towel was his daughter. I thought of my mother's giant scale of life, anything good always being balanced by something bad. I wondered if it had been good with him, if Wanda had been happy, and if this wasn't the way she'd been made to suffer for that happiness. I was afraid my mother might be right. He held the bundle half under his arm, half against his chest. He said, "She's lucky, actually, that she's not dead." And he walked out of the house.

The kids came home from a neighbor, and I said that I was going to be their babysitter. I put them straight up to bed. They were exhausted anyway, tumbling out of their clothes and into their pajamas. The older one asked where her mommy was. I told her she went to a movie and that I didn't know which one. I called my mother and told her the same story. She sounded surprised that I was calling, surprised by the sound of my voice. I wondered how long it took her to forget about me once I was out of the house. I wanted to tell her Wanda's story and about the doctor, but I knew she'd have no sympathy. She'd say that a woman should know better, that I should know better.

When Wanda woke up, she said, "Don't tell me what happened. I don't want to know. He came though, didn't he? He took care of everything?"

"Yes," I said.

She told me to get an envelope out of the desk drawer with my name on it. She said she had written it to me in case she died. She didn't let me read the note. She crumpled it up, but pulled a locket out of the envelope. It was inscribed to Wanda

Sorenski, Runner-up Miss Bayonne 1963. She put it into my hand and pressed my hand shut. She said, "Look at me, Pix." And her chest heaved a little, but she didn't cry. She took a deep breath and told me about the Kiwanis Club, that she knew a member, a bricklayer down the street, who said he'd invite me to compete. She'd already explained that I'd need an invitation like this, how she'd been nominated to go to the Miss Bayonne pageant because her dad had been a member of the Kiwanis—a men's club—way back. "I wanted to surprise you with the news. Anyway," she said.

"We shouldn't talk about that now," I said. "You should go to sleep. The doctor said that you're lucky you're not dead."

"That's right," she said. "Go home, Pixie. Go on home."

I walked out of her house, locking the door behind me, but all the way home I was reciting the end of Cliff's letter, that he could still hear the dog moan, no matter what, no matter that he shot that dog in the head, he could still hear it moan. I didn't cry anymore. I decided not to cry ever again, not to think about my dead father, or the man, not to think about Cliff anymore or my sad mother or Wanda and that baby, not to give in to all of what the world seemed to want from me, that it was trying to wring out of me. And so I said to myself over and over, "That's the end of it. That's that."

Ezra

Rule #6: Don't keep guns in the house.

I went from being the Pinkerings' gardener to being my mother's chauffeur. She hated going to visit her mother every afternoon. It made her pale and shaky, too nervous to drive although nobody said this out loud. Plus she said it was still a good idea for me to get to know my grandmother even though it wasn't really her anymore at all. The idea, too, was that it was a good excuse for me to practice driving with my new permit. I was sixteen after all, and just as Janie had to start thinking like an almost-college girl, I had to start thinking like an almost-driver, even though I knew that once I got back to school there'd be no cars, no driving, nowhere to go.

I liked driving to the hospital, because we had to take I-95 and I loved to be behind the wheel, going 65, weaving in and out of traffic as much as my mother would allow. "Slow down. Please, Ezra! My God!" It was a giant step for my mother to let

me drive. She hadn't let me play with Legos for fear that I'd
swallow one until I was much too old to actually enjoy Legos.
But Dilworth had insisted I get my driver's permit. "Like all
the other young American boys in the nation, he may want to
take someone out on a date one day, and use a backseat like
everyone else." He was still a little proud of my conquest of
"the Pinkering girl."

But when I wasn't behind the wheel, I was mostly miserable, sulking, sighing with my chin in my hand just staring
out the window, alone in the bungalow. Helga would come out
to clean, touching things with her dust rag, grunting each
time she bent over to lift something off the floor. She'd say,
"Oh, you are lof sick. Look at you. Anyvone could tell." She
tried to muscle the story out of me now and then. "Tell Helga,
wass is wrong. I know everythink about men unt women unt
lof. I've had many lof affairs. Tell me."

But every time I looked at her, the butterfly Band-Aid
keeping the loose skin of her eyelid from sagging over her eye,
her red elbows, and dumpy apron, I knew it was all wrong,
that she'd never understand someone like Janie. I'd shake my
head and eventually she'd waddle away. I did, however, wonder
what advice Helga would have and the idea that I could get a
different perspective made me think that I could have been
wrong about Janie. I began to imagine that she'd given me the
polite brush-off because her mother had been in the room, that
Janie was now a hostage of sorts. Maybe she'd tried to give me
a message, maybe the water being perfectly warm was a kind
of secret message that meant that things were really perfect
between us, but that she couldn't talk right then. I had these

kinds of daydreams, worked on perfecting them, until they started to seem plausible.

I hated the time that my mother and I spent actually inside the hospital. We usually visited during lunch hour so that my mother could feed my grandmother and feel useful. I hated the smell of that place with its stale recycled air-conditioning and plastic-wrapped meals of square meat, congealed vegetables, the little cups of juice and jiggling Jell-O. I wasn't eating it, of course, but the idea that someone had to was disgusting. And there was always the Lysol and urine, a voice screaming down the tiled hall, the piped-in elevator music, playing an all-instrument version of "Oh, What a Beautiful Morning."

My mother didn't say much. Occasionally, she'd talk about the lack of rain. Since the end of my relationship with Janie Pinkering, it had stopped raining altogether even though it was still sticky and the sky seemed heavy, as if it wanted to rain. In the evenings, it would grow cloudy and windy, a high wind kicking up in the tops of trees, even far-off thunder, but as much as it seemed like the beginning of a storm, it never was a storm. I knew that it was the kind of symbolism that would not be lost on Miss Abernathy. I decided that in the fall I'd try to get into her creative writing class and write out the whole affair with Janie Pinkering in beautiful prose, chock-full of her much-loved symbolism.

My grandmother hadn't said my mother's name since that first visit. Aside from the occasional stream of mixed-up words, she'd been very quiet for a couple of days in a row. My mother said that the words were a lifetime of all of the things she'd never said, but in random order, which seemed to frustrate my mother, who was blind to the fact that she, like her mother, never said much that was really on her mind. But my grandmother was improving. When she did talk, asking for something, usually more salt or a straw, she got the words right, for the most part. My mother fed my grandmother, wiping her chin, giving her sips of juice, while my grandmother eyed her suspiciously. My mother seemed to think this meant that my grandmother was in the process of becoming herself again.

"She's trying to place me," she said. "Even though she knows that I'm her daughter, she hasn't felt it yet. And now she's beginning to *feel* that I'm her daughter." My mother wasn't doing much to jog her mother's memory. Aside from my mother's announcement that first day that we were her family, and the fact that she'd seemed, at least then, to know exactly who my mother was, and maybe the nurses asking about how her visit was with her daughter and grandson after we'd left, there was no mention as to who we were exactly. But still I didn't think that my mother was wrong. I thought that something had changed and that my grandmother was gearing up for a breakthrough of some kind, and my mother certainly wanted something from her. "She needs me, Ezra. You can tell by the way she looks at me," she'd say. "She needs me."

One Wednesday, my grandmother looked a little weak in her eyes, tired. My mother was feeding her, talking about how in past summers there'd been water restrictions and how she and most of the other neighbors had watered their lawns at night when they thought everyone else was sleeping—not the goody-two-shoes Worthingtons, of course, who'd never sin against the environment like that—but all the other sprinklers in our neighborhood, ticking and rotating all night, stealing precious city water for their plush green lawns.

My grandmother pushed the tray away with her hand. "You make me tired," she said. "All of this that I've swallowed. I'm tired of the boiling, the boil, boil."

"Oh, well, we'll go then, so you can sleep," my mother said. I was relieved to cut the visit short. I wanted to be out in the sun, back in the car, the warm air pushing in through the windows.

My grandmother put her head down on her pillow, tugged the sheet up to her neck. I could see the outline of her long thick legs. She pulled them together, curled them up. She rubbed her hands over her face, dry skin on dry skin. Her body became hard in that position. She braced herself and said, "I'm going to die and all I can hear is the struggle of springs, the muffle of someone dying, the tub water filling. Do you remember the tub?"

"You're not going to die," my mother said.

"I remember it, you know, his feet in the hall, how he opened your bedroom door."

"You heard someone open *my* bedroom door? When was this?" My mother shook her head, bewildered.

"It was my fault. It's the way the world works. I'd had pleasure, Pixie, with the butcher. I'd been so alone for so long, and he loved me. Anyone could see it on his face, how much he loved me. I untied his blood-stiffened apron one night after the store was closed, the blinds drawn. Just once, that's all it

was and then I never went back. I never saw him again. But for
that pleasure, there was suffering. I thought it would be my
suffering, though, Pixie, not yours."

"Mr. Graziano? Are you saying you had an affair with Mr.
Graziano, the butcher with the pug-faced wife and ugly
daughters?"

"You can't deny how one thing follows another. Mr.
Graziano, yes, and then just a month later, not even a month,
I'm in bed and I hear it."

"What?"

"I wanted the sound to become another sound, the neighbor's restlessness, Mr. Gunsellman back from the plant, late
shift. It became muffled, the sound of crying. Clifford hears it,
too. He picked up the bat. He was just a boy, really. He
couldn't do anything. A mother should be able to go to war for
her son. Only a good mother knows how to kill; the baby's
born and suddenly there are talons, claws, teeth you never
knew were there. Mothers can kill. And Cliff can only scream
like a kettle. Hear the kettle? It's going off, the high-pitched
whistle." There was no whistling kettle, only the over-
intercom music and an occasional patient shuffling down the
hall with an IV on rollers.

"What are you saying?" my mother said, no longer smiling. She put her hand on the sheet. She made a fist and the
sheet twisted. Her face was pale and slack. "What did you say?
Heard what?"

"There was no other man. I made him up later," and she
looked up at my mother, "for you to have. Later, after it all, in
the tub, the water filling up, all of the water tinged pink with

blood, I made up the story of the man breaking into our house. But I was the one. I took the bat. It was in my hands, suddenly, like a miracle I couldn't explain and I brought it down on his head."

"Whose head?"

"Your father's. See him? Is he dead? No, he's not dead. I raise the bat again, but Clifford pulls it from my hands. *Take him out, Cliff. Drag him out.*" And my grandmother closed her eyes. "I didn't kill your father, but I could have. Two weeks later he fell through the front door. Remember? That night he drowned himself. It might be the one thing, the only thing, that redeemed him." She swallowed air, two or three gulps, and then breathed normally. "I gave you the stranger. It was a gift. And you accepted the gift."

"What?" my mother kept repeating it. "What gift?"

But my grandmother was breathing deeply then.

My mother stood up and let go of the sheet, a wrinkled star now slowly released from her fist. She turned around and stumbled into the chair where she'd been sitting, but caught herself on the armrest. She stood, picking up her pocketbook. She unsnapped it and took out her sunglasses. Her eyes were round and soft, with fine wrinkles stitched between her thin eyebrows. She put the sunglasses on.

"Let's go," she said, breathless. And, as usual, I followed her, and we left.

That afternoon my mother set up the old reel-to-reel in the living room without saying a word. Mitzie was at one of her carpool-driven activities. Dilworth, having finished up work where I now imagined him mismeasuring bridges and mangling fillings, had gone for a round of golf with someone other than Bob Pinkering. He'd not only fired my stepdad as his dentist but also as his golfing buddy. I stood back for a while in the kitchen doorway, but slowly I moved into the living room with her and sat in a chair across from the sofa where she'd curled up. It was dark, the curtains drawn, lights out, the film's shadowy light, the clicking reel. She was drinking from a bottle of scotch, straight, no glass even. I didn't know what had happened that night in her house with her father and mother and Cliff. Someone had been hit over the head with a bat. There was bathwater, pink with blood. But that was all I understood. It went so quickly in a whisper. But I knew it wasn't good. I knew that my mother looked smaller, shrunken into herself, with a pillow pressed to her chest. I could tell that what had begun to come undone in her the night I found her ironing in the kitchen had continued to lose its hold and now all of those small but essential hooks-and-eyes that kept her together were gone. She said, "I remember the parade, too, earlier in the week. A parade right down the Atlantic City boardwalk, all lit up at night. It was a misty night, just enough water in the air to make the streetlights look like shimmering globes. It didn't ever really rain. There was a Planters' Peanuts man, a giant peanut with his top hat and cane, and advertisements all over the place for a diving horse, but I never could figure out where that was or why anyone would want to see such a thing. We rode on the backseats of Oldsmobiles, each girl from each state, waving away. I remember people calling out. A bunch of boys on top of a phone booth, chanting, *New*

Jersey, New Jersey." And the reigning Miss America on a parade float, the crown, the scepter, the robe. We were a family, you know. That's what they called it: the Miss America Family. They'd tell all us girls, 'Welcome to the Miss America Family.' And even though I knew it wouldn't really last, the words would echo in my head. It was like I'd been an orphan and was now suddenly adopted. In my interview, I talked about the terribleness of war, the hope of peace, but do you want to know what my true cause was? The one thing I really was hoping for as Miss America?"

"What?" I asked.

"I was hoping for a real family. The real Miss America family of my own making. The perfect family, Ezra, smiling faces around a steaming pork roast, a bright, happy kitchen always freshly scrubbed clean with S.O.S. And it would seem like I have that, wouldn't it? It'd seem that way."

We watched the roaming spotlights, Glenn Osser conducting in his headphones, Bert Parks, too, in his pale yellow tuxedo, and the dancers in their ruffled shirts skipping through dry-ice smoke. There were ads for Toni's hair products, Dippity-Do and White Rain, and Oldsmobile "Escape from the Ordinary," all excited about their auto windows and locks, "a new wiper and washer control at your fingertips." And then my mother quick-stepping down the runway in her blue dress with its gold medallions, her Miss New Jersey banner across her chest. Bert Parks saying, "Miss America is a composite of positive wonders," like he'd just made that up and didn't it sound good? It was in color, but new color, not what we've got today. This color was always just a little off, her cheeks too pink, her forehead too pale, her hair a loud yellow, but she was beautiful, her face filling the screen.

When we heard Dilworth's car in the driveway, Miss Colorado in her red leotard with its sequins, boa collar, and fringed bottom was twirling a baton to the tune of "Moon River." Dilworth had obviously not had a good day on the golf course. His new partner, I figured, was more of a challenge than old Bob the podiatrist, distracted by the thought of his chickie in New Orleans. Dilworth slammed the back door and walked into the living room.

He said, "Pixie? Oh, Pix? Are we going to eat tonight?"

My mother didn't answer. I kept quiet too.

He charged over to the screen, stood in front of it, to get our attention. Miss Colorado was twirling across his broad chest, his pink polo shirt. She could whip a baton over her shoulders, tip back her head, and roll the baton over her mouth. "Do we have to relive the glory days? Some people are hungry, you know, in need of nourishment. In the here and now. Do you think you could handle making dinner? Do you think you could handle that?"

My mother pointed at the screen. "She went on to Radio City Music Hall, twirling double batons on fire for their Christmas show." Her voice was flat, expressionless. I couldn't understand why Dilworth couldn't see that something had changed, something serious had happened, and I wondered why I could see it so clearly, why it was so obvious to me and whether it was normal or not, this desire I had to cradle her in my arms and promise to take care of her forever, because that's really what I wanted to do.

"Pixie," he said. "Pixie."

"In a little while, Miss Nebraska is going to be voted Miss Congeniality. She's going to thank God for all of us."

Dilworth said her name again, angry now. "Pixie!"

She looked into his eyes, not daring him, not pushing him, but showing weakness.

But he didn't read her right, or maybe he did and decided to take advantage. "You know that beauty pageants are a joke. You know this, don't you? If I told someone you were Miss New Jersey, they'd laugh. Right? Am I right?" He stood with the beauty contestants on his beefy ex-quarterback's chest, including my beautiful mother, in the background now, just over Bert Parks' shoulder, Bert Parks, with his white bottom teeth always showing, his serious eyebrows. Dilworth looked down, finally seeing what we were seeing. He marched from lamp to lamp, turning on each little switch, the overhead ceiling fan, too, mistaking one chain for the other. And suddenly the room was bright and windy, and I could just barely see the ladies on the screen, their hips pivoted to one side, waving their cupped hands. I could no longer tell which one was my mom. They all looked the same, suddenly grainy, faded, old.

Dilworth stood his ground, the dark hair on the back of his head flipping up in the fan's breeze. My mother walked unsteadily up to bed, still clutching the bottle of scotch. She'd flipped off her shoes, so she was barefoot, the thin bones of the backs of her ankles so delicate. Now, looking back, that's what I see most clearly, her delicate ankles, the pink heels of her feet.

Once she was out of the room, Dilworth turned to me. "What are you looking at, runt? See how you upset your mother. See? How is it that I have to deal with you, you snotty shit-for-brains."

I wanted to yell at him, to tell him that he was the asshole around here, that one day my mother wouldn't just whisper when she thought he was asleep that she was going to leave him, but she really would pack up and go, maybe shouting at the top of her lungs, but I didn't. I said, "Shut up," in this quiet voice.

"What did you say?" He paused. I was quiet. "I didn't think so."

I never yelled back at Dilworth. I always just took it, because I've always been a good kid, and if I fought back, what would my mother do? Dilworth stomped off to the kitchen to warm up some of Helga's leftovers. I sat in the living room for a long time, watching the faded women on the screen until there were only two left, holding hands, Glenn Osser's orchestra buzzing their violins. Finally, Bert Parks announced the winner, Miss Michigan. She covered her mouth with her gloved hands. She got the scepter, the red fur-lined robe, the crown clipped to her hair. And then the film unwound, its tail rattling behind it like a tattered, wind-beaten kite, exhausted. I shambled back to the pool bungalow, leaving the reel-to-reel and the screen in the middle of the living room.

Once in her bedroom, alone, my mother took her pills, I assume, the two white pills that help her sleep, and went to bed. When she woke up in the middle of the night next to her husband in their queen-size bed, she took the gun out of her bedside table, the gun she'd bought years before in that pawn shop in Bayonne, and before Dilworth had the chance to wake up, she shot him.

Part Two

Pixie

How to Play the Role

I didn't kill Dilworth Stocker," I said. "He isn't dead. I only nicked his shoulder, really, and no one can expect to go through this life without some sort of scar. Dilworth now has a visible scar. Perhaps he won't ever sleep quite as deeply. But, trust me, he'll be just fine. He's Dilworth Stocker!" Dilworth's mother left him and his father beat on him, even in the back room of his furnace shop with customers waiting, listening in, but he never let it bother him. Dilworth became a dentist, an American triumph. I wasn't confident about much, but I never worried about Dilworth's ability to bounce back, not for one second.

At my first therapy session, I talked to a young woman, a quiet psychiatrist peeking at me from her wire-frame glasses that magnified her eyes and their dark circles. "I am a dentist's wife, simply that. Just look at me!" I told her. "I certainly don't belong here." I was serene, perfectly rehearsed. I'd been playing this role for years. She nodded, expressionless. It was a dark room, wood-paneled with a fake floor plant in the corner, its leaves dull and dusty. I wondered if there had been a real one that had dried up under her care. She didn't seem the least bit nurturing. I took the fake plant as a bad sign. I was skeptical.

Honestly, shooting Dilworth was a mistake on my part. I admitted this, and that I had terrible dreams, although I didn't go into the dream itself. I didn't tell her that my mother had had an episode, a breakthrough, of sorts, in which she told me certain things. Nor did I mention anything about the past, how I'd shelved it for years, that I'd thought I could ignore my memories, fold them and tuck them away, my brain a linen closet of things I didn't want to think about. I'd practiced this to near perfection, but the closet door had opened and the sheets were jumping off the shelves, springing open, gusting like sails. No. I was moving step by step, slowly, deliberately.

I concentrated on explaining, simply, that the night before last, lying in bed next to Dilworth, I'd woken up from one of those bad dreams with a scream stuck in the back of my throat. And I'd wondered at first where I was. The air-conditioning was off and the windows were open. I liked the house tightly sealed in all weather. I liked to control the temperature. I'd read somewhere that it was better that way for our health, as well as for the wood furniture and floors. In Delaware, there's a lot of undue humidity. Dil liked to keep the windows open. He liked the fresh air. Especially in winter, he insisted on sleeping with the window cracked, to breathe real air and prove his heartiness. He's originally from western Pennsylvania where heartiness is a virtue. The psychiatrist nodded in a way that made me think she knew people from western Pennsylvania or somewhere like it.

When I looked at Dilworth in the light through the window from the streetlight outside, he didn't look like himself. He looked like someone else, someone who resembled Dilworth but was not exactly Dilworth. I thought of waking him, testing him with questions on how I met him in the electric dental chair, my teeth "a marvel of science," he'd said, his highest compliment, how he'd helped me back and forth from work to the hospital where poor Ezra's lungs were filling up again, my sickly son, pneumonia. I thought of asking him about Mitzie, our little girl who looks just like him. And why not resemble Dilworth? Who needs to be all that pretty, my mother would say, it's only one more thing to be taken away, like everything else. And, perhaps, I agree. Maybe I should have asked him to explain our marriage, never a love affair to begin with, but his perspective on the cold that settled like arthritis into a bone and how it was we stopped touching each other.

But then Dilworth rolled over, the streetlight outside casting weird shadows on his face, and it was at this moment in talking to the psychiatrist that I felt like I could go on talking forever, that there were a million things that I'd never explained to anyone, ever. I'd known he was not Dilworth Stocker, not even a little bit, but someone else altogether.

This made me panic, "as it would you," I added to the young psychiatrist, "or anyone for that matter." I wondered when the stranger had taken over. "Imagine sleeping next to someone you've known for years and years, someone you trust and find that they are not themselves, but someone else," I said and then I asked the young doctor if she was married although it was quite obvious that she was not the marrying type. She was a dedicated professional, the kind who thinks of her patients as her children. One day someone will ask her if she has kids and she'll say, "No, but as a psychiatrist I've brought a lot of people through to maturity."

"No," she said. "I'm not married."

"Well, you can still imagine!" I told her. I went on, realizing now that I hadn't talked this much in years, that my throat was actually ragged from all this chatter, but I couldn't stop. I couldn't even slow down. I thought of my mother in the hospital, the stream of words pouring out of her, tumbling one after the other, like a paper-doll chain from her mouth, and I imagined it must have felt a little like this, a breaking open and then no stopping, like the flooding of my memory, but suddenly out loud, a script set to all of those images. I admitted that I could have phoned the police. I could have woken the stranger up and asked him what he was doing in my bed.

"But Dilworth is a big man, a quarterback in his heyday," I said. "And I'm petite, a woman, but I am a woman with a gun. I believe all women should have guns, only women. The world would be a better place. I believe this very strongly. Every woman should have an escape route. I always have. It's the way I've gotten from one place to another."

The therapist took note of this, scribbling something on a pad.

I went on and told her the rest, that I took the gun out of

my bedside table where I've had it for years and have never, ever disturbed it. I picked it up and took a few steps back. My hands were shaking, my heart seizing in my chest like my mother's heart, her angina. I felt like I couldn't breathe even though I was breathing too much. The windows were open and there was a breeze in the room, but there wasn't enough air for me. I pointed the gun, shakily, and I took a deep breath and closed my eyes. I fired two shots off, quickly; one burrowed into the pillow, the other hit Dilworth in the shoulder. I dropped the gun then, to my feet. Dilworth woke up howling, cursing. He rolled on the bed like an angry bear, blood now pouring onto the sheets. Mitzie stumbled into the room, still sleepy, and started screaming, and I could hear Ezra running across the backyard, calling out for me, not his sweet cry but something deeper that I almost didn't recognize, and soon he was there, too, in the room. I looked at him, so big, so fully grown. Suddenly, it was clear to me now that Dilworth was Dilworth and that this was my life, something truly happening, something finally happening, if you know what I mean, and although that was a relief, this action, the blood, the screaming, a relief in a way, if you can understand that, it was terrifying, too. Because suddenly everything in the world, my world, was as wrong as I'd always felt it was.

The psychiatrist asked me what was so wrong with my world, but she asked the question without saying a word. She was silent, her eyebrows raised.

I said, "Let me ask you this: is your world perfect? Is everything just the way you think it should be? My mother has always said that people think they can see what's coming when

they can't. I'm saying that you can mistake the most obvious
things for the most obvious things, that we go through this
life nearly blind, even with our eyes open and our hands desperately searching out every corner, the coming of every sharp
edge, our feet reaching in front of us for the point where the
path drops off."

"And did your path drop off?" she actually said it out loud
this time.

"Well, of course, but what kind of path was it? Making sure
the toilet water was a bright blue? Changing the trap on the
bug zapper? Where does that path go anyway, only in a circle,
I'd imagine, like riding an upsy-down horsey on a merry-go-
round. Are you following me? Do you know what I'm saying?"

She looked at me intently and nodded, most reassuringly,
"Yes," she said, "blue toilet water, the bug zapper, the merry-
go-round. Yes, of course."

Ezra

Rule #7: Always carry your own bags.

It's not as exciting as you'd think, your mother shooting your stepdad. It's a lot of busywork and maybe that's a good thing. Dilworth made arrangements from the hospital. Helga was to come and stay with me and Mitzie until Mitzie's chain of carpool mothers could be reached and my father could come and pick me up. The plan was to shuffle Mitzie from house to house until my mother came home. Dilworth used his bum arm as an excuse not to be in charge of Mitzie. She would end up at the Worthingtons, where she'll probably spend a lot of time from here on out, leading a very wholesome life, probably turning into a very decent and upstanding individual. The Worthingtons can almost guarantee something like that. As for my dad, it was around the time of year that he usually showed up anyway. And he showed up so quickly early the next morning—in a total of maybe seven hours—that it confirmed my suspicion that he was a lot closer more often than he let on, that California was a cover, an excuse not to come.

Helga soaked and washed the sheets, the rug in the master bedroom, the towels, and the bloody handprints on the walls and doorknobs and sinks. I don't want to go into detail here. There are just a few facts anyway. Our neighbor, Jim Worthington, drove Dilworth to the hospital, where he got bandaged up. It was really a small flesh wound, but Dilworth is so pumped with blood, so alive and all-American in that blood-pumped way, that it seemed like a lot of blood. I was to call my mother's psychiatrist, at home, in the middle of the night. Dilworth told the Worthingtons that my mother had been cleaning the gun, because she often cleans when she's awake in the middle of the night, and that it accidentally went off. (A story he'd stick with.) But that she was too upset by the accident to drive Dilworth to the hospital herself, and, he added, perhaps too embarrassed. And the Worthingtons, being polite, pretended that this kind of thing happened all the time. At the front door, I heard Mr. Worthington say, "Well, you owe me one," and "Hey, what are neighbors for?"

I'd said to Dilworth while he was waiting at the front door for Mr. Worthington to get dressed, my mother still upstairs, that I didn't know my mother had a psychiatrist. It seemed like a silly thing to bring up at that moment, what with the recent gunfire, but it surprised me. My mother wasn't the type to go in and bare her soul. She always seemed bored by self-awareness, annoyed by people who indulged in it.

Dilworth answered, "How else would she get the drugs she likes?" He was holding a bloody towel to his shoulder.

I'd been masturbating, if you want to know the honest truth, when I'd heard the gun go off. I'd been remembering what it was like to be inside Janie Pinkering, and I had a bottle of my mother's almond-scented hand lotion to help me along, which was confusing because the lotion reminded me of the smell of my mother's hands. But I knew what the sound was right off. As soon as I heard it, I realized I'd been waiting to hear the gun ever since my mother bought it when I was five years old. I zipped up a pair of shorts and ran across the yard, my chest bare, calling for my mother, into the house and up the stairs.

When I found her, she was already moving toward the vanity, where she sat down, her ankles crossed politely, and swayed her legs to one side. She was putting on makeup. I remember the shakiness of her hand as she applied her lipstick, only the slightest of wobbles as she stood on one foot to put on her linen pantsuit. The gun had already been put away somewhere, hidden by Dilworth, so she couldn't do any more damage to herself or, again, to him. I remembered how it was when I was a little kid. I felt the same way I'd felt then, the same way I'd felt when the men started showing up at our house, night after night, the men greenishly reflected in the kitchen table, the men behind her locked bedroom door. I remembered in a flash the way I often imagined her during that time, her voice so feverish that she could catch fire, standing in front of me, not knowing that she was on fire, acting as if everything were normal, everything in its place, but something so basically wrong. I could still smell the gun smoke in the room. I wanted to save her and I couldn't and I hated her for it, for making me feel helpless. I didn't move.

Mitzie went right to her. She stood beside her. She said, "Everything's okay, right?"

And my mother said, "I shot your father, but he seems to be fine." We could hear Dilworth talking on the downstairs phone, the wince in his voice. His blood marked things here and there around the room. Mitzie's eyes were wide, taking it all in. She hiccuped a little sob but didn't cry, not really. She started talking in her screechy voice about swimming and her friend Bonnie's new bike with pom-poms streaming from the handlebars.

My mother said, "That's nice," and "Would you like pom-poms?"

Mitzie said she would, in fact, but she could wait for a birthday. "Are you going somewhere?" Mitzie asked.

"I believe so," my mother said. That's when she got up and dressed in the pantsuit and started packing her bag. "Someone will come for me. That's what happens in a case like this. Some sort of professional. I'm not sure, really. It's my first time." And so my mother finessed shooting Dilworth. In fact, the more she talked to Mitzie about the novelty of the evening's events, the calmer she got. Mitzie, too, calmed down, buying my mother's explanation that things like this happen, that it was new to us, but that it's something that's almost bound to happen eventually to every American family, like the death of a beloved pet, but maybe not even that tragic, maybe just the breakdown of an old car.

I walked downstairs where I found Dilworth and followed his orders. I called my mother's psychiatrist. It was obvious from his craggy voice that he'd been asleep, and who wouldn't have been? It was the middle of the night. I said, "I'm Pixie Stocker's son and we've got a situation here."

"What kind?" the doctor asked.

"The serious kind," I said. "I don't want to say that my mother shot her husband, but it seems like my mother shot her husband, in the arm, only. He's on his way to the hospital right now. Maybe she was just cleaning the gun out."

The doctor said that he'd be right over, and I waited on the front stoop. I could hear Mitzie through the open upstairs window, chattering about the sag of her ballet tights at the crotch and how much the Worthingtons' cats seemed to like her, that Mrs. Worthington said that maybe she'd give Mitzie a kitten one day, if her parents approved.

The doctor was old and bowlegged. He walked up the path like a rocking bowling pin just about to tip over. He had some other people with him, two stocky men in jeans, T-shirts, and white coats, like sloppy scientists, and he told me that he was going to take her to the hospital, that it was where she needed to be. I pointed upstairs, but I couldn't go up to watch. I couldn't stomach my mother's sweet disposition, the way she'd say, "Oh, just one moment please," as she remembered her toothbrush or eyelash curler.

My mother didn't take long. But before she walked out the front door toward the waiting car, she said, "Ezra?"

"Yes?"

"Will you be here when I get home?"

I nodded, because I was choked up all of a sudden, scared, I guess, because nobody else was. And then I said it out loud, because I knew she wasn't really looking at me. "Yes," I said.

"I'll be here." But even as I said it, I knew that I probably wouldn't be there, that Dilworth would probably start working on farming me out, and that I'd be working hard to get farmed out. I felt naked and folded my arms across my bare chest.

She said, "You know, it's already done. There's nothing to do now but let it play itself out as gracefully as possible."

The doctor took her arm. They walked together to the car. The door was open. Its interior light lit the brick path. The two stocky guys sat in the front seat. The doctor sat in the back and my mother was seated beside him, her soft, blond hair lit up on top of her head, and then someone closed the door. The light went out. Headlights flared and they pulled out of the driveway. I was standing with my empty hands at my sides.

Mitzie said, "It'll be okay. Everything's going to be fine."

Across the street, I could see Mrs. Worthington in her bay window. Her living room was dark, but there was just enough light from the dining room to show the outline of her body, shoulders hunched, one hand up to the window to cut the glare, a cat stretched out on the sill. I tried to imagine what she saw: my mother taken away in the dark car, and me and Mitzie alone on the step, my skinny chest and Mitzie in her nightgown.

I said, "No, Mitz, it's not all going to be okay. Everything is not fine."

"What do you mean, Ezra? Mommy said so. Didn't you hear her?"

I glanced down at Mitzie, her eyes filled with water now. It was hot enough out, but she looked like she was shivering; the hem of her nightgown shook. "I must not have heard her say that," I said. "I must have missed that. I guess you're right." I felt like I was going to cry and I didn't want Mitzie to see me crying. "Go up to bed. It's late."

"Not till you say it, Ezra. Not till you say it's all going to be all right."

"It will," I said. "Everything will be all right."

She turned away and trotted upstairs. The wind was warm. I wanted to believe what I'd said, but I couldn't.

As Dilworth had requested, Helga arrived soon after in her trusty red Ford Escort with its bent radio antenna. She helped Mitzie fall asleep, humming what sounded like patriotic German marches, even though Mitzie could have fallen asleep just fine by herself. She now seemed more fine than she'd ever been, as calm as Mitzie Stocker gets. I fell asleep on the living-room sofa for a few short hours. Helga had me up early, pushing her meaty hand into my thigh, bouncing me into the sofa cushion. She had already packed a bag for me.

"Your father is comink," she said. "He's on his way to pick you up and take you to Baltimore with him."

I'd been to the city a number of times before with my mother on shopping trips and once with Dilworth to an Orioles game, where we wore matching hats and pretended to like each other. But I'd never been anywhere with my father, really, much less to a different city. "Are you sure?" I asked. "I mean, he usually just takes me to the Columbus Inn for crab and corn bisque."

Helga was firm. "He will take over your care for a while. Until Mrs. Stocker iss home and running her householt again."

Sure enough, my father pulled up in the driveway and

beeped the horn of a shiny silver convertible, top down. I wouldn't even ask because I knew it was not his. He hopped out of the driver's seat, wearing a pair of small, round sunglasses, faded jeans, a one-pocket T-shirt. He wasn't tan as much as he was even. His wavy hair was receding just a little up front but was longish and curly in the back. He was handsome, embarrassingly so. It made me shrink.

He said, "Hello, Mitzie. Helga."

Mitzie waved and Helga nodded.

My father took my bag for me, gallantly, like I was a girl and I let him. I mean, I wasn't going to hold on to it and get into a tug of war. "Here we go. A road trip!"

Helga and Mitzie had followed me to the door. "Be careful," Helga said, eyeing my father.

Mitzie said, "I wish I could come with you, Ezra." She hadn't been remotely invited. "But I've got a lot to do here."

I said, "I know. But don't take it so seriously."

"I won't," she said, but she seemed determined. I wondered who was going to visit my grandmother and if Helga was really taking care of her birds. I remembered suddenly the dead bird in the Nescafé jar hidden in the Pinkerings' pachysandra—unfinished business.

My father threw my bag in the backseat, and we climbed in, buckled our seatbelts, and zipped out of the driveway and down the street, passing by the neat lawns and stone walkways. It looked pretty, manicured, delicate.

"So," he said. "I hear your mother shot the old tight end." His tone was cavalier, but there was a nervousness in his eyes, a flickering, that led me to believe he was concerned.

"Yep," I said, but I felt a little defensive. My father always started out too chummy. I hated that, and I was feeling bad for Dilworth. I remember how he'd been with me alone in the kitchen, proud of my conquest of "the Pinkering girl." "You don't know him," I said, but I think I meant, *You don't know me.* "He's not so bad."

"No, not now," he said. "I mean, he got shot. He didn't deserve to get shot."

"He was a quarterback," I said.

"Right. That's right." My father drove with only one wrist on the wheel, his hair whipping around on top of his head. "I blame marriage," he said. "It's not a healthy way for people to live. Especially not your mother."

"I think she liked being married to you," I said.

"Oh, God, no! Who would want to be married to me? I turn into Clark Kent, always trying desperately to stay Clark Kent. I lose my cape completely. I'm no fun and then, well, I screw it up. One day I just can't pass another telephone booth." He smiled at me but could tell I wasn't interested. "That's a bad analogy, though. I mean, I'm no superhero. We all know that."

"I'd hate to be Superman," I said. "No pockets. You can't be casual in a getup like that." It wasn't my joke. I'd heard Christopher Reeve say something like that once.

My dad laughed. "So, you're okay?" he asked.

"Yeah," I said, but I wasn't so sure. I was still thinking of my mother, how I couldn't do anything for my mother, how I'd done what Dilworth told me to do, and I felt like I'd betrayed her. On top of that, I'd told her I'd be there when she got home, and here I was gone already. I imagined her in a white hospital room with the bowling-pin–shaped doctor at her side and then I remembered Pete Duvet describing the particulars of being crazy, talking to puppets, doing crafts, being asked how he *felt* about everything. I wondered if my mother was doing any of these things, if they were making her take pills coated in peanut butter, and if these pills made her talk about that night in her parents' house when she was just a kid my age, with her mother screaming and her dad and her dead brother, Cliff. I was thinking the words, *My mother shot her husband while he was asleep in bed. My mother's in an insane asylum,* even though nobody had called it that or called it anything, for that matter. But saying it over and over didn't make it any more real.

My father told me where we were headed. "We're staying with a friend of mine, with his parents, actually, where he's been staying since a messy breakup. It's not the best circumstance. It's not optimal, but I promised we'd visit for a little while. I promised I'd stop by, and explained your situation to him as well." I wondered how he'd done that: *Poor kid's mother shot her husband. Poor kid's mom's in the nuthouse.* "Plus, there's an opportunity in Baltimore that I can't pass up, a big one. My ship's coming in." He turned to me and smiled, showing all of his white teeth, and flicked his eyebrows up and down. I was tired of all of his little schemes, lofty in their vagueness. He went on, "Plus, the way this guy puts it, his parents could eat him alive." I pictured monsters. He paused. "You tired? You look tired. You can sleep if you want to."

I couldn't sleep, but I didn't feel like talking. So I tilted the seat back and stared at the blue sky, the clouds, swag after swag of black power lines. I looked up into the cabs of eighteen-wheelers, the tanned arms of truckers, their elbows cocked out of windows.

When we started to wind through the city, I propped the seat up. The stop-and-start traffic made it hot, the sun beating down on the top of my head. People noticed the car and stared at us, disappointed, I thought, in just seeing me in the passenger's seat, not a blonde to go along with my father, not, for example, an exquisite beauty like my mother, but just some pip-squeaky kid.

I watched people clumped at an intersection, a girl adjusting her underwear by reaching up under a short pink skirt. We drove away from downtown, the harbor, the Domino Sugar sign, up Charles Street, past Johns Hopkins and some big stately homes with yards. Finally, we ended up on York Road. We passed a WE BLEACH TEETH billboard, a check-cashing store, a Chinese restaurant with its string of plastic colored lanterns and plate-glass storefront painting of a red dragon.

"This isn't the most direct route," my father confessed, "but I think we're getting closer." And then, changing the subject, he said, "I should warn you that Richard—that's the guy we're visiting—he's very gay. I forget to warn people. He'll look tame today because he's with his parents, but he's very flamboyant. I don't know how many gay people you know, I mean besides me, and so I thought I'd just warn you." And so this was how my father told me he was gay. Quite simply, he told me only when he *had to* tell me, when he was about to get busted; I'd realize soon enough that Richard was a loose cannon, capable of saying anything. My arrival had come up unexpectedly. My father hadn't had time to figure out another plan. In his defense, he probably hoped that I knew, that by sixteen, I'd put the pieces of the puzzle together, or somebody had just come out with it. In any case, I hadn't known, and it was shitty timing, wasn't it? The worst timing of all. I mean, my mother had just shot her husband, for Chrissakes.

"What do you mean, *besides you?*" I said, because I had no idea what he meant.

"I mean that besides me I don't know if you know *any* gay people." The car was slowing down now. My dad was looking up at house numbers, trying to be casual, as if it were just a glitch, a momentary miscommunication in our little chitchat. But he was nervous, too nervous for someone just glancing at doorways. He was gripping the wheel tightly now, and there were little bubbles of sweat on his forehead.

"You mean you're gay?" I said.

He pulled the car over in front of a fire hydrant and looked at me, both hands still on the wheel. "Of course!" he said, incredulous, but fake, too. He knew that I didn't know. He had to make sure I knew before I met Richard, before Richard let it slip somehow, and this was the way he did it, by pretending not to know that I didn't know. "Didn't you know that?"

"I thought you were in *politics.* I thought you were like *a politician!*"

"Is that what your mother told you?"

I nodded.

"Your mother romanticizes me. I gave up politics years

ago, like everyone else. Back in the '60s everything was political. But that doesn't work. I mean, I can't very well be out with everyone I meet. I'm a businessman. I always figured you knew, though. I mean, how couldn't you!" He was a little breathless, his eyes exhausted but lifted up by his raised eyebrows as if still flabbergasted, in a complete and utter state of shock, almost as if it were my fault for not having been told.

I was pissed that I was the last to know. I thought of how my mother always spoke of my father, all of that business of "He is who he is" and "You can't change somebody," that he was trying to buy some life for himself. I thought of how Dilworth never talked about him at all—which I suppose was a real act of restraint, a kindness almost, since Dilworth was the type to use all his ammo. But at the same time, I remembered Dilworth hadn't thought I'd had it in me to *umph* Janie Pinkering. I now realized that he'd thought I was gay, like my old man! I decided that *British* had been one big code for *gay,* the same way Dilworth would say, "He's a *little* man, very intelligent," meaning Jewish. Even Helga that morning had eyed my father suspiciously. She was probably in on the secret. Everyone knew! I was disgusted.

"I know plenty of gays!" I said, indignant. "Plenty." But I didn't really. I'd only heard rumors about the teacher at St. Andrew's with his homemade rockets, the one Rudy *thought* was gay, and that time in the high weeds when Rudy got real weird. I turned away from my father, looking at the neighborhood, the gutter littered with glass and plastic bags. It was a shitty part of town. Broken-down row houses, a Dunkin' Donuts, and a pancake house up the street. We were the only

white people in view, at the bus stop, the flag-happy car deal-
ership across the street. I thought, *I could get shot here in the silver convertible. Shot and killed with my gay father.* It seemed to me
now that everyone had guns and were just itching to use them.
I imagined the L.A. girls I'd always pictured him with,
blondes in bikinis, and suddenly their chests grew hard, their
jaws square. They grew Adam's apples and muscled arms. I
imagined my father kissing one of them, his perfect face kissing a man's tough lips, the coarseness of his stubble, my
father's hands running through another man's hair, and I wondered, although I had some pretty sick ideas, what exactly my
father did with his lovers next, if they had sex and what kind,
if my father had ever taken it. I thought, *My father's a fucking
faggot, an L.A. fag,* and how I could just add that on to *My
mother shot her husband. She's in the nuthouse.* That the two went
together nicely; it was just perfect! I thought of that day Rudy
and I'd gotten stoned and spied on some supposedly naked
women, and Rudy went crazy, really, and pulled out his dick in
the high weeds all lit up with sun. I thought about opening
the door and throwing up on the street. I wished I hadn't let
my father carry my bag to the car for me.

"We're here," he said, regretting it, but not really regretting it either. I mean he'd timed this thing so he could weasel
his way out of it. He pointed to a house, slightly tilted forward
from the row, like a bucktooth. It was a quaint house with
flower boxes and the typical Baltimore fresh-scrubbed front
stoop. I figured they'd held on to the place even though everything changed around them.

The door opened and Richard bounded down the stone

steps. I would pick up soon enough that Richard was a bounder, that he nearly galloped wherever he went, like a boy with a new toy pony, a head on a stick. He was a little younger than my father with a mop of Miss Clairol red hair and a lavender shirt and thin tie, and he was agile and strong. I wondered if my father had ever done it with Richard, if he was an ex-lover. I figured he was. Why else would we have to be here? Why now?

A blanched old couple stood in the doorway. Richard rounded the car, glanced at us and gave a quick smile, and held out his hands, showing us his parents. He was very gay, combustibly gay. And his parents looked like little expressionless parchment cutouts of people in contrast. I felt sorry for them. I felt like we were compatriots losing the same war. I wanted to tell them that there were normal kids in the world, like me, who could just sit in their den and learn the strategies of chess, popping the old lady's homemade tarts.

Richard leaned into the car, over my lap. "What took you so long?" he said. "I thought I'd asphyxiate on normalcy and all that plastic-covered-furniture tension. God, that lingering odor of mothballs and soup!" He sniffed his jacket. "I don't know if it will ever come out!"

Pixie

How to Fake an Inkblot

Another doctor escorted me into the same small wood-paneled office, a man this time, but he was also short with the same dark circles under the eyes and frizzy hair as my first therapist. He could have been the first doctor's brother, and I wondered for a second about their mother—although they weren't really siblings—and if she'd taught them anything about personal grooming. Above his white coat pocket there were a hundred pen marks, as if he couldn't remember to cap his pens before tucking them away. There was mustard on his collar, a splotch now crusted over. I wondered if anyone was taking care of these people. And what about Ezra? Mitzie? (I admit I think of Ezra first, don't I? Sometimes when I think of my family, I think of Ezra alone for just a split second, before Mitzie and Dilworth flood in. It's like he's purely mine, a part of me, that he's always been with me, long before he was ever

born.) I decided that maybe my kids were better off now without having me right there in front of them, but at the same
time absent, lost. Wasn't it better to have me really be absent?
Wasn't that at least less confusing?

I'd gone through all the interviews by this point. I'd taken
the long test, filled in the bubble sheet of true and false.

The sky is blue. <u>True.</u>

I've always loved auto-mechanic magazines. <u>False.</u>

Animals talk to me. <u>False.</u> et cetera, et cetera.

And now these inkblots. I laughed when the doctor pulled
them out. "I thought the profession had given up on those old
things! I thought they'd be antiques by now. I mean each one
is a Jackson Pollock painting, and who would comment on a
Jackson Pollock?"

He was not amused. He held them up, one after the other.
What good was an inkblot going to do me? Anyone can outwit
a black splotch on paper. I said the sweetest things like,
"Butterfly, two tilted irises, horses kissing." But sometimes I
saw bubbles rising in water, and I thought of the tub and my
father dying. It made me feel sick. I tilted my head. I stared
and stared until at last I could think of something nice . . . a
seal, the kind with the big wet eyes. Finally, I told the doctor
that I'd rather talk to a woman again. "No offense."

He said, "None taken."

And soon enough, the other psychologist shuffled in again,
the young woman with the raised eyebrows and wire-rim
glasses who thought she knew what I was talking about. She
was wearing woolly slip-on clogs.

I told her that I'd thought about it and had decided that I

might have something worthwhile to share with others. "I've had a varied life," I said. "I could really write a how-to. The chapters of my life would go something like: How to Survive Not Being Miss America, How to Survive Finding Your First Husband in Bed with Another Man, How to Be a Pimpless Whore, How to Marry a Dentist, How to Shoot Your Husband, things of this nature." I was trying to keep things light. I was joking, but she took me seriously. It's her job to take people seriously. With all the weirdos in this world, I've no idea how she can keep a straight face.

She nodded solemnly.

I told her that the first chapter would have to be about my childhood, planning my escape route. "But I don't want to dwell on my childhood," I said. "My childhood was spent trying desperately to get out of my childhood." I didn't tell that I hadn't been able to shake it, that it had been there in my mind so much that I'd almost been living two lives, neither very successfully. I didn't tell her that for years I kept Wanda Sorenski's knitting needle, the one she used to break her water and induce a miscarriage, and that I remembered the small weight of the baby on my chest, barely alive, tiny, blue, how its little breaths finally stopped. After Wanda's doctor left, after I got her kids to bed, I washed the needle in her kitchen sink and put it in my pocketbook. My life went on, but I kept it for a long time, because life is ugly, because I knew something, and I was going to hold on to knowing it. I think I knew that memories could leave you, if you wanted them to, if you'd let them. "I'm better at reinvention than I am at dragging around the past," I said. "It did my father no good to try to relive the past, jumping into the Kill van Kull like he did when he was a kid. It killed him, didn't it? I'm lucky I have a terrible memory. I've never wanted a good one." But as it turns out, my memory is good and bad, spotty. I know this. It's keen and then evaporates.

I went on to explain that when I was Miss New Jersey, after having been Miss Bayonne, I didn't know that I was already a whore. I hadn't yet decided that there were only three types of people—whores, pimps, and johns. I didn't think it was a groundbreaking realization. I knew it was an inkling, maybe, that all people have, the kind of thing that might come to you after finding your first husband in bed with another man. I told her that was how it happened for me, and I hauled Ezra back to a dump in Bayonne where I lay around for a week or more on a nappy sofa, thinking about large, philosophical things like that. Supposedly, this type of talk would make me a feminist. (It's obvious the doctor is a feminist, complete with her woolly slip-on clogs. She'd have been one of the protestors on the boardwalk, burning her thick-strapped A-cup bra.) But I am not a feminist, because feminists, in my opinion, true feminists, won't compromise their ideals. I believe that as a woman you must play dirty; you must take advantage of every so-called weakness. I think that feminists confuse equality with women becoming more male. And look where that's gotten us: now women have to make $30,000 a year and still we've got to raise the children. "Feminists don't deal with unalterable truths," I said. "They're optimists; to be a true feminist you have to be. I am not an optimist. I'm honest."

I was only vaguely aware that I hated men because they

took my beauty personally, like I'd done something to please them, and I hated the fat, self-satisfied way they sat back and watched me like sultans. I remember a certain summer Saturday crowd of them in the chain-link fenced-in yard near the apartment my family lived in. They soaked their feet in metal tubs filled with water, ice slivers, and cans of beer, not to mention the Billy Trexler types, hanging out the windows of borrowed cars. I was used to being paraded. I was used to being expected to smile, to wave. If I wasn't smiling, people would stop me and tell me to smile. "Smile!" they'd demand. "Hey, where's your smile?" Sometimes I would turn to them and demand that they do something to entertain me, to earn the smile, but often I would simply show my teeth and get it over with. This is what the world wanted from me all the time, and I longed to have the distinction that the stage afforded me. So the world wasn't just people wanting me, but an audience appreciating a star. I realized that it was a false distinction, but I needed it.

And the wives from the Kiwanis Club, although they were envious of me, almost scornful, they promised me that I could go all the way to the top. If you are not going to be Miss America, I recommend spending time with wives of the Kiwanis Club. It's another option and one that you can slip into without knowing. How else would someone become a wife of the Kiwanis Club but unwittingly? It's something to be aware of.

I remember when I confided in one of them, during a card game, that I didn't really have a talent, she turned to me and said, "In 1949, Miss Montana rode her palomino into the orchestra pit. Darling, this is not about talent. It's a tits-and-ass show."

I said, "I kind of play the accordion a little."

Another answered, "Miss America doesn't kind of do anything a little bit. From now on you're an aficionado!"

And another added, "If my husband wants accordion music, he'll play his polka records."

Wanda was there, too, nodding along, taking it all in. Wanda would have liked to have been a wife of the Kiwanis Club—I suppose it suits some people—but her husband was not around enough to be a member.

I spent a lot of time in smoky parlors, listening to the Kiwanian wives discuss beauty contests, pathetic talents being their favorite topic—archery with balloon targets; fly-casting; reciting the Lord's Prayer in Indian Sign Language; a speech on sewing, complete with a slide show; and an endless line of flaming baton twirlers. But they paid for everything—my dresses, hair fixings, makeup, swimwear, even the masking tape to cinch my waist and hoist and center my boobs. Meanwhile I learned to play the accordion in a way that didn't block my cleavage, on an angle still showing off my ass.

In 1970 there had been only one Miss New Jersey who became Miss America, Bette Cooper, 1937. She'd started out as Miss Bertrand Island—named after an amusement park at Lake Hopatcong. She'd been dared by friends to enter the pageant. At that time, there was no talent competition; that would come along the next year, with Miss Ohio winning, amid controversy, because of a tap dance routine to "The World Is Waiting for the Sunrise." In any case, Bette Cooper won and panicked. Some say it was her boyfriend who was the driving force, a local guy named Lou Off. She blamed her father, who wanted her to finish school. Her father claimed that it was just too strenuous for Bette to be Miss America. In any case, she disappeared.

Like Bette Cooper, I didn't want to be Miss America, really. I didn't want to be shuttled around the country, cutting ribbons at car dealerships, posing next to prize-winning pigs at the New Jersey State Fair, signing "I love you" to deaf schoolchildren, not that I have anything against car dealerships or farm animals, and especially not the deaf. However, if I'd really wanted to help deaf schoolchildren, then I'd have taken the whole Miss America thing more seriously, like a supreme calling, or I'd have skipped it all together and taken sign language at Monmouth College instead of interior design, classes I eventually dropped out of. I wanted the crowning moment, the crown itself. I got myself so geared up for it that I expected it. I expected to win. But I didn't win.

During the talent competition, I was playing the accordion beautifully, smoothly, and it was almost like making something dead breathe. I thought of my father, because he'd drowned, and it was like I was trying to keep him alive, the bellows inflating and deflating like his lungs, my father, in my arms, singing, his sad voice carried throughout the large hall, the audience making him even more alive. I wanted to keep on playing forever, and when the end of the song came, I couldn't recall it, and somehow I was back at the beginning. Everyone was staring at me. I knew that they'd heard the fumbled keys. I was going over my time limit, but I wanted to keep playing, pumping my father's lungs. Finally I found a note, right in the middle, and I held that note for as long as I could. The crowd clapped politely, but I knew that it was over. My name wasn't called for the final ten. All of the leftover girls were sent off-stage to our dressing tables, where we sat in our evening gowns, watching the rest of the pageant on TV monitors, no different from everyone else in America in their living rooms. I convinced myself there, in that room of overwrought women, slumped in shimmering gowns, that I would have been a Bette Cooper. I'd have walked down the runway, Bert Parks singing his heart out, and I'd have looked out into the audience and seen my mother, in her unfashionable button-down dress, bewildered, suspicious, scared, wondering exactly how all of this good luck and happiness would turn ugly, and Wanda, jumping up and down, her heavy breasts bouncing, her small hands clapping wildly. There was also the clot of women from the Kiwanis Club, still scornful but applauding in white gloves. I'd think of Cliff, maybe hearing about it over some foggy Vietnamese radio station just for GIs, his buddies clapping him on the back, whistling at him as if he were the winner, not me. And then I'd have walked out of the building with the flowers, the crown, down the boardwalk, down the sandy beach, right next to that giant rolling ocean. I wasn't always afraid of water. On that family vacation to the shore, I remember playing in the ocean, and I used to swim in a public pool with my father, but after he drowned, well, I've been afraid of water ever since, but this time I wouldn't have been afraid. I'd have just walked and walked and walked. So, it didn't really matter that I didn't win.

I'd always really wanted to be Miss America so that I could have the perfect family. Who else would eventually be the perfect American wife and mother other than Miss America? She'd eventually become Mrs. America, right? In being the perfect wife and mother, I could erase my mother, my father, my brother and me and start over, proving that there was higher ground, that I'd built it, and that I could reign over it. I could erase my childhood by perfecting someone else's. This is a tragic flaw in thinking, I know now. But I wanted to have the Miss America family—that's what I called it—with a husband named Steve, one son and one daughter, Troy and Wendy. I imagined we'd have a dog, too, a collie named something like Scout or Lucky. I reminded myself of this dream and the fact that Miss America's crown was not necessary in making a family, not even the perfect family, and certainly not a prerequisite for doing a better job than my mother had. I was sure I could outdo my mother by picking a husband from a paper bag—not that I didn't love my father, I truly loved him, but he was imperfect. And so I got married. It's what people do.

"But this isn't what you want from me," I whispered to the psychiatrist. "Is it? I'm very good at knowing what people want. You want to know the secret, you want to know why I did it. I've confided that I realized on that nappy sofa in Bayonne after leaving Russell that I believed we were all pimps or whores or johns. I boiled that down to two categories, then, the powerful and the powerless, and decided that we didn't need to be divided into rich and poor, black and white, not even men and women. That there was no other division besides the powerful and the powerless. I believed this for a long time. But now I would say that there is a more accurate division: those who know and those who don't, that the world is divided by secrets. And when a secret is revealed to you, you become a different person, sometimes more powerful, sometimes less." And so, you see, I knew, but I didn't know. My mother had told me something, but I was still trying to pull down those billowed sails, those wind-gusted sheets and shove them back into the closet. I was beginning to remember the moth smothered by the cottage sheet, too. I was starting to sense the breeding, the coming swarm. And why bed sheets? Why all of these particular linens? White, domestic, ordinary. Now, of course, I know why.

"I'll tell you this: the dream I had the night I shot Dilworth was an old one, my father coughing up keys. The man is always in the dream, swimming toward us, but this night there is no man and, for the first time, I actually catch a key. I held it so tight it was sharp in my fist, its little teeth almost biting alive. I unlocked my father's arms and I climbed on his back with my arms around his neck, but instead of swimming with him to safety, I was choking him, my arms forever tightening around his neck. I killed my father and that's when I woke up. Does that help?" I asked the therapist. "Does that tell you anything?"

"What does it tell *you?*" she asked. "How does that help *you?*"

"Oh, please!" I said. "How did you get to be a psychiatrist anyway? Did you get someone else to do your homework for you? If you think I'm going to provide you with all of the answers, well then you're crazier than I am."

She said that I sounded angry and she wanted to know what that anger was about. "Where is it coming from?"

"The food here is atrocious. I wouldn't feed it to a dog, and my roommate, by the way, pulls her hair out strand by strand. She sits on the edge of her bed, picking at scabs on her scalp, humming "The Star-Spangled Banner." It's irritating. Really and truly. And you, you look a mess. You need to defrizz that hair. Get out of the cardigan. It's summer, for God's sake. Wear some color other than gray. It only brings out your dark circles."

Ezra

Rule #8: Make things clear right from
the get-go.

Richard was right; the house smelled like soup and mothballs. It was old and musty and the sofa and matching wing-back chairs were covered in plastic. There was a piano pushed up against a wall that was cluttered with old round-framed photos. Doilies were dripping off all the furniture, as if naked furniture were lewd, and there was tons of furniture, old polished dark-wood stuff. There were little crystal dishes filled with fossilized pink candies and sappy music playing on the radio, a giant ancient thing on a table in the living room. My father had to duck into the house. He was too big for the furniture, the small room. He hunched forward, looking miserable, with a weak smile.

"Hester and John Pichard," Richard introduced. "Ta da! Russell and his son, Ezra." I thought *Richard Pichard,* and that his parents kind of deserved some sort of punishment for having named him a rhyme.

Mr. Pichard was wearing a light blue cable-knit cardigan, the kind Mr. Rogers was so fond of. He was built close to the ground, hunkering yet spry, like if you tried to take anything he'd get there first, and I had the feeling that he was waiting for me just to try it. He had a crooked nose that veered off to the left, as if it was impolitely pointing out the hump on his left shoulder. His wife was also short, but she was thin with little breasts swung way down by the thin belt of her plaid summer dress.

Mr. Pichard looked at me and then to his wife. "I bought toy trucks. You said he was a boy! A little boy!"

"He's sixteen," my father said.

Richard piped up, "I told you he was sixteen. I told you he'd more likely appreciate a subscription to *Penthouse* or a bouquet from Condom World. Can't you remember sweet sixteen?"

Mr. Pichard ignored his son, which, I'd come to realize, was the only way that he dealt with him. "Well, what will I do with all these toy trucks!" he said. "I bought a shitload of toy trucks!"

Hester said, "Remember when you overordered the buckle shoes? This is like that time he overordered the buckle shoes. Remember? We had too many buckle shoes for years and years." She smiled at me.

But I wasn't really there. I could only think about being gay, my father's gayness and mine, possibly, also. I'd taken biology, for God's sake. I knew about genetics. Maybe Rudy was gay and he saw it in me, too, and that's why he took me out into the high weeds after we'd gotten stoned. I was afraid now that it wasn't my webbed toes at all that the girls at St. Andrew's School had instinctively been warded off by, but my deeply rooted gayness, so deeply rooted that I was unaware of it. I wondered if Janie Pinkering had suspected it or noticed it right off like I had Mr. Pichard's nose, and if that wasn't the transformation she'd been striving for, the transformation into heterosexuality, the transformation that, even after having had sex with her, I'd failed to make. Obviously, my father had failed in just the same way with my mother. I wished that I could talk to my mother, to ask her how it was possible that she'd neglected to tell me that my father was gay, a giant snag in their marriage, no doubt. I wanted to ask her if she'd thought I was gay, too, like Dilworth had. But I assumed that it wouldn't be possible to get in touch with her for at least a few days, maybe weeks. Who knew how long it took to get over shooting somebody? There were a lot of questions to ask. I thought about the slight trembling in her hand as she applied her lipstick, the small wobble in her step, how I'd told her I'd be home when she got there. I felt sick about it all over again.

As if he'd heard what I was thinking, Mr. Pichard said, "Who knows who plays with trucks anymore these days? Maybe he plays with dolls. You can't tell."

"Look at the three of them," Richard said, gesturing to Mr. Pichard, my father, and me, touching his mother's sleeve. "You can't tell gay from straight. Will the gay man please take one step forward." Mr. Pichard glanced nervously at my father and me and then back at Richard. "They all look so charmingly straight, don't they? Lemonade, anyone?" Richard asked, swooping out of the room.

"I *am* straight," I said. "I mean, I don't just *look* it." I wanted to get that cleared up right from the start.

"Of course, you are," Mr. Pichard said. "I bought you trucks, didn't I?"

"Too many," Mrs. Pichard reminded him. She lifted up a crystal bowl of candies and offered them to me. "Like the buckle shoes."

"I'm sixteen." I picked up one of the pink candies but it was stuck solid to the others. I shook my head. "Thanks, anyway."

"He's sixteen," Mr. Pichard said. "Of course."

"Oh, yes," Mrs. Pichard added.

My father clapped my shoulder. "That's right."

But I couldn't stop. "I'm not gay," I said and then rambled on, "I've been umphing the Pinkering girl. I was their gardener, but I'm learning to drive now. I've got my driver's permit."

They all stared at me nodding and smiling. Richard stepped into the room with a pitcher of lemonade and a stack of waxy, flower-printed paper cups. "Lemonade!" he sang sweetly.

"Your barn door is open," Mrs. Pichard said to the three of us, ignoring Richard. We all looked down, and Mr. Pichard zipped up.

Pixie

How to Find Your Husband in Bed with Another Man, Gracefully

Hopefully," I told the little psychiatrist at the next session, "you're learning something from all of this. I'd hate to think that you aren't paying attention. It's for your own good."

She ignored my comment, but I could tell she'd thought about our last session. Her lips had a shine to them, like she'd put on Chap Stick, a big step for her, and her hair was clipped back, still frizzy at each side and one poof on top. Her sweater was navy blue, not exactly feminine but a step in the right direction. She wanted to show me pictures. "Just ten," she said. "And you can tell me a story about what you see." She held up a black-and-white picture of a young woman carrying books. In the background, a strapping young man was working on the farm with his shirt off, and an older pregnant woman was leaning against a tree.

"I suppose you want me to reveal my own story, to cast my own family in these parts?"

"You can tell any story that you want."

"Okay, fine. Here it is. I'm the girl, right? She'll leave, but with no guidance from the pregnant woman. I mean, she's incapable of guidance, stuck as she is, only nagging advice on what not to do. A.k.a. my mother. And the farmhand isn't exactly going to take her away from all of this, but it's hard to say who he is in the story. Should he be my father? Just about to die on everybody? My brother about to go off to war? Or my ex-husband? The farmhand could very well be gay."

"What would make you think he's gay?"

"He's handsome. He's unattainable. It's just a distinct possibility. I've learned these things the hard way." I explained to her that I married a gay man. Actually, I fell in love with him. I didn't particularly care for sex, so he suited me. That's one way to marry a gay man without knowing it. Your libidos will appear to be similar. Russell never looked at me like the men from that chain-linked yard, with their feet soaking in metal tubs, never lustfully, like a chieftain of some shabby yard tribe in Bayonne. Sex had bad implications for me, and Russell was tall, and even though he was thin, his body was heavy. I hated the heaviness of it, the way it could press the air from me. But sometimes, and not often, just every once in a while, it was different, and I wasn't like St. Christina the Astonishing, hovering above the bed, looking down from the ceiling's corners, but I slipped into my own body and could feel my skin touching his skin. It felt the way I'd always imagined it should feel. I thought how silly I'd been to think that I was dirty. I almost forgot why I'd come up with that idea in the first place. He'd look at me like I was an innocent angel. Even in the most ordinary moments sometimes I'd catch him gazing at me the way a sinner gazes at a statue of Mary, someone who could save him if only he had enough faith, and he was acting like he believed, acting his heart out. I thought he was beautiful, and he thought I was beautiful. We admired each other. We often kissed in public. His arm slung around my neck, he'd stop walking just to kiss me on the mouth and we'd smile at each other, then continue on.

I met Russell one afternoon while I was teaching an at-home dance lesson. My client was an older man, a retiree of some sort, with clumsy, wandering hands. His wife was upstairs, dying slowly, and so sometimes a nurse would bustle into the room to ask him a question. He'd sigh, pulling the needle from the record. "I don't know," he'd say. "Can you leave me be for just one hour? Just one goddamn hour?" And then he'd sit in his chair with his head in his hands, and it would take him a while to become light again, to be ready to cha-cha. He was recovering from one of these moments, and I was pointing at a foot chart, talking him through the chase step when there was a knock at the door. He said, "You can get it." And I did, and there was Russell with his white teeth, his long hair pulled back and hidden under his suit collar. He had one finger on the trigger of an all-purpose cleanser like a cowboy in a western, someone come to save me.

I said, "It's not a good time."

And he agreed, "No, it's not a good time. I'm not having any fun at all."

"I mean, the man of the house is, well, not feeling right."

"Me neither," he said, sighing, looking up the street at the line of houses that had shut their doors on him, or worse, had invited him in out of sympathy, buying only the $1.25 sampler. "I'd love a doughnut. That's what I want. If I have to spray one more fucking demo strip, I might shrivel up and die right here on this guy's front stoop. You know?"

And I did know. I was tired of the endless count of one, two cha-cha-cha, steering the old man through the foxtrot, the rhumba, while reigning in his wayward hands, tired of being the person I was. Russell and I left together, the foot chart still on its easel, the cha-cha record still on the turntable. We ate doughnuts, and got married two weeks later.

My mother came to the wedding at the justice of the peace. I'd invited her but hoped she wouldn't come. She helped me attach my veil. I remember her clenching the bobbypins in her teeth, whispering, "I thought I taught you better." But she'd never taught me anything except the merits of not being happy. If I'd known then that she'd fallen in love with a butcher, Mr. Graziano—which I think now may have been the case—I'd have told her to run off with him, to claim some happiness, but she was afraid of love, petrified of it. I, for one, wasn't going to repeat her mistakes. I was making my life up as it came to me.

Russell and I were excessively happy. It was what we wanted to be. He was out most of the time, but that wasn't too unusual, I thought. My father hadn't been home much either. But when he was home, I wasn't like my mother, stern and unforgiving. I always remembered the cottage vacation and the fight over the beautiful hat, and so when Russell was home, I made sure that I was happy, that we were all happy, that if he ever decided to buy me a hat I would pull it from its white tissued box and wear it all around our small apartment. There was no hat in a tissued box, though. Sometimes there was some dope to smoke from his bong, and I'd smoke it with him while he strummed guitar, his eyelids heavy and red. He was in college to avoid the draft, and he'd try to look studious. He'd read his books sometimes and tell me what he thought of it all, philosophy and physics, and he usually agreed with his teachers. He'd say it was all common sense, though, like he'd have been smart enough to figure it out if the old dead guys hadn't beaten him to it. He wore little glasses, even though he didn't need glasses. He was faking it, and I let him fake it because I wanted to believe him. I was confident that we were happy. I was sure of it. And Russell played along when he was there. We thought we were happy and normal because we didn't know any better.

We didn't have much sex. Despite the times that it felt good and right, I still thought, in general, that sex was dirty, and love was pure. But I knew that I wanted a baby, to begin my perfect Miss America family, and I knew what I had to do to get one. Still, we did have sex occasionally. It was the early '70s; sex and birth control were political acts that we believed were our rights, and it was our duty to claim our rights.

One night while lying on our mattress on the floor, I brought up the idea of a baby. Russell was reading, hunkered toward a dime-store lamp. I was looking out the window, the ledge lined with a dusting of snow and shuffling pigeons. I said, "I'd love to have a little baby." And that's what I wanted, a little tiny cooing baby.

"I don't think that it's necessary to have a baby," he said. This, in retrospect, was a clue. A child wasn't necessary to prove he was straight. Marriage seemed to have taken care of that just fine. But I wasn't picking up on clues.

"Of course it isn't necessary!" I said.

"There are a lot of people in the world already," he said, taking off his glasses and looking tired and serious. "In good conscience, I don't think we should add to the population."

"Well, somebody's got to have the kid who's going to discover the next cure, negotiate the next peace accord. We won't be raising an idiot! I think other people should stop having kids, but not us."

"Still," he said.

"It's necessary," I said. "It's absolutely necessary. It's what I want."

Now he was sitting straight up on the mattress. "I don't know," he said, sighing, looking up at the ceiling. "Do you want to be one of them? You know, them?" He was talking about our parents, his father, in particular, a dairy farmer who talked to his cows with more tenderness than his children, a man he was always disappointing. We'd both agreed that our parents had screwed up most of the things they'd ever tried to accomplish, raising us being one of those things. We didn't talk about family much or anything really that wasn't about the here and now. Russell liked to say things like, "Let's stay in the moment," and "The past is the past." This suited me perfectly, as you could imagine. He helped me fold the sheets, you could say, stuff the closet to maximum capacity, and press against the door till we both heard the safety of the knob's click.

I said, "Becoming a father isn't becoming *your* father. I won't become *my* mother just because I am a mother."

He did love me, you know. Not the same way that a man loves a woman, but maybe in a better way. He pulled me to his chest. He stroked my hair. "Okay," he said. "Okay. Let's make a very little world peace leader."

I got pregnant easily, and being pregnant was almost like being Miss America, not the nausea in the beginning, not the throwing up, the backaches, my belly tightening sometimes into a hard ball. But the way people regarded me, suddenly, not only as someone who was going to be a mother but almost like their own mothers. I'd always wanted the stage to be this barrier of respect, but really my belly worked even better. Men opened doors for me, carried my grocery bags. I forgot that there'd be pain, that there could be complications. Wanda's knitting needle was still in the bottom of my pocketbook. Wanda, however, had done everything wrong. I, on the other hand, was powerful.

But Ezra's birth was difficult. I bled all the way to the hospital, gushing through towels onto the front seat of our beaten-up Ford six weeks ahead of my due date. There was nothing the doctors could do to stop it. Ezra's head was already crowning when they spread my legs for the first time. The nurse yelled for the doctor. I pushed only twice and he was there, too little, born early and weak, the fluid in his lungs not fully squeezed out during the birthing process. My body gave him up too soon, my muscles not woven tightly enough, my bones not holding him in. I blamed myself, my body, for betraying me, the way it had always done what it wanted, taking charge of my life.

In the recovery room, I begged the nurses to let me hold him. They said he was stable enough for a short visit and so one of the nurses brought him to me, wrapped tight with a knit stocking cap on his head. The nurse left the room and I grew weak, my arms heavy, becoming numb. I was afraid I'd drop him. I said to myself again and again, in a desperate whisper, "Don't let go. Don't let go." That's how soon it began and last summer it had come back, that smallest of whispers, a tightening in my chest, like a balloon filling with water. Whenever I was with him, I wasn't sure, moment to moment, whether or not I might reach out and clutch his shirt. I could almost hear myself say, "Don't leave me. Don't become a man. Do you still love me?"

My mother came to visit me in the hospital wearing her ancient thick coat with its oversize buttons, her pocketbook clutched in her fist. She'd peeked in on him in his incubator. She'd asked the nurse to show her his feet. "He's one of us," she told me later, in regard to his webbed toes. "But he's not a healthy child," she said. "There's something wrong with him. Don't get too attached." This was my mother's philosophy on everything, not to get too attached because it would just be taken away, better nothing to begin with than something and then nothing. She was talking about her parents, of course, and I think she was talking about my father, too. She'd loved him once, because if she hadn't loved him she wouldn't have turned so cold. She'd have been indifferent and remained indifferent, right? And, maybe she loved the butcher, too. She certainly needed him, and who can really distinguish true need from true love? From what I could tell, she believed that she paid for that love, that small happiness, that it was the reason so many bad things happened. My mother looked at the world this way, and I wanted desperately not to.

"He's fine!" I said. "He's beautiful!"

Finally, we were allowed to bring Ezra home. It became harder to live near the ocean. I could feel it out there, the pull and drag of it, like an animal clawing the beach. I was afraid of its rising up. Every night I dreamed of my father drowning, and sometimes my father was so small, just the size of Ezra, four pounds, a body that could fit in the palm of my hand. I felt that if I lost Ezra, I'd lose everything. I remembered Wanda's baby, the homemade abortion, the baby born alive who died in my hands and how it only reminded me of my father and the skinny sailor on the dock. I didn't want to live in a world that was always giving you things only to snatch them back.

But Ezra lived. Even though his lungs would fill up easily, he was alive. He was pink. His cheeks almost fat, and I felt like I'd taken something back that had been mine, that had been taken away. I felt justified, and my role in life was to keep him alive, to keep what was rightfully mine.

I didn't get to name him Troy. Although the picture in my head of the perfect family had changed considerably, I still liked my names. "What world peace leader's named Troy? Donahue?" Russell asked, and so we named him after Pound. Russell didn't know much about Pound at the time though. He only knew he was a great figure in literature. Only later did he learn that he was a Fascist, not a peace leader at all. By then it was too late to change it. Ezra was a very bright baby, and at five months he knew to look when someone said his name; sometimes he'd clap his finger-splayed hands. Nobody knows much about literature and Fascists anyway. There's no need for Ezra to ever know. Sometimes I'll introduce him as being named after the great literary figure when I know the other person doesn't know too much about the world, and to make Ezra like his name. Anyway, his middle name was John, after Lennon. You can't really go wrong there.

We had no money to speak of. Eventually, I would get a job at the Dairy Queen, handing out soft-serve while teenage boys came on to me, Ezra sitting on the floor behind the counter, an angelic kid sticking to his coloring book, staying in the lines. But early on we relied entirely on Russell's income. He got financial aid from school, but we still had bills. He was always getting jobs selling things door-to-door, but he usually resented the capitalist organization's underpaying him and thought that his product was overhyped by a greedy sales force somewhere far away from honest middle-class Americans. He often took the opportunity to sit down with a lonely housewife, not to show off his wares but to discuss politics, to talk about the evils of the war and our repressive society. He came home tired, his feet sore. He reminded me of my mother when her angina acted up and her chest seized as if she were being pressed to death. As I look back on it now, he was lonely. And I was lonely, too, but I didn't know any better. Maybe he didn't either.

And Ezra was sick off and on, often on the verge of drowning, in fact, his little lungs filling up with fluid. It made me sick with worry. Sometimes I would have to run from a room and throw up. I didn't eat much. I only wanted to save him. I was maniacal about his health from the very beginning. When he wasn't in the hospital, which we couldn't afford, I kept him wrapped up in blankets and never took him outside. I remember our small, dingy apartment, the smell of shit, especially when summer arrived and I was still too frightened by a sudden chilly breeze to open the windows more than a crack. I laid him on the bed in a sun square from the window and baked with him.

And then my mother called. She said, "Cliff stepped on a mine. He's dead." Her voice was flat. There was no expression, not even a hitch in her breath. I wondered how she'd perfected it, this detachment. She didn't want a ceremony. There was no real body to speak of, anyway, left to bury. She started buying caged birds and stood hunched in front of their cages saying, "Hello, pretty, pretty, pretty."

For me, it seemed that the whole American military had collapsed, that there was nothing left to protect us in this world. I thought of the last letter from Cliff that I ever got, how he didn't sound like himself anymore. It was the one about the moaning dog, belly filled with stones, and how he shot the dog out of mercy, and he started to hear the dog's moan everywhere he went. I started to hear that dog, too, a sound that I didn't understand, like a hand over someone's mouth, the whine that comes through their nose. I saw danger everywhere. I worried that Ezra was going to choke on a peach pit, tip over in a chair and crack open his head. I was afraid he would suffocate on his own pillow. For years I went on like this, hovering around Ezra, his thin body, his skin so fine I could see the pale blue veins etched beneath it, smiling at Russell when he drifted in with a paycheck and bounced Ezra for a minute or two on his knee. And I felt almost dead, because, I guess, I was so afraid of life. I'd learned that tragedies could happen when you least expected them, so I tried to always expect them. For years I stared at the furniture, remembering how once my accordion had become my father, his air-filled lungs, his voice rising up, and I wanted the chair not to have to be a chair. I wanted the table to get up and walk away from this place. I wanted the waxed fruit that my mother had given me as a wedding gift to become real, filled with its own sweet juice. Looking back, I think I wanted most of all to be myself, not this wooden version, but really alive. For years, though, nothing changed.

When Ezra was five, my mother called again one afternoon out of the blue. She said, "Soldier wrote me a letter. A fellow named Jamison. He sends his condolences, a couple years late, I'd say. And he says if either of us want to talk to him about Cliff that we can travel to him in Perth Amboy. He says he's injured and can't travel well. Who would want to go to Perth Amboy?"

"Don't you want to know what he's got to say?"

"What's there to say? Cliff's dead. It won't bring him back."

I decided to go. I told Russell that I'd be gone overnight, that Ezra and I would take the bus and get a hotel room. I'd sent a letter on ahead of me, and even though I didn't hear back, I decided to arrive when the letter said I would. I packed our suitcase. It was the middle of the day, a Sunday in spring, the weather warm enough for just a light sweater. The bus was crowded and dirty and made too many stops. The kid in the seat across from us threw up in a paper lunch bag, and, for a minute, Ezra turned greenish, but I said, "Please don't throw up." And he was such a good kid that he didn't.

Once in Perth Amboy we had to catch another bus, a local. Ezra was five, but very small for a five-year-old. He sat on my lap, just the size of a wooden dummy, the suitcase between my feet. We were actually underdressed, because everyone else had been to church and the ladies were all wearing hats.

An old woman said, "You need help? You lost?"

"No, I don't think so," I said. I pulled the address out of my pocketbook and she told me it was just two more stops.

"Don't stay too long. That's not the nicest part of town."

"I don't think I will," I said, but I wanted Jamison to tell me as much as he could. I'd hated Cliff when he died, and I wanted Jamison to tell me something that would make me forget that I hated him at all, ever.

The building was brick, old. Jamison's apartment was on the first floor and when I knocked, I heard a woman's voice, "Just minute please." A small Asian woman answered the door, Vietnamese, I figured. "You Cliff sister?"

"Yes," I said.

"I figure because we don't see door-door Avon-selling women around this place."

"Is Jamison here?"

"Jamison always here," she said, and she pulled me in the door, closing it behind me. "Jamison, it's Cliff sister with her child." She took my suitcase and put it next to the door and quickly shuffled out of the room.

The apartment was small and smelled like medicine and sleep-breath. There was a bed in the living room when you first walked in, and Jamison was sitting up in it, pillows stuffed behind his back, wearing a T-shirt that was too tight for his broad chest. "That was my wife. She likes to be called by her American name—Almaz. I told her there's no American by that name, but some English teacher in Vietnam called her that. You can't change her mind about anything," he paused. "You're just like he said you were. Is that your boy?"

"Yes, this is Ezra."

"I didn't think you'd come all this way. But I promised Cliff I'd talk to you. We made a deal, a long time ago. Cliff could have just as easily been standing in a room with someone from my family right now, if things had worked out differently. Sit down." He pointed to a folding chair next to the bed. "I'd get up, but my insides came out. I've got a scar that runs up my side into the pit of my arm. I still don't move around much. It's been years now. I've had twenty-two surgeries. So these doctors might never get it all straight. They don't know a damn thing."

Almaz came in with cups of tea and juice. "Here, for you," she said. "And the boy."

I said, "Thank you," and Ezra did too, his eyes too big for his head.

"You not going to talk war stories, are you?" Almaz said to her husband in a scolding tone.

"I'm going to talk about Cliff," he said.

"Not too much war, you know. That too much." She looked at me. "Too much for him."

Ezra drank his juice quickly and put it down on a bedside table covered with pill bottles. "I've got to pee," he whispered as loudly as his little voice could whisper.

"I take him," Almaz said, grabbing his hand and leading him out of the room.

"No," I said. "I'll take him."

"It's okay. He not going to fall in."

I let her take him, out of politeness, but it made me nervous.

"Cliff was a good kid," Jamison said.

"Yes, he was," I said.

"I'll tell you, Cliff had the idea that you'd needed him and he hadn't come through. We don't have to get into it. You know what I mean? That he hadn't been man enough."

At first I didn't know what he was talking about. Then I thought maybe he'd wanted to be the one to have come to my rescue, that he was talking about the man, the stranger in my bed. I had the impression that Cliff had been there, standing by, but my father had taken charge, my father had perhaps stolen Cliff's heroic moment. You see, I didn't really understand, but I said, "I guess I know what he was talking about."

"Good," Jamison said. He seemed relieved, like he'd said what he'd had to say without having to say it. "He always felt bad about that, about not having been a better brother. He felt so bad about it that I think he wanted to be everybody's brother. He wanted to save all of us. He wanted to save the whole damn country. He wanted to be an American hero, even though America didn't want a hero."

I thought about poor Cliff with his sweet girlish mouth, that maybe I'd read him wrong, that maybe he didn't want to just go over there to kill people but to save some, too. "How did he die?" I asked. "What was it like?"

"No, you don't want to hear that crap."

"I do," I said. "It's why I came."

Jamison looked at me carefully. He rubbed his nose and then looked down at his hands. He said, "You know, I used to keep everything to myself, but then after part of what was once inside me was busted open, I got different. They stitched me up all right, but I don't keep everything inside me like I used to. I've sprung some kind of leak," he said and laughed. "You know?" And then more seriously, "Do you know what I mean?"

I nodded. "I do," I said, but only now do I really understand him. He stared at me to see if I was telling the truth, and I gazed back, convincing him, I guess, that I was sincere. He started talking. "Cliff was out ahead of me. There were lots of us. Lots of soldiers didn't make it. It wasn't good. Shit," he said, "people were just being blown up. The VC came out of nowhere. They just came right up out of holes in the ground, and there we were in with the nipa palm trees, trees filled with red ants, and the red ants come at you, crawl down your back. I saw a guy strip naked, screaming his head off, in that fire fight 'cause of the red ants from a nipa palm tree, and the VC just coming right up out of holes in the ground."

"Did you see Cliff die?" I wanted a picture, I guess. I wanted Jamison to paint a glorious death scene.

Jamison looked down at his bedside table, his eyes darting from bottle to bottle, but not really looking for anything, it seemed. "One guy was blown away next to us. And Cliff looked at me. He said, 'Fucking shit.' I couldn't hear him, only see his mouth, wet with rain, and somehow I knew he was spooked, that he wasn't going to make it." I could see Cliff's mouth, too, drops falling off his full lips, spraying off him as he turned his head toward the crashing noises. "Then there was a bright flash," he said, "a thundering noise, but not thunder, and rain. Our uniforms almost black with all the rain. His body was blown to pieces, really, nothing left of him but broken pieces. I started after him, crawling on my elbows and knees. I started to look around for something to put back together. I tried, but there was nothing all around me, but pieces of his body and other men's bodies. I turned and turned. I walked on my knees, my gun to my chest, but I could hardly see. My eyes were so wet, rain beating down on my face." He looked out then, across the bed, the floor. "But everywhere I looked there were just pieces of us. How could I put anything back together? Arms and legs, blood, the ground red with it." His face was clouded over, his eyes now all over the room, the walls.

Almaz was back. She pushed Ezra toward me and sat on the edge of the bed. She grabbed Jamison's hand and started rubbing his arms like he was cold, and he looked cold. "Too much," she said to me. "I knew it. Too much. What I say?"

"I'm fine," he said, but he wasn't fine. He was still distant, his eyes still bleary, glazed. I felt suddenly lonely. I wondered when the last time was that Russell had touched me, really touched me. I envied their tenderness.

I stood up and took Ezra's hand. "We'll go," I said.

"Yes," she said. "You go."

"No," Jamison said. "You don't have to go."

There was more I wanted to ask, like when Cliff shot the dog and Jamison sang like his autistic brother in the tree. I wanted to ask if his brother was still alive. For some reason, that seemed suddenly important. But I knew I couldn't ask. "We should go," I said and we did.

I didn't get a hotel room. There was no need. It was still light out. We rattled home from one hissing bus to the next. Ezra fell asleep on my lap. I carried him from the bus station to our apartment, finally dark, the suitcase beating against my knees. He woke up as I climbed the steps to our floor. The apartment was quiet. It was late by now, after midnight. I went to fix myself a drink in the kitchen. I told Ezra to go see if his daddy was there, and he tottered off down the hall. Soon enough he called back to me, "Daddy's in here, waking up with his friend." I walked to the bedroom and saw it too— Russell sitting up in bed, foggy and disoriented, the kid next to him, a little younger, but not much, wide-eyed, both of their bare white chests almost glowing.

"Go make a peanut butter sandwich," I told Ezra. "Go!" and he ran down the hallway to the kitchen.

I don't remember much—what I said exactly or what he said, or if the kid next to him even moved the tiniest bit. I think I stood there for a minute, just taking it in, letting everything wash over me, things suddenly making sense. I think I said, "Fuck you." But I didn't even mean it. Russell looked beautiful just then, innocent really, the most innocent I'd ever seen him, even though that sounds wrong. He looked pure; he looked like the angel. I backed out of the room.

"Pixie," he said; maybe he only whispered it. He stood up, grabbing one of Ezra's stuffed toys to cover himself, an oversize rabbit, white and furry with pink satin ears, one floppy and one upright. He looked ridiculous. I actually thought of Cliff and how what he went through was real, and this, well, how could I take it so seriously? I started to laugh, my hand up to my mouth and then I thought I might cry, so I stopped laughing. I thought about all of Russell's sweet gazes and I knew that they weren't real, that they were out of some sort of guilt, and I was flooded with all my girlish feelings of dirtiness. I remembered the man and all of that, what I thought was the truth. I thought about how Cliff had said he was more an American than he was a Kitchy, but you can't ever shake who you are. I knew that if Cliff had come back, he'd have to be a Kitchy again. He'd have had no choice. It would come back to him when he least expected it. And I knew I'd never have tenderness, not the kind I was looking for, that it wasn't possible for me.

He said, "Wait, Pixie."

I turned and walked out of the room. I closed the door behind me. I picked up the suitcase that I hadn't unpacked and I yelled at Ezra to come on, to hurry up, to bring the sandwich, and we left.

"How did you feel?" the psychiatrist asked.

"About what?"

"About your visit with Jamison, about finding out your husband was gay and having an affair, about leaving with your son?"

"I didn't know much except how to be an escape artist. My mother was right all those years ago when she said a woman can't chain her hands behind her back and jump into a river like my father did, but still I was getting pretty good at leaving. I disappeared. I became a woman in a slip on a sofa. I stopped feeling. I needed a plan and I made one up."

Ezra

Rule #9: Good people buy your peanuts
and bad people don't.

Rule #10: Always send in the lamb first.

Mrs. Pichard served meatloaf and whipped potatoes with
gravy—a dark beefy gravy with round oil slicks on top.
She offered ginger ale and whole milk. I chose the whole milk,
something I hadn't tasted in years. It was too rich and sweet,
almost buttery. For dessert, she laid out small yellow-trim
plates, each with a canned pineapple slice topped with mayonnaise, cheddar cheese bits, and a maraschino cherry. My father
didn't touch his. Richard whispered, loudly enough for everyone to hear, like he was whispering in a school play, "I've
gained a zillion pounds and I've been here six days. But if I
don't eat, she thinks I don't love her."

There was something intolerable about mayonnaise and
fruit. It reminded me of the stuff they passed off as food to my
grandmother at the hospital, something my mother would
have unwrapped from plastic and spoon-fed her. But it seemed

very normal, excessively normal and therefore heterosexual, even though Richard was eating it for all the wrong reasons. I decided to eat it for all the right reasons, in the name of American red-bloodedness, the way Dilworth would, I thought.

I said, "This is delicious, Mrs. Pichard. A real treat!"

She smiled.

Halfway through his pineapple surprise, Mr. Pichard said, "I made my money in shoes. What about you?" he asked my father.

"I'm a dabbler. I used to be in politics." He glanced at me. "I'm an entrepreneur. I'm always seeking opportunities." And he repeated the last statement, because it sounded best. "I'm always seeking opportunities. In fact, I've got a deal I'm working on now. We're looking for investors." I wondered who "we" were. It wasn't me and him, and I got the impression that it might just be him. "It could be the kind of investment deal you've been looking for," he said to Mr. Pichard. All I could picture was a ship, even though I knew it was just an expression, but I pictured my father's ship coming in, a cruise ship with confetti and streamers. Mr. Pichard never responded to my father's proposition. My father still looked too big, the silverware like play silverware, the cup not near big enough to wash things down his throat. He had to duck down to see people below the chandelier, a fake thing with lots of sparkly glass that was hung much too low and was too dim, anyway, to really show you clearly what you were eating.

"I was a Manhattan housewife," Richard said. "But now I own a convertible. That's it." And then he whispered to me, "I stole the convertible, actually. I'd drive it into the river if it weren't the only thing I had."

"Family shoes," Mrs. Pichard elaborated. "Shoes for the whole family."

"And I don't mind the blacks," Mr. Pichard added.

"Oh, no, of course not," Mrs. Pichard said.

"They need shoes, don't they? Come Easter, the blacks will buy the finest shoes in the shop. Jimmy Carter once said that by eight years old he could tell a good person from a bad person. The good ones, he said, bought his peanuts and the bad ones didn't. That's a motto to understand, to take to the grave." Mr. Pichard winked at me. I thought about rules, how everybody must have them, stupid rules that nobody really lives by.

"I think that statement was taken out of context," my father said. "I think he was in a church, making a very different point, and had been misunderstood."

"I understood him," Mr. Pichard said. "Some things I don't understand." He glanced at his son. "But that I understood."

"Yes," Mrs. Pichard said. "He's fond of that story. He is. He tells it often."

Richard said, "I'm trying to take this setback in my life as a time to reflect on my circumspect childhood. I could be living in New York still, you know, with friends of friends of friends, but I need to regroup, to relive, and renew." He turned to me. "You see, Ezra, there's no conversation to follow here, really. You can say whatever you want. Tell them about your mother shooting your stepfather in the arm, anything at all."

This got Mr. Pichard's attention. He looked up at me across the table quickly and returned to his plate. "It doesn't matter here," Richard went on. "You just talk and talk and talk some more."

Mr. Pichard grumbled. "He shouldn't have gone to college. That was the problem, Hester. Our son should have sold shoes."

"My father doesn't really speak to me," Richard said. "Have you noticed that? My mother is in denial. No one here is paying attention."

"I am," I said. "I think."

"When my son was a boy, he needed too much attention," Mr. Pichard said. "Not like Ezra here. A good young strapping boy who knows to sit quiet, eat, and listen. Like me, when I was a lad," Mr. Pichard said. "Our boy had an unnatural need for attention, and Hester gave it to him, as best she could."

"He had the loveliest assortment of shoes a boy could ever want," she said, her fork clattering on her empty dessert plate absently.

"I dressed up once as Betty Page for Christmas dinner, in the leather thigh-high boots," Richard said. "But he still didn't talk to me. He doesn't talk to me. He blames my mother." He took a sip of ginger ale. "We only speak through her. It's odd at first, but you get the hang of it. Like right now, if I wanted the salt, I'd say, 'You know, mother, if I had a father who spoke to me and if he were sitting right there, I'd ask him to pass the salt.' And often enough, miraculously, the salt arrives. There's all kinds of love."

Mr. Pichard didn't look at him. "It's time to go upstairs. I need a soak in the tub. Hester, leave the dishes." He pushed his chair from the table and let his napkin fall to his plate. He walked to the stairs and used the banister to pull himself up. Mrs. Pichard placed her fork diagonally across her plate, nodded to us all sweetly, and followed her husband, disappearing into the dark at the top of the stairs. The dark almost seemed to swallow them up as if they no longer existed.

The three of us stood up and started stacking plates.

Richard said, "It's a show, really. All of that business of me needing so much attention, it's his way of acknowledging my sexuality. And, to him, it's the nicest way to say it. If you looked into their hearts, you'd see that they both love me."

"I'd go back to living in New York," I said.

"I have no money," Richard said. "Nothing. You can't just be depressed, getting fat eating Ho Hos on someone's sofa, watching soaps all day. Except, of course, here. It's awful, but they'll take care of me until I'm on my feet again." He was trying to be bright, but his face crumpled for a minute as he looked around the room. His eyebrows rose, eyes moist, and then he smiled. "Nothing has changed here. Nothing. It's like walking through a museum of your shitty life. Each room should be roped off with red velvet rope." And then he brushed us away with his hand. "I'll take care of these. You two go on to sleep. That door right there opens into a bedroom."

It was a small room. The double bed took up most of the space. It had an adjoining powder room. My dad went in first to take a piss. When he was done, I went. The toilet water was blue, reminding me for a moment of home, my mother's sparkling toilets, and Ty-D-Bol commercials, a man in a boat in your toilet. The toilet lid was covered in a yellow fuzzy toilet-lid hat to match the hand towels. On the wall were two wooden plaques, one of a little girl sitting on a pot and one of a little boy peeing into a pot. There was a little calligraphy note framed on the wall that read IF YOU SPRINKLE WHEN YOU TINKLE, PLEASE BE SWEET AND WIPE THE SEAT.

When I walked back into the bedroom, my father was slouched on the far side of the mattress, a weak old thing that pinched and squeaked under his weight. He began untying his shoes, taking off his thick blue socks. "I'm sorry about all this, Ezra. I didn't know it would be this bad of a scene."

"It's okay," I said.

"Mr. Pichard reminds me of my own father," he said. "When I was your age, my dad gave me stock tips. That was his idea of relating." I remembered seeing my grandfather only once, at my grandmother's funeral—I don't remember her at all. He was a practical man, concerned more about the supply of napkins and ice chips at the wake than with grief. His family had made money from cows and they had a lot of it. I've thought ever since that he was unemotional and practical because he was midwestern or Scandinavian—they'd come from Scandinavia—that Scandinavians from Wisconsin were unemotional and overly organized by nature, and that it had to do with all of that cold weather. It had been winter, the house surrounded by two feet of snow. "Once when I'd been in the city awhile, attending NYU, but before I met your mom," my dad continued on, "I went home for Thanksgiving and my dad, who was out on business somewhere, met up with my train. We rode the last leg of the trip together. We ran into an old friend of the family, another from the old country, who'd moved with his family two or three towns away. He asked my dad a lot of questions about who'd died and that kind of thing. Then he said, 'So, does anyone in your family make love anymore?' It was a really strange question, because the man was strait-laced like my father, but I said, 'No,' just like that, because I knew that no one did. But my father turned and stared at me, my uptight father who hadn't even loosened his tie. 'Of course we do,' he said. 'The women, at least, Aunt Jude and your mother and grandmother.' I was shocked, really. I said something like, 'They do? With who?' My father was really calm. 'By themselves,' he said. I said, 'Well that's hardly making love.' My father's whole face went red. He stared at me. And the old neighbor almost died. 'Glogg!' he cried. 'Do you still make glogg!' Glogg's an old Scandinavian drink with vodka and grain alcohol. The old guy looked like he was going to cry. My father just cleared his throat. 'We have glogg for the holidays,' he said. 'For special occasions.' And we were all quiet for the rest of the trip, not a word. It's the closest my father and I ever came to communication. And see? It wasn't communication at all." He was undressed down to his striped boxer shorts. He pulled back the covers and slipped under the sheet. His chest had that same evenness as his face, a soft tan, and he was trim, muscled. There was almost no hair on his chest and so he looked even younger, his nipples pink like painted dolly cheeks, like Mitzie's Barbie hats. He put his arms behind his head and crossed his ankles under the sheet, like someone lying down on a picnic blanket.

I looked away from him, getting undressed on my own side of the squeaky bed. I clicked off the light and curled up, my back to him.

"I'll tell you this, Ezra, I never hand myself over first. I can't. I always offer a lamb version of myself to see if the person will slaughter it and if they don't, well, then slowly I'll hand myself over, very slowly. Even then it's a rough road. It's the only way I know to be."

I'd have asked him if he did that with me too, if he'd always offered me someone else, but I knew he did. "Why did you and mom get married?"

"It's a curse, heroism, the curse of a boy who read too much Robin Hood. I wanted to be a hero. Then I ruined everything, because I couldn't save myself from myself. But you remember that part. You must remember that? Don't you, Ezra?"

"What part?" I had no idea what I was supposed to be remembering.

"The mind can be so perfect," he said. "It knows just what to throw away." He paused. "Tomorrow, you know, I've got business to attend to. I don't know what in God's name you'll do here all day, but I've got important things going on in Philly. I'll be there until after dinner probably. I'd bring you along for the ride, but you'd just be bored."

I didn't say anything. I knew that this trip wasn't a good-will mission to help out a friend going through hard times. It wasn't about some promise he felt he had to keep. He was pawning me off, unloading me on strangers. It was typical my father, quintessential him.

"Look," he said, "this is temporary. Your mom will be in

charge again soon. We'll figure this thing out." Like my whole life was just one fucking algebra problem.

Later, I listened to him breathing, a rattling breath in the dark, a figment just about to disappear again, and maybe that was best. I didn't know anything about him, still, even after having learned his lousy secret and it was a secret, too. He thought my mom should have told me, that she'd have let it slip somehow, but it was his secret to tell, and he's the one who let it stay a secret, year after year in his friends' convertibles, eating crab and corn bisque at the Columbus Inn, making fun of Dilworth and the waiters. It was always the lamb-version of my father, the one he handed over in place of the real thing, and he'd only given me a glimpse of the real thing when he'd had to, when he was on the verge of being exposed. I imagined him out in the silver convertible, picking up men in restaurants or riding around with old lovers. I imagined the silver convertible parked outside some apartment and him and some other man inside, in bed together. I could almost imagine them, their naked chests, the rustle of their bodies under the sheets.

I tried to shake it off and listened instead to Mr. and Mrs. Pichard upstairs, padding around in their bare feet, the intimate noises of two people getting ready for bed together, brushing their teeth, gargling, murmuring. Richard, I assumed, was up there too, in a bedroom decorated for an eight-year-old boy, probably cluttered with all of the toy trucks that Mr. Pichard had supposedly bought for me. I lay there with my eyes wide open, staring at the ceiling. I tried to imagine Mrs. Pichard having scrubbed her husband's humped back in the tub. I romanticized them, a tottering pair, still in love, maybe him brushing her white hair while she sat in the chair of her vanity. I thought Janie and I could be like that one day. But it was hard to hold on to. I doubted that they were happy at all. I mean, to some people, my mother and Dilworth may have seemed happy together, prior to her shooting him, that is, the shooting being a pretty good indication that their relationship had its wrinkles.

I was afraid that my father would roll over in his sleep and touch me or, worse, that I would wake up with my hands on him. I remembered the summer before with Rudy in his dad's boat, how, after we got stoned, Rudy said, "You up for a peep show?" He had to shout it over the music blaring from his dad's stereo system, Led Zeppelin's "Black Dog."

I asked him what he meant and he told me that just a few blocks from the dock there was a commune or something where the girls sunned themselves, naked, that all we had to do was follow some old train tracks. "You want to go?" He took a comb out of the inside pocket of one of his dad's jackets hung over the back of the captain's chair and ran it through his blond hair.

I said, "Sure."

He shoved the comb in his dad's pocket, picked up an empty Coke bottle, and spit in it. Smoking pot always made him want to spit, he said. His dad was still inland. Rudy said that he was probably getting drunk and wouldn't be back until dark.

We headed down through some high grass that bent over a pair of extinct railroad tracks. Rudy was carrying an old battery-operated transistor radio that his dad kept on the boat. I'd taken my shirt off on deck and still had it off. I don't usually go around without a shirt. My skin was real white, but it was hot out and the sun felt good. Rudy had this galumphing walk, like he was always ducking something, except when he was balancing on the tracks. With his arms straight out from his shoulders, his back stiff and head tall, the transistor radio dipping and swaying in his fist, he was graceful, almost dainty, like a girl carrying a basket.

He pointed out two white sheets billowing on a line tied to two posts and a skinny center tree about 200 feet away in the backyard of an old house. He turned off the radio and put his finger to his lips. "That's the place," he said, stepping off the other side of the tracks. We crouched low in the weeds and tried to peer between the sheets. "Did you see that titty?" he asked.

I nodded, but I hadn't. All I could see was a woman's shadow on the sheets and her ankles and feet on the other side below.

"I'd love a piece of that," he said. He looked at me. "You would, too, wouldn't you?"

I nodded but he kept looking at me so I punched his shoulder. "Sure!" I said.

The sun lit the sheets up bright white. The woman's shadow on the sheet didn't move around much, just stood, hands on hips. She was talking to a bunch of girls I couldn't see and they laughed all at once. The sheets rippled in the wind and then rose so I could catch a glimpse all the way up her thick thighs. I decided that they could be hippies or even just regular people standing in their backyard.

"I haven't seen much of anything," I said. "They could be wearing bathing suits."

"They're not wearing a thing. I guarantee it." Rudy unzipped his pants. "I guarantee it." I glanced at Rudy. He was rubbing himself with one hand, and still crouching in the grass, he steadied himself with the other. I looked away quick, but still I saw him in my head, his hair bright as the white sheets, his braces shining. The tip of his pecker was almost rose, almost blue. I kept my eyes straight ahead, and he started talking fast, "You know she's built like my cousin's friend, you know the one I told you about in the basement, almost fat like that, but really muscle, almost bigger than I am, but not really. I found this place on my own. It's a gold mine, I tell you. It always delivers."

I stood up, looked around for my shirt, even though I knew I'd taken it off on deck. I imagined the women, rising up from behind the sheets. I felt lightheaded when I stood up, everything tunneling to black for a minute, and then wondered how many times Rudy had sat here in the weeds, jerking off by himself.

"Why aren't you jerking off?" he asked. "Go ahead." He smiled, his eyes pinched, looking up into the sun at me, his head cocked. "Want to touch mine? Go ahead."

I turned around fast, and then I took off running. Weeds stung my legs. The sun made the world too bright; glass glittered up from the dirt. The world was so bright, it looked almost wet, shellacked, painted a loud new color.

Rudy stood up and shouted after me, in a hoarse yell so that maybe the naked girls wouldn't hear him. "God, I was just fucking around with you. You took it all wrong!"

But Rudy's pecker flashed in my mind, the bright prick and the women for some reason rising up, circling his head. I'd never thought of anything like it in my life, ever. Then I heard Rudy's transistor radio. He must have turned it up real loud, but I was already far away. I tried to catch my breath but couldn't. When I got to the dock, I bent over with my hands on my knees. It was like a giant clock sat in my stomach, ticking too loud. Each time I shut my eyes, women danced around Rudy's head, naked. They had sunken white bellies and small powdery breasts that jiggled, their thin arms swooping as they circled faster and faster, bobbing until Rudy's head was lost in a blur of their bodies: pointy elbows, skinny rumps, knobby white knees, and over and over again, Rudy's dick, its reddish blue tip all sunlit. At the time I thought it was all Rudy, that he was the one acting like a faggot somehow, but now I wondered if he hadn't seen something in me that I couldn't see or didn't want to see.

Lying in bed that night, I felt sick all over again, and I hated my father for making me think of all this stuff. I was angry at him for not saving my mother the way he'd set out to do, but leaving all of that to me, and what could I do? I was his son, after all, maybe just as much of a fag as he was. And it dawned on me that I should have shot Dilworth, that maybe for some reason he deserved to be shot, and that I should have been the one to do it, not my mother, but me. I worried about not saving my mother the way she needed to be saved, about not understanding that night when she was young, the screaming and the wooden bat. I wanted to save someone, to save little Mitzie from the Worthingtons' good healthy

American living, to save maybe Janie Pinkering from her parents or Miss Abernathy from a dull life as an old maid English teacher—despite the information that she might be having fuck-me sex with her fiancé. I thought of saving Richard, in his thigh-high leather boots from his parents and his parents from him. I thought about saving my father. I imagined walking in on my father and his lover, the slow turn-around of their faces, the surprise of it. I imagined telling my father he was wrong, that he'd done everything wrong, but that we could fix it. It was fixable, if only he'd be willing to try, for me. And I imagined him saying, "Yes, Ezra, for you." Finally, I lay in bed trying not to think of anything but Janie Pinkering's peach-like knee and, on it, the blue butterfly, the hinges of its wings slowly opening and closing.

Pixie

How to Become a Pimpless Whore

"Do you have a gun?" I asked the psychiatrist, the windowless room artificially cool.

"No," she said. "I don't."

"First, you should buy a gun," I told her. "It's the best way to keep order and balance." I told her the story; how I'd bought mine in a pawn shop on Avenue C in downtown Bayonne where Ezra and I were living at the time. The owner was a little Italian man, and Ezra, a big-eyed child with a curly head of hair and a little sunken chest, stared at him without blinking. The glass case came up to the owner's chest. He had to get up on his tiptoes to lean over the glass case, and when he did, he held out a yellow lollipop wrapped in cellophane. But Ezra was a perfect child and the man was a stranger offering candy. This was back in the days when the only thing anyone knew about bad guys was that they were strangers with candy, before we were willing as a culture to admit that bad guys could be with you day in and day out, someone you trust. I nodded. Ezra took the lollipop, unwrapped it, and shoved it in his mouth. Then he pulled it out and said, "Thank you, sir." Ezra was a good kid, really. The owner asked me what I wanted a gun for and I said, "Personal protection." I didn't go into the particulars. He showed me a little handgun, and as soon as I held it, it felt so good, the weight of it, the black shine. I bought it.

This was after I emerged from my two weeks on the nappy sofa in the Bayonne apartment with little Ezra, where I lived on the peanut butter sandwiches that he made for me and Dixie cups of water. I stared at the wallpaper until the water stains became shapes and then the faces of my family—my mother, Cliff, Russell, Ezra, even my father, smoke-darkened, bubbling from the wall. Russell had taught me many things in a bungled secondhand way, Buddhism and Hinduism and Marxism. But I was tired of men, of how each culture seemed to have its version of how man created mankind, how we came from Manu's head, hands, thighs or feet, or how we were lice on Pangu's body, or that old white rib of Adam's, a story my mother never really much cared for, what with her strong belief that we come from fish. I know how people came to be, the way they still come to be: a woman's body swells up, the belly hardens, there's blood and pain, and finally a baby. This obvious fact gets overlooked. In the stories men have made up and handed down you'd think that they were the ones to give birth, that they can create a human being with almost any part of their bodies until one day they'll think each sinew, each blood vessel, each of their little cells can procreate, until they shrug and infants drift to the ground around their feet like snow, when really their only contribution is a grunt and a cupful of sperm, those invisible tail-flicking fish, more like my mother's theory after all.

After failing to become Miss America and after having found my husband in bed with another man, I was tired of people not being what they'd set themselves up to be. Russell hadn't wanted what I thought he wanted, but he'd wanted something all the same, not me, but the idea of me, because it lent some credibility to a certain idea that he wanted to have of himself. I decided that I would become pure, but in a new sense of the word—that I would be honest in my society, a society based on sex and money. I was actually thinking these words in my head: *I want to live like Thoreau, truthfully, essentially.* I thought of myself as a country almost, one that had existed and had been ruled by natives in a way that I'd come to see as barbarians, and I was claiming that land, forming my own newly empowered government, writing my own constitution. I was philosophical about it all, talking to myself in the mirror, giving little speeches while brushing my teeth. I was deluded, if you want the honest truth. I was in some kind of dream. I decided that I was a whore and that the best way to be a whore was to be in complete control, to be a pimpless whore. It was the truth of my life. And so I exploited the native in me, I suppose. I exploited myself for the ideals in my new self-made government. I wasn't Miss America. No, I'd given that up. I was my own United States of America, just starting out, though, with its fledgling colonies. And I had a dizzying spirit, a relentless pride. I walked around like a conqueror, having conquered my native self. It was convoluted at best.

I never had to pull the gun out and take aim, not until recently that is, and as I've said, that was a mistake. I was careful in the men I chose. I was after a certain kind of man. I didn't care if he was married or not. Marriages had become trivial matters and personally none of my business. I hadn't vowed anything to a stranger's wife. Sometimes it was a pinky ring, or a chain necklace, something to indicate pride. But also I looked for a weakness in the eyes—not too weak; the weakest men are the most capable of cruelty. The expression I wanted was something closer to surprise. I had to decide right off that I could shoot them if I needed to. The answer always had to be yes without hesitation. When I went looking for them, sometimes there was more to it than that. Sometimes there was a clitoral twinge, like a forked stick, a divining rod trembling when it's held over a spot of water underground, the right spot for a well if you were willing to dig. It was about the picking and choosing, the surge of control.

I never went to crowded bars where the men were so immediately up close and too hard to discourage if they weren't quite right. I chose quieter places. I never had to wait long. I let them make the first move, sidling up, elbow on the bar, one foot on a rung of my bar stool. Eventually, I'd tell them what I proposed, always making it sound like the idea was just dawning on me for the first time. I'd explain to them they could wine and dine me, perhaps entice me to a hotel room at the Chalfont. They could spend X amount of money, maybe $25 or $30 back then. Or, I'd say, we could just be straightforward. "It's money and sex, isn't it? Let's just make it a fair exchange without the middleman—the waiter, the door-man—without strings attached."

Some of the men would say that it sounded illegal, because these were the types of men I chose. I'd shrug. "It's my body. It's your money. What could be illegal between two grown-ups? Why would they make a law like that? To keep the restaurants, the flower shops, jewelry stores, and hotels in business? Sounds like a conspiracy." I remember their smoked-down cigarettes, the way they tamped them in a quiet bar's crystal ashtray before taking my arm. I know that some people would wonder if I wasn't just interested in degrading myself, perhaps only subconsciously, but really, I'll say that I was doing what seemed only extremely sensible at the time.

When we got to my apartment, I'd pay the sitter, a sweet kid watching TV on the sofa. I'd make the man a drink, and sometimes Ezra would stumble from his room in his baggy pajamas. He'd ask for a glass of water. I'd give it to him and carry him back to bed. The men would get nervous. They'd sit at the kitchen table with the drink I'd poured them and say, "Maybe I should go." I'd hear them from Ezra's bedroom. But when I came back into the kitchen, I'd take off my itchy sweater, pull it off over my head. I'd unclip the pins from my hair, letting it fall to my shoulders. They'd follow me to the bedroom, where I lit candles and played soft music on the record player . . . It was that simple. And when I was in bed with them, I'd listen for Ezra. I wasn't a good whore. Sometimes if I heard Ezra cough, I'd tap the man on the shoulder and excuse myself to check on Ezra. But sometimes, too,

I'll admit, I was caught up in it, and I was just a woman, not a mother, and it was like that spot with the twitching stick but beneath it, there wasn't water but longing, something that I had pushed from my mind, and when I was having sex, it was like just beginning to dig.

I walked the men to the door after it was over, wearing my long satin Asian robe, the folded bills left on the kitchen table. Sometimes they'd say they'd want to see me again and I'd say, "A deal's a deal." But I was good at picking the ones who wouldn't come back, drunks banging at the door till I called the cops, and a lot of the time, they didn't really want to come back. As I said, I wasn't very good at being a whore anyway. Once they were gone, I'd go into Ezra's room, brush the hair from his forehead to see if he was hot. I'd smell the sweat of men on me, the smoke in my hair, and I'd think, somehow, that it made sense, that this was a real world and a real woman living in it. I hated the world and the woman, too, I guess. But I felt it was the only truth, in all of its ugliness, my thighs, for example, still wet. I could hear my brother's Vietnam dog, moaning inside me, a low aching moan and nobody to save me. And maybe I was waiting for someone to save me, in some way, although I'd have said the opposite then. I was waiting for my father, as I thought he once had saved me from the stranger, or Cliff; how Jamison had told me that he'd wanted to save me and the whole world while he was at it. I admitted to the psychiatrist, "I didn't know then what I know now."

"And what do you know now?" the psychiatrist asked.

I looked around the walls, thinking that there should be a window in one of them, some way to see outside. I didn't tell her that Cliff wanted to kill my father, that my father never saved me, although this is when it started to change, the moment that what my mother had told me in the hospital started to become true. But instead I said, "Ezra, my sweet son. One night I was with him after a man had left, to check on him, as usual, and his head was hot, his chest laboring. I walked quickly to my bedroom and rummaged for the thermometer in my bedside table alongside the gun, note paper, pencils. 'Ezra,' I was calling out, 'Wake up, wake up.' The sleeve of my Asian robe caught a candle, flame still lit, as I turned back to his room, but I hadn't noticed it. I smelled the small scent of something burning, but I thought it was Ezra, his hot body against the sheets. I wasn't paying attention to anything else. I ran back to him, sitting up in bed when I walked in.

"'Mommy,' he said, his eyes blinking and then wide. 'You're on fire.' And I looked down and saw my sleeve, like a flag catching, like the limb of a tree in full bloom. *Do you know what I mean?*" I asked the psychiatrist. I'd started to cry, talking about it, real tears sliding down my cheeks, splotching my silk top. "And the heat seemed to be coming not from the fire but from my chest, a fire that had been there for a long, long time, who knew how long? But now it was true, suddenly, spreading out from my heart, a bright, hot flare."

Ezra

Rule #11: It's better not to try at all
than to try and fail.

When I woke up in the morning, my father was already gone, his side of the bed neatly made. He was out in the world, I supposed, trying to find a way to finance gayness. I got dressed and went to the bathroom. When I stepped out, Richard and his mother jumped up from the sofa and began bustling around in the kitchen. They were both in waist-tied cotton bathrobes, Richard, a thick version of his mother. Mr. Pichard was watching a commercial—a family extremely happy about margerine—on an old tube-run TV. He had a satchel in his lap and a cardigan slung over his arm, obviously ready to go somewhere.

"Here's orange juice," Richard said, handing me a small glass, a jelly jar from the '70s.

Mrs. Pichard gave me toast wrapped in a butter-stained napkin. "Mr. Pichard has decided to invite you to his gym," she said.

Richard nodded. "It's an honor. I've never been invited."

Mrs. Pichard gave me a satchel, too. "There are a pair of Richard's swim trunks in there from when he was a boy your age." I was curious if she'd ever caught on to what my age was exactly. There'd been such strange confusion about that fact. I imagined that the swim trunks might fit an eight-year-old who'd love a roomful of toy trucks. "And goggles, too." She called to Mr. Pichard, "He's ready!"

I hadn't said a word.

"You swim?" Mr. Pichard grumbled.

"No, sir, not really. I tried to learn once but didn't, and then my mother filled our pool with dirt."

"It's not important," he said. "C'mon."

We drove to the gym in Mr. Pichard's enormous Buick, so big and black I felt like he was driving his own hearse, and I wondered what it would have been like if my mother hadn't just hit Dilworth's shoulder, but instead if she'd lodged a bullet just a few inches over, into his heart. I was scared not only of what things were happening in my life but also of how I had no control over anything. I was suddenly aware that any assortment of strange combinations of unknown things could collide on someone at any moment with no warning. Mr. Pichard and I didn't talk.

It was an ancient gym that smelled like old paint and dirty laundry. Mr. Pichard signed in at the front desk with a pen tied to a string, the string taped to the desk. He paid a few bucks extra for me and then walked stiffly to the locker room. It had open-stall showers in a row, their giant industrial-looking nozzles of scalding water spraying down on the mole-covered, wrinkled and pocked backs of two old men at opposite ends. It was an old man's gym. That was obvious.

Mr. Pichard opened a curtained changing stall for me and stepped into the one next door. The curtains, thick white with blue stripes, hung on a metal curtain rod with metal curtain clips that screeched each time someone tugged them. Luckily, Richard's suit wasn't for an eight-year-old, but he'd obviously been a chunky kid, because it was wide for me. The trunks were also much too short, exposing the whites of my upper thighs that hadn't gotten tan in the Pinkerings' deck chairs because of my long swim trunks. I imagined that Richard had wanted to show off his legs, could see him strutting around some pool. I pulled the drawstring tight, left the goggles in the satchel, which Mr. Pichard put in a locker, and followed him to the pool with the towel Mrs. Pichard had packed draped in front of me.

It was a greenish indoor pool. A group of older ladies in rubber swim caps, some ornamented with rubber flowers— which embarrassingly reminded me of Janie Pinkering's father's French tickler—were finishing up an aquacize class. One by one they heaved themselves out of the buoyant water. I waited by the ladder.

Mr. Pichard walked around to the deep end. His elbows cocked at his large ears, he dove in and swam a few slow strokes underwater, his humped back making him look like a giant sea turtle before surfacing. We were the only ones in the pool area except for the aquacizers now disappearing behind the women's locker room door. I looked down at my webbed toes and sighed, thinking of Janie and her dad, and how close I had been to becoming a Pinkering myself—although I knew I hadn't really been that close, not really—and wondering if I'd get a second chance. I stepped down one rung of the ladder, but I didn't go in.

"What's the matter?" Mr. Pinkering asked, his voice echoing.

"Too cold," I said.

"It's piss warm! It's a baby's bathwater!"

"I guess I just don't feel like it," I said and I padded to the bleachers while Mr. Pichard did laps. I've always felt strange in water, out of place, awkward as a frog on land. I was feeling out of place enough. I didn't need to remind myself that I couldn't really swim, how vulnerable I was, bested by an old man with a humped back. I wrapped myself in the small faded bath towel and sat on a short row of bleachers while Mr. Pichard swam on his back, pulling down armfuls of water, so evenly that it seemed like he was flying, not swimming. And then Mr. Pichard, back-floating, began to sing, a soft hum at first, but then slowly louder, richer, a beautiful Italian operetta, his voice bouncing around off the ceiling, the walls, the water's rolling surface. It was a sad song, and I wondered if this was the reason that he'd invited me to the gym, if he was telling me something, a secret that no one knew about him. His arms pushed him through the water; it rippled over his bony body, past his slowly kicking feet. He was graceful and beautiful, his voice pressed from his lungs to the ceiling and back again. He held one long note, so sweet that my eyes stung, and then he stopped. He reached the edge of the pool in the shallow end and climbed the ladder.

He said, "Let's go. It's time to go."

But he didn't take me home. Instead he drove a couple blocks and parked at a metered spot near PJ's Pub where, he told me, he was a regular. It was a dark bar, a couple of steps down from the street. It was mostly empty, except for a few college kids, eating french fries and drinking beer, and a few older men watching TV at the end of the bar.

"I've got a guest with me today, Hiram," he told the bartender. We sat at the bar, and he ordered us Reubens and gin-and-tonics. The bartender glanced at me and then back at Mr. Pichard. He didn't say anything, though, or ask for ID. I imagined that he knew that Mr. Pichard could raise his voice, could cause a stink, that he was the type to start yelling about lukewarm soup. The drinks were clear with lots of ice, a small straw, and a chunk of lime. I stirred mine like Mr. Pichard and the pale green pulp rose up and swirled. It tasted sweeter than I thought it would, much better than the drinks Janie concocted at her dad's bar. We ate the sloppy sandwiches and drank, both of us sucking on the limes. I felt old, almost like an old man myself, like Mr. Pichard and I were buddies from high school who'd walked to school with our books held together by a leather belt.

He talked about local sports and local politics, neither of which I knew too much about. He was still sore about the Colts sneaking out of Baltimore and the talk that they were going to tear down Memorial Stadium to build some ritzier stadium somewhere, probably out by the highway.

The bartender brought two more gin-and-tonics. "This one's a little weaker for your guest. He should go easy, right?"

Mr. Pichard nodded, and once the bartender was down at the other end of the bar, Mr. Pichard turned to me and said, "You know, you and I have got something in common."

"We do?"

"What Richard said last night about your mother shooting your father. My mother shot mine, too," he said. "I never told anybody about it, but, well, it's not something you forget easily."

"My *step*-father," I corrected. "He's my *step*-father."

"I know, I know. Not the fella with the big opportunities, who doesn't eat my wife's dessert, someone else. I can follow these things."

I wasn't interested in talking about it, really. It hadn't come up since the first few minutes with my dad in the car, and that was fine with me. But this explained why the old man had invited me out with him for the day and the look he'd shot me across the dinner table. He had his own secret to get off his chest. "I didn't see it, you know," I said. "I think she was just cleaning out the gun. I don't think she meant to."

"A woman always does what she means to do," he said. "Mrs. Pichard, even after all these years." His eyes were bloodshot. He looked into his drink. "You know she's the reason he's that way. Richard, you know. I've read up on it in books. They say it can be the fault of a strong mother."

"Do you think that's all true, Mr. Pichard?" I said. "I think you can just be born that way."

"I don't want to love him, you know that," he said. "But sometimes your heart doesn't let you choose. People think you can predict who your heart will and will not love. But they can't." He paused. "I'm not that way, you know. If he was born like that, it wasn't from me."

"I'm not that way either," I said, thinking of Janie Pinkering, her long legs under her swishing tennis skirt. I was a little woozy drunk on gin-and-tonics, but I couldn't help but be a little nervous about homosexuality too. I mean, I'd just found out that my father was, in fact, that way. I couldn't be sure about much.

"Good," he said.

"Did your father die?" I asked.

"No," he said. "She was an excellent shot. It was a warning. He was leaving her, and she shot him in the leg."

"Oh," I said, in a tone that seemed to say, *Well, that's only fair.*

"It was a mess. You see," he lowered his voice, "she was a strong woman, my mother, and I loved her. But I'm not that way."

"The books are wrong, Mr. Pichard. Dead wrong. About you and me and maybe Richard, too." I left my father out of it. Mr. Pichard was confused enough as it was.

"Yes," he said. "You're right. What do some college guys writing those fancy books know anyway? Nothing. Nothing."

And then I said, "I don't really think my mother was just cleaning out the gun."

"No," he said, "Of course you don't. Who would?"

I felt close to Mr. Pichard just then. I wanted to say something else but was suddenly heavy, a little drunkenly sentimental. I thought of him singing while floating on his back in the pool. I said, "Man, you can really sing." But as soon as I said it, I wished I hadn't. I mean, it wasn't exactly a macho thing to say.

His face cast over, stern again. "When I was your age, I wanted to be an opera singer. But it's better that I went into shoes. It's better now to think I could have done it, better than having become a failure." He drained his gin-and-tonic, mostly ice water now. "You didn't hear anything. You got me?"

Pixie

How to Marry a Dentist

I wasn't receiving visitors, but I got a call from Dilworth. He told me that he forgave me, that he wanted me to get better. He was seeing a therapist himself, at the behest of my psychiatrist, the older man who'd given me my sleeping pill prescription for years without asking a single question, not even if I was chatting with animals, if, for example, the neighbor's cats occasionally struck up a conversation. I told Dilworth that I agreed that it was a good idea for him to talk to a therapist, and that I'd been faring well, although I wasn't so sure, having cried so much in the last session. My therapist had been proud of me, though. She handed me tissue after tissue and rubbed my back gently in a small circle. I wondered if she'd learned the small circular motion in school. I couldn't imagine what they taught. Wasn't it a Ph.D. in listening? In any case, she said the crying was good for me and that there might be more to come.

Dilworth informed me that he'd told our friends and family that I was on a vacation visiting an old friend in Massachusetts who had cancer and might not see the fall. He added, "Of course, I haven't told your mother anything. She wouldn't realize it if you were on the moon."

I might have said, "Actually, she'd prefer it," but I didn't have the energy.

He said, "Mitzie is living with the Worthingtons."

"Why can't you take care of her?"

"Not with only one arm. Maybe if my good arm was the one that still worked, but it's not, Pixie." He took a deep breath. "Look, the Worthingtons are wonderful! Natural-born parents."

Except that they weren't natural parents, I wanted to remind Dilworth, and they weren't related to Mitzie at all. But I didn't feel like getting into it any more than necessary. "Is she okay? What did you tell her?" I asked.

"She knows it was an accident, that you were just cleaning the gun, you know. And I've told her about your friend with cancer," he said. "She eats with me on Tuesdays and Thursdays when Helga's cooked earlier that day. She says she thinks you're great for taking care of your friend. As usual, I've got everything squared away."

"I know Mitzie," I said. "I made Mitzie. She's lying to you, to make you feel better. She knows exactly what's going on. You should tell her the truth, Dilworth. It's not good to lie to kids. One day, she'll be with Ezra in a restaurant when they're both grown and he'll say, 'Remember when Mom went crazy and shot Dilworth.' And everything will come crashing down and she'll remember that she was really there, and what it was like when I left the house that night. See? Do you see what I mean? How could she not know? She just wants to make you happy." I wanted to go on to say that I'd failed Mitzie, that I'd been raising her in preparation for *my* life, all that *I* know, and I didn't even know my own life.

"You're not well," Dilworth said. "It's hard for you to be away from home, from us. I shouldn't have called. It only makes things worse. I can see that. But you need help and help is what I'm getting for you! Look, Pix, you're a fragile person, but we'll get you all back together. You know, Mitzie likes your friend with cancer. She prays for her."

"You realize, Dilworth, that I don't have a friend with cancer. I've never even been to Massachusetts. You know that, don't you?"

"You're still not yourself yet," Dilworth said. "You'll bounce back though, soon, I can feel it. You'll be your old self."

And I knew why he wanted the old me back, the one who couldn't do anything right, who was a mess, who took her sleeping pills and went to bed, and didn't shoot him. "Where's Ezra?" I asked. "I want to talk to Ezra."

"He's with Russell in Baltimore."

"I need to talk to him. Tell him that. Okay? Don't lie to him."

Dilworth agreed, but a halfhearted agreement that made it clear that Ezra wouldn't get the message, and then he hung up.

When I married Dilworth, I threw away Wanda Sorenski's knitting needle. I decided that I was a dentist's wife, that I had no need for it anymore. Who wants to dwell on the ugly things in life? When we were standing in the empty living room of the house he'd bought for me, a nice house in the heart of the suburbs, Dilworth told me about his mother running off and his father beating him in the back room of the furnace shop. The real estate agent was out in the yard—a perky woman in a lime green suit, tacking a SOLD emblem over the FOR SALE sign. And Dilworth said that we didn't ever need to talk about it again, because he'd survived it and, "Look," he said, sweeping his arms around the room, "look at what I have now!" You can see how I understood Dilworth and, although I didn't dwell on my past, he knew things about me, too. We understood each other in that way. Dilworth wasn't all bad, you know. He gave me the yellow kitchen, the one I'd always wanted, sparkling S.O.S. clean, a whole house of matching mahogany furniture. He gave me the daughter I wanted to complete my set, at a time when I was still trying to picture my family as the perfect family, a symmetrical family photo, mother and daughter in matching dresses, father and son wearing identical ties. Marrying Dilworth was an insurance policy for my sickly Ezra and a way to rise up into the predictable, uncomplicated, happy, pastless world of Dilworth Stocker.

I'd say that there's only one trick to marrying a dentist: be attentive to your teeth, that dentists admire well-structured, sturdy, clean, white teeth. They notice these things. These things are important to them. But that wouldn't be fair. There's more to it than that. On my part, I was tired of all of the men. The government I'd created was crumbling, its constitution had never really been written anyway, and the natives were exhausted, desperate, sickly. And the conqueror had been bit by something and had no built-up immunities and was fevered, deluded. I was the native, the conqueror, the entire wild vast landscape, see? And, in the real world, Ezra was in and out of the hospital. There was Dilworth with his shiny teeth-cleaning tools, his little spit cup and sink. To marry a dentist you have to need the dentist.

But really Dilworth couldn't help me, not the way I needed. I was alone again, married, once again, to another lonely person. Loneliness doesn't really have anything to do with the person you're with, although we were no company for each other, not really. Loneliness is personal. It happens inside of you. Self-insulation. It can be its own religion. For me, I guess it was. I was good at it, faithful, a devoted parishioner. If I saw my attempt at being a whore as governmental, as self-colonization, then my marriages turned out to be religious excursions, a religion of loneliness, and I was evangelical, my husbands converted.

Ezra

Rule #12: Trust no one.

My father didn't come home that night. He called from Philly. I could hear some sort of party going on in the background, or a bar, maybe a gay bar, I thought. I was trying to get a picture of what his life was like, anything at all.

He said he was at a banquet. "I'm caught up here. I'll be there tomorrow." But he didn't come the next day or the next, despite his calls, which always included an excuse and a promise. Richard would talk to him, too. I could hear Richard saying, "Don't pull this old trick." And I knew that my father was who he was, like my mother always said, you couldn't change somebody, and that maybe it wasn't my father's gayness my mother had been warning me about, but this. The way he was there and then not there. But I was used to it. I felt as though I could have predicted it, and, at that time, predictability was good, any predictability, and so my father's consistency, at least, was almost a relief, a strange comfort.

The days went by in a blur of dark greasy gravies and canned fruit and television. Richard and I played gin rummy and canasta. Usually once a day, he would leave the room in a huff over something his parents said, but I wasn't paying much attention. He was right; you got used to the aimlessness of the conversation and stopped trying to piece everything together. I moped about Janie Pinkering. Once, I said out loud that I was in love with her. But no one responded. Once I said that I hoped my mother wasn't going any more crazy, cooped up like that. Again, nothing. The three blank faces stared at the TV, dipped cookies in tea, and the next comment was always something else altogether about the neighbor's asthmatic dog or the detergent not really being as lemony as the announcer claimed. That's how it was.

I'd given up on trying to find a Rule to Live By, but something kept coming to me over and over, something about always being in control and never counting on someone else, especially not someone you wanted to rely on, someone you wanted to pull through for you and who, for whatever reasons, just couldn't ever pull through. The idea of it came from my father's having left me stranded at the Pichards', but every time I really thought about it, I came back to hating my mother. At least, I'd figured out that I couldn't rely on my father, but good old Pixie could give you the impression that she was there for you, and then suddenly she wasn't.

One night I went to bed early but then got up and walked toward the kitchen to get a drink of water. Richard and his parents were all in the kitchen. I heard Mrs. Pichard say, "Why did you give him your car?"

Mr. Pichard added, "I don't trust him. Where do you suppose he is? All that business of opportunities. I don't buy it."

Richard was defensive. "He'll be back. He hasn't *stolen the car*."

Mr. Pichard said, "My son has always given in to people. Weak. Remember the boys who stole his Halloween candy when he tripped over his dishwasher costume? Those boys who were supposed to have been his friends."

"I was a robot!" Richard hissed. "Not a dishwasher."

"That's right," Mrs. Pichard said. "I remember the shiny buttons."

"He'll come back," Richard said, emphatically. "He has to come back." I imagined him motioning through the wall, back toward my bedroom, mouthing, "His son? Remember?"

Mrs. Pichard said, "Yes, the boy."

Maybe they were nodding or maybe shaking their heads, sorry for me. I couldn't be sure. Would he come back? I'd heard of an Indian princess traded for a gun. Would he trade me in for a convertible? Would he consider it an upgrade? I wondered what Mitzie would say to me. I remembered how she told me everything was going to be all right, and I'd believed her. I wanted her to start talking in that screechy voice about handlebar pom-poms and shit like that. I wanted to hear about stupid things, the stupid little things that can make a kid happy.

I went back to my room and came out a few minutes later, coughing loudly. Richard was now the only one left downstairs. He was alone in the kitchen drinking coffee at the counter.

"Can I use the phone?" I asked.

"Sure, go ahead."

I dialed the number and kind of stared at him to let him know I meant privately. But he didn't pay any attention. I got the machine. It was Dilworth's voice. "We can't come to the phone right now. Please leave a message. If this is a call for Mitzie, she can be reached at the Worthingtons, temporarily." He gave their number, but he sounded weird, out of touch, like a stewardess giving crash instructions in that smiley, chipper way.

"I need to use it again," I said.

"No problem."

Mrs. Worthington answered.

"Hi, it's Ezra Stocker. Is my sister there?"

"Yes, but she's sleeping."

"I need to talk to her."

"Yes, but I'd hate to disturb her."

"She's my sister and I need to talk to her."

"Hold on," Mrs. Worthington said. "Hold on."

I wasn't feeling polite anymore. "Do you mind?" I said to Richard, my hand over the mouthpiece.

"Oh!" He picked up his coffee and swished out of the room.

"Hello? Ezra?" Mitzie sounded a little groggy.

"Mitz," I said. "What are you doing at the Worthingtons?"

"Mrs. Worthington doesn't have any kids, Ezra. She can't. Did you know that? Isn't that sad?"

"So?"

"So what?"

"So, you're going to be her kid now?"

"No, not really, but it's nice for her, you know? They take pictures of me and send them to friends."

"The Worthingtons are weirdos, Mitz. They're not right. They're too good." It was their goodness that made me suspicious of them. I don't believe that people can really be like the Worthingtons. I believe they can only pretend to be that good, but that really there's a whole lot going on, just under the surface.

"Mr. Worthington tends a garden and we get our own vegetables from it. And Mrs. Worthington had a tea party for me and my friends. She doesn't like crowds so she orders stuff from catalogues. And she only lets me watch PBS and *Waltons* reruns."

"I'm not comfortable with this," I said. I imagined Mitzie cut off and swirling away from the family, but there was no family left. I remembered how I'd wanted to be a Pinkering with unattached toes and how that didn't seem the least bit possible now even though I still hoped it was. I was jealous that the Worthingtons had her and, too, that she had them, a shot at something good.

"Where are you?"

"I'm not even really sure."

"You know what, Ezra? It can be good if you want to look at it that way. You just have to decide to see it that way."

I wanted to say, *Yeah, and our mother's in a loony bin. She shot your father.* But I wasn't sure what happy face Mitzie had put on that one and I didn't want to disturb her.

"Ezra, it's late." And then she whispered, "Mrs. Worthington looks worried. She wants me to get a good night's sleep."

"Wait, Mitz, you haven't told me anything yet about anything. How was the tea party?"

"I've got to go. I'm very important here, Ezra. It's hard to explain. It was nice talking to you."

"You too," I said and then Mitzie hung up.

I walked to my bedroom, passing Richard lying on the couch, his hands behind his head. "Are you mad at him?" he asked.

"Who?" But I knew who he meant, and I said, "Are *you* mad at him?" I guess I figured that he'd been such a staunch defender of my father in front of his parents that he'd convince me that my father was coming back, but away from his suspicious parents he had a different tone.

"You can't trust men," he said.

"I thought you couldn't trust women."

"You can't trust anybody. Even the good ones."

"And my father's one of the good ones?"

"Your father, Ezra, is one of the great ones. You can't see it, but he is. Deep down, he really can love people, really and truly."

I thought of what Richard had said about his own parents, that he knew they loved him in their hearts. I thought that would be a terrible way of having to go through life, having to imagine everyone's love for you locked away someplace just out of sight, and it wasn't the way I wanted to live my life, but also I was jealous of how easy it was for Richard to accept things this way, and I wished I could love my father in that uncomplicated, easy way, to take his love on faith.

I spent a lot of time the next few days thinking of my mother locked away and me locked away and how we were both in asylums of sorts. I wondered if she was making puppets or spilling her guts. I wondered if they'd gotten her to cry. I thought of Mr. and Mrs. Pichard as little puppets in my hands and how I could learn to talk for them, Richard, too, his puppet in a boa. I imagined my father as a puppet, just my hand with a tissue over it, my father, the ghost.

When he finally did show up one morning a little after eleven, he was wearing a Phillies baseball cap. It was new, the white still white, the red stitching still tight and bold. We were all huddled around the TV watching *Oprah,* a reunion show, a real tearjerker. When he walked in the door, everyone started to get up, Mr. Pichard to be polite, Mrs. Pichard to start fixing up dinner, and Richard to look annoyed with his hands on his hips.

"No, no," he said. "Don't get up. Ezra and I have to head back to Delaware. We'll take the train."

"Oh, pish posh," Mrs. Pichard said. "You can stay another night, surely. It's getting dark." It wasn't close to dark.

"No, I've talked to Ezra's stepfather. He just needs to get his bag. Sorry it's so abrupt."

"Oh, no," Richard said, "don't worry about me. Just leave me here again."

"If they've got to go, they've got to go," Mr. Pichard said. "I'll give them a ride to the station."

"No," Richard said. "I'll give them a ride. It's the only thing I *can* do."

"And thank you," my father said to Mr. and Mrs. Pichard.

"Really, one day I'll repay you when you least expect it. That's a promise."

"Oh, you're very welcome," Mrs. Pichard said. Mr. Pichard grunted, probably not too convinced by my father's promise.

I went and got my bag from the bedroom. It was sitting already zipped up on the white fringed bedspread as it had been for days, waiting for my father to pop in and haul me out of here. I didn't want to stay, but I didn't want to go either.

When I walked back into the living room, Richard and my father were already out the door. Mr. Pichard slapped me on the back. "What shoe size do you wear?"

"Excuse me?"

"What's your shoe size?"

"Nine and a half," I said.

"Get him some shoes from the closet, Hester," he said, and she scurried back into the kitchen where I imagined there was a pantry filled with shoe boxes. She came back with a dusty box.

"Try these on when you get home," Mr. Pichard said.

"They'll never wear out," Mrs. Pichard added.

"Thanks, for everything," I said. I held on to the shoe box. There was something enticing about the idea that the shoes would never wear out, that some things could last forever and never change, like the Pichards' whole world, nothing like mine.

They smiled and walked me to the door.

Richard beeped the horn. "We'll miss the train!" he shouted out.

My father was in the passenger's seat now, looking up into

the porch light. His face looked slack, tired. I figured things hadn't gone well, that the big ship hadn't docked.

I ran down the steps and slouched in the backseat.

Richard put the car in gear and pulled a U-turn in the middle of the street. "They gave you shoes," he said.

"Yep."

"I bet they've got buckles," my father said.

I opened up the box and there they were, navy blue with a big buckle on top. But I didn't want to give my father the satisfaction of thinking he knew them so well. "Nope," I lied. "They're lace-ups."

"Really?" Richard said, like he suspected I was lying, but he didn't push it.

"If I'm going back to Delaware," I said to my father, "where are you going?"

"On to New York."

I'd figured as much.

"Is the mother all better now?" Richard asked.

My father answered as if I'd asked the question, looking back at me over his shoulder, with his other hand holding down the brim of his baseball cap. "She's almost herself, the old tight end told me. I can't imagine what *that* could mean. I think your mother is unknowable, a beautiful mystery, always."

My father filled me in on his conversation with Dilworth. It was a given that it was "impractical," as my father put it, for me to go with him to New York and then back to California, and, he said, Dilworth didn't seem too keen on the idea either. He said the word *keen,* which, not being the type of word he'd use, led me to believe that it was a direct quote from Dilworth, which made me picture Dilworth again as that happy stewardess. Mitzie was at the Worthingtons and my grandmother was recovering.

"Ezra should stay here," Richard said. "Look at me! I'm perfectly prepared to take over the helm of motherhood."

"You're a regular captain of motherhood," my father said.

"I'm Captain Motherhood!" Richard said in a deeply cartoonish voice. He zipped around potholes and flew into the station. "All aboard!" he said. "You better run."

"Thanks, Richard," my father said, both of us hopping out of the car.

"For what? The freak show that is my parents?" he said. He turned to me. "Your father's a good man," he said. "He's a son of a bitch, but the good kind."

"Thank your parents again for the shoes," I said.

"Watch out," he warned. "If you put them on and click your heels together, you'll end up at their dinner table, in hell, forever."

On the train, my father and I found two seats together. I settled in next to the window. We each shoved our bags under our feet.

My father said, "You must want to ask me something. You know you can ask me anything."

"I don't have anything to ask," I said.

"Sure, you must have something," he said.

I was pretty sure he wanted me to inquire about his lifestyle, a heart-to-heart, a father-son heart-to-heart bonding,

the kind you read about in books, as if he were capable of that
sort of thing. But really, when you come right down to it, I
don't care that my dad's gay. I couldn't give a shit. What I
couldn't stand about him was that he was a child, he was child-
ish. He was supposedly the father, but I could have taught him
a thing or two about how you show someone that you love
them, the kind of commitment a real relationship takes, that
you can't go around being squeamish about it all, disappearing
the first chance you get. "You go to a ball game?" I asked.

He paused and then laughed, "Oh, this," he said, tightening the curved bill with his big hand. "Yeah, there was a game.
A business acquaintance had an extra ticket. Work-related."
There was a pause. "But that's not what I meant. I thought you
might have a question about me."

"If you have an answer you can tell me, but I'm not going
to ask a question."

"Okay," he said, "let me think. It goes something like this:
a history of my life," he said. "I've been scared to do what I
wanted. I've done what I've wanted. And now I try not to
want."

It almost sounded like a rule to live by, but I hated it. I
hated it for what it was on the surface: it could never include
passion or Janie Pinkering. And I hated it because it was a lie.
I was sure that my father still did whatever he wanted. "I don't
believe you," I said.

"Well, you're a smart boy," he said. "Anyway, I didn't say I
was succeeding."

There was a long pause, and I had the feeling that he was
thinking, working something through. Then he said, "You

know, you were born because of our repressed society. You're a direct result, if you know what I mean. And when I think of the things that I hate about repressed societies—hate crimes and rows and rows of identical tract housing—my mind doesn't whir for long before I think of the good you. My relationship with your mother was something of a miracle of repressed society. What I'm saying is that if I'd been raised in a pure environment to be who I am, I wouldn't have married your perfect mother and I wouldn't have had you, and you are the best thing that I could have ever created." He paused. "And so you should feel lucky. That's the way to look at it, Ezra. Good fortune. There are worse things than repressed societies to be born because of."

"Yeah," I said. "I'm just such a lucky kid." I thought of all of those speeches I'd been given my whole life, the ones on starving kids in China and what it must have been like to have been Anne Frank, and how I was supposed to be happy all the time or I was a spoiled jerk. All that crap. "What were you born out of?"

"Catholic duty and, probably, a love of the Yankees. It was baseball season. And drunkenness, too much glogg." He laughed. "See? We're getting to know each other better already."

"Yeah," I said. "Right."

I got off in Wilmington. My backpack already over my shoulder, my shoe box under my arm, I stood up in the aisle, and my father did too. He gave me a hug, a firm hug, with two strong thuds on the back, but I just stood there. He said, "You're such a good kid. But you show too much, you know?

You've got to remember that sometimes it's better to send in the lamb. You'll know what I mean. I forget sometimes how young you are."

It was easy to hate him, to think he was saying that I should learn to fake it, to make his life easier. He might as well have told me that life was bullshit, that I had to grow up and learn to bullshit and be more like him. He walked me to the steps leading to the platform as if the train was his house and he was walking me to the door. I stepped down and walked into the glass enclosure toward the escalator. When I looked back, my father was still standing there, leaning in the opening. He was warped by the glass. He looked tired, but as soon as he saw me he waved, just his hand in the air. I wished it was an old train, one with steam, one just about to set off into a fog. I wanted to lose my father in a cloud, but he was standing there, with his heart beating in his chest, blood running through his veins, his lungs pulling and pushing air. I preferred the ghost. There was a gust of wind, a hot breeze, and the Phillies baseball cap flipped off my father's head, backward, behind him, into the train and he turned around to go after it.

Pixie

How to Shoot Your Husband

I'd been at the hospital long enough. There was no need to keep me any longer, what with certain insurance concerns, and I'd passed every test. I needed no medication. I'd have to keep up regular sessions with a counselor of some sort, but I was free to go. This was what the little psychiatrist told me. It was our last session. She said, "You're well on your way to recovery."

I looked around the wood-paneled room, the diplomas hung on the wall.

She said, "Do you want to tell me?"

And I knew what she was asking for, the real story, the one she could sense always lying just beneath the surface of everything else.

I told her.

I didn't want to shoot Dilworth. I wanted to shoot the

stranger in my bed. But, you can say to yourself, *Aren't we all strangers?* And I would agree. Yes, even to ourselves. For me, there's always been a stranger in my bed, a man always coming for me, a secret so old that the man has become an ordinary shape, something as common as my husband's broad back, one shoulder dug into the mattress, the pillow pressed flat beneath his giant, squarish head. It's something every day, a noise you know but that's also out of place, like the birds that night. I remember them, twittering in the dark. And sometimes someone says something, and it's immediately true; although you fight it, some part of you knows it's the truth. And you've always known it without knowing it. It's like finding something that you didn't know you were looking for, a covered button years after you've thrown the dress away. My mother had pulled back a sheet in my mind, a bed she'd made years before, and there was Dilworth's body, the length of it, naked, down to his thick ankles and wide stumped toes. It was not Dilworth but a stranger, and then it was not a stranger at all but my father, a slick lock of hair on his forehead, wet and black. And I remembered that my father had become a stranger in my house before that night, like the men on the street who watched me, the press of their eyes on my body, and how my mother knew, said, "She's too old to sit on your lap." And to my father, "You're too old, too." She hated him and stirred the beans at the stove, the ash of her cigarette growing long. Wasn't my mother's lie almost the truth, a stranger in the house? That night was hot, too. There was no air-conditioning, just the thick breeze from the window screen and then the body on top of me, heavy and hot, wet with sweat. I'm not really there, but above, circling the ceiling of my room like that old saint who flew around church rafters, my arms flapping against the ceiling looking down on the struggling bodies. There's screaming down the hall, and muffled in my own throat. And, yes, there's a figure back-lit in the doorway, tall and thin, arms raised and the bat, too. My mother. Cliff standing behind her, his hands shaking like two alarm clocks at his sides, and then the heavy blow, the deep drum of wood and skull, my father's body limp on mine. My mouth fills with blood, the rustiness of it. It's easy to mistake one thing for another. The shot rings in my ears. The gun's recoil stings my hands. Dilworth rears from bed. The blood is real, the sheet bright with it. Ezra this time, not my mother, shouting out across the yard. Mitzie now the one in the doorway, her little white nightgown showing her red knees, not Cliff. The room is filled with white moths, blurry, so thick with wings that I can barely breathe. I would whisper to my brother now, if I could, that my father was not the enemy, that I was not a country to be saved. *Stop here*, I'd tell him, *with everyone as they are.* And I try to stop, too, looking at my kids, my husband, stumbling down the hall. We are all real, suddenly obviously ourselves in a room. The moths escape through open windows. And it's like looking through the curve of clear water in a glass jar. I slip into my body, the tight fit of being stitched into this skin.

No matter what happens, no matter what comes, you stand up. This is what my mother meant when she said once during an argument, "One day you'll understand, you'll know that I never once gave in, not even in the smallest way." My mother this time takes my arm and leads me to the tub. I can remember that, too, now. The water roaring from the faucet, the red swirl rising up from between my legs. She's talking, her words pouring over me, the sponge soapy, wrung out in her rough hands, the tub now pink with blood. She says that she's afraid to love too much, that she knows I'll be taken away from her, like this, she says, this way. See? She's always tried not to love too much. She says, "Don't disappear, Pixie. Don't disappear on me, girl." She's crying. She's scrubbing me down. She says, "There was a stranger, remember him? There was a man . . ." And she washes it all away.

Part Three

Ezra

Rule #13: Disregard all previous rules.
They're complete bullshit.

Helga was parked in the loading zone down the stairs outside the station. Because of her fear of birds, we had to drive home in 100-degree heat with the windows of her Ford Escort just barely cracked open, so no birds could accidentally fly in.

She said, "It hass only gotten worse. Your grandmother's birds are green monsters with sharp beaks."

The car's air conditioner, of course, was busted, if it had ever existed in the first place. Helga sat snug in the driver's seat, her rump squared by the seat's edges, her belly pressed against the wheel so much so that I wondered how she could make a turn. But if the seat were pushed farther back for breathing room, I supposed her short legs wouldn't be able to reach the pedals.

"So," she said, "your father's okay."

"He's gay," I said.

"Yes," she said. "It's a shame because he's a handsome man. There wass a boy like that in my hometown in Germany and all the girls were in lof with him and I wass too. Men usually lof me. I have a certain charm, but not with him."

I leaned my forehead against the window, so hot I wondered if I could die like this, of suffocation with Helga in her Ford Escort, her big mouth sucking in all the oxygen, only miles away from home and Janie. I wasn't sure if it seemed so hot and stifling because of where I was coming from—the tight confines of life with the Pichards and my father on the train, or where I was going—back to my mother and Dilworth and God-knows-what. I only knew that maybe if I got to Janie's without dying, I might be able to breathe again. I sighed. "But you can't love all these men, can you? I mean really fall in love with them?"

Helga turned to me and smiled broadly. She stopped at a red light and folded her short arms across her bosom like a sturdy German Buddha and said, "I am like Jesus. I lof them all." Helga's pink dress was stained dark under her fat arms, her face shiny with sweat. It seemed like she meant it. I felt like I knew nothing about love, whether it was real at all or just something that might or might not swim inside each of us deep down, unseen, something Richard had no problem believing in.

The light turned green and she shoved the car into gear. "Your mother," she said, "iss no longer in the hospital. She iss staying at your grandmother's apartment and has taken over the birds. Thank Got. She wants to see you, but she's been sleeping. It wass a bad place to sleep, she told me, and now she iss sleeping in your grandmother's spare bedroom. She wants you to call."

"Why isn't she at home? She should be at home, shouldn't she?" Sweat trickled down the insides of my arms.

"She isn't going back home. Dilworth does not know this. He thinks she iss beink too embarrassed to see him, but that she'll be back soon."

"And my grandmother?"

"In hospital still. But improvink!"

By now we were driving down our tree-lined street. I felt like I had been away for years. I stared into each house, wondering who knew what and what rumors were being whispered among the neighbors, over fences and telephone wires, at poolside cocktail parties at the club. Mrs. Worthington was out front, weed-whacking behind her bushes. The yard was filled with kids, playing some sort of tag, as many kids as there usually were cats. There were five cats perched in the bay window, their heads zigzagging back and forth as if they were watching mice from behind the glass, not children. Mitzie was with the kids in the yard. She was wearing shorts and her knees were dirty; her hair was pulled into short ponytails over each of her ears. She looked like a regular kid, not like the Mitzie I knew at all who'd always been so together in her matching outfits and hair-sprayed hairdos. "Mitzie is still living at the Worthingtons, I take it."

"Too bad she couldn't have her own babies. Mrs. Worthington iss such a goot mother," Helga said.

And my mother was not, that's what Helga meant. I was

covered in a thick film of sweat. I felt dizzy, and as she pulled into the driveway, I already had a grip on the door handle, popping it open as soon as she came to a stop.

"My mother can do all of that stuff," I said. "Mrs. Worthington didn't invent motherhood, you know."

Helga didn't seem to listen. She said, "Go inside. There's thinks for you to do," she said. "Your mother wants you to call her. She needs to ask a favor."

I swung my backpack over my shoulder, grabbed my shoe box, and ran up to the front door. I was nervous about calling my mother. I wanted her to be fine, because I was planning on seeing Janie Pinkering. I was thinking that Janie was probably waiting for me to stop by, that's how much I'd convinced myself. That's what I was actually trying to believe.

Dilworth was in his La-Z-Boy. He had the contraption tilted all the way back so he was lying flat. He was wearing a T-shirt with one of the arms cut off and a big bandage wrapped around the meat of his shoulder. I could make out that the bandages on his shoulder were connected to a network of bandages that strapped around his chest for extra support. The TV was on, a car race, the roar, roar, roar of each engine as they made their laps, and a newscaster's dull monotone, but Dilworth wasn't looking at the TV. He was staring out the side window that overlooked nothing but the driveway and some shrubbery, a short glass of scotch resting on his stomach, held with the hand of his good arm.

"Hey," I said, quietly.

He turned his head. "Ezra!" he said. "Come on in. How are you doing, there? Good to see you. Beautiful day. Sit down and stay awhile. What do you have to say for yourself?"

I sat down on the edge of the sofa, facing him, still holding on to my backpack, my shoe box. "Not much," I said.

"Well," Dilworth said. "Too bad. That's a shame. A pity." He wasn't making sense. He was like a thesaurus of clichés, Dilworth set on autopilot.

"How are you doing? Your shoulder?"

"Just fine. Can't complain. No golf, the doctor said. No dentistry. Good news: full disability. I'm okay. Taking it day by day."

"You mean no golf or dentistry *ever*?"

"Oh, well, hard to tell. Can't say for sure. It's uncertain. There's nerve damage. I can't really clench my fist. I have to drink with my left hand. It was my right, you know, where I took it. So, tough luck. Could be worse, right? Can't cry over spilled milk."

"No," I said. "I guess not." There was a pause and Dilworth looked back out the window. I stood up. "Well."

"Okay, then. I can see you've got things to do. Excuse me for not walking you to the door. See you later. Thanks for stopping by."

"I'm going to be staying here, I guess, you know, well, out at the pool bungalow, until school starts," I said, although I wasn't really sure about this. I didn't want to live with my grandmother and my mother in the small stinky apartment, but I wanted to be as far from Dilworth as possible too. Staying put in the bungalow seemed the best bet.

He looked at me then, glassy-eyed, tired. He scratched his head, closed his eyes, and nodded. "Of course," he said.

"Certainly." But I wasn't so sure he knew what was going on at all.

I went to the kitchen to call my mother, pulling the phone cord as far as it could go like the last time I'd used it, to call Janie in my Hispanic accent.

My mother answered on the third ring. She didn't believe in snatching the phone up too quickly. She'd always said it made you seem anxious and made the caller nervous. I took this as a good sign, and I was right. My mother's voice was calm. "Hello, Mrs. Kitchy's residence."

"It's Ezra."

"Oh, Ezra. I'm so happy to hear your voice. Are you all right?"

"I'm fine. How are you?"

"Just fine, really. There's been such a big fuss, and I'm just sitting here, absolutely fine."

"Well, everything's a little crazy on this end. I mean, things have gotten a little off. Mitzie is living with the Worthingtons. Is that okay by you? I mean, the Worthingtons! They only let her watch PBS, wholesome TV with no commercials. And Dilworth is just staring out the window. He can't play golf or fix teeth. And how come you never told me that Dad's gay? You know that, right?"

There was a long pause. My mother sighed. "It sounds fairly normal to me, Ezra. People think that life is supposed to play out just so, but it doesn't. And anyone who doesn't believe that your life, Ezra, is a normal life, as normal as anyone can expect, well then, they simply aren't following along. They simply aren't paying much attention. Because what's normal is that life is completely, unforgivingly odd. We *are* a normal family, Ezra. You should know that by now."

I didn't believe her. "I disagree," I said. "I couldn't disagree more! What kind of wife shoots her husband?"

"Oh, please, Ezra, this sort of thing happens all the time. Lots of husbands and wives want to shoot each other."

"But they don't do it."

"That's because they're not being honest. In any case, it was a mistake. I've admitted that. Don't get so excited. This sort of thing happens to everybody, Ezra."

I let out a gusted sigh.

My mother dismissed the discussion. "I want you to borrow Dilworth's car and pick up your grandmother. She's ready to be released from the hospital. You can bring her here to her apartment."

"You're not coming? I can't drive without a licensed driver."

"It's no big deal. I'm trying to clean up bird cages. Helga gave up on the birds. She paid a little kid to come in and sprinkle bird seed in the cages and that was all. It's filthy. You can go alone."

"Sorry, I can't do it."

"What do you mean?"

I didn't feel like being at her beck and call. "I've got pressing business." I was being my dad, giving her the lamb.

"What are you talking about?"

"My ship's about to come in."

"Four-thirty, Ezra Stocker. You will pick her up at four-

thirty. And stop talking like that. It's unbecoming." She hung
up.

I cut through the Pinkerings' neighbors' yard to the
Pinkerings' wooden fence, which was just high enough that
I couldn't see over it, and the horizontal support boards were
on the inside, so there was no way for me to climb up. I walked
the length of it and finally found a knothole. It was a low
knothole, and I practically had to lie down to see through it.

Janie was there with Elsie Finner. They were sitting by the
pool, not in swimsuits but in raggedy shorts and T-shirts like
the one that Kermit's girlfriend had worn to the tennis match
where she played drunk and laughed at everything. There were
three cars in the driveway—Janie's blue convertible, Elsie's
Saab, and a tan Mercedes. So, I figured that at least one of her
parents was at home. I couldn't risk going to the door.

I'd unpacked quickly, throwing dirty clothes into the
hamper to be picked up by Helga on wash day. I shoved the
shoe box under my bed, showered, and changed into fresh
clothes. I was wearing khaki shorts and an army green shirt,
sneakers. My hair was still wet, and I wished now that I looked
more ratty. Evidently, it was the new style. I'd brought my
swim trunks and that alone proves how optimistic I was, how
willing I was to do whatever it took, and how hopeful, too,
just living on hope.

I called out, "Janie," just above a whisper at first. But she
went on yakking with Elsie, giggling, sipping fruity drinks.
Finally, I yelled it, "JANIE!" And she looked up. I could see
her glancing the length of the fence, her ponytail whipping,

landing curled around her long neck. "IT'S ME! EZRA! OVER HERE!"

"Where are you?" she said.

"HERE!" I threw my swim trunks up in the air a couple of times so she could see where I was exactly, and then got down again to the knothole to watch her walk across the yard, to see if she was running, maybe, to come to see me. But it was really a stroll, her tan face still a little mystified by my voice and the appearing and disappearing swim trunks. She walked up to the spot, so close that I lost her face and then her soft breasts under a yellow tank top, and then from the bottom, her unlaced Nikes, pointy ankles, and, finally all I could see were her shins and her sweet knees, like soft fruit.

She knocked on the fence. "Ezra?"

I stood up and knocked back. "Yeah, it's me. I'd have come by earlier, you know, for that swim, but I've been out of town." She didn't say anything, and I couldn't see her face to read her expression. "I've been off with my father." I thought, *Be personal, be personal,* Janie loves personal, but I couldn't tell her that my mother shot my stepdad or that my dad was gay. I thought, *Send in the lamb.* I thought, *No, it's unbecoming.* I said, "I was out seeking opportunities with my father." She didn't say anything. I panicked, "He's gay."

"What kind of opportunities, then?" Janie asked, sarcastically. "Opportunities to be gay?"

"No, of course not. Business opportunities, really. He's a businessman."

"I thought he was a politician. You told my mom he was a politician."

"Well, that too," I said.

"Sounds like a blast, Ezra, but, you know, now's not the perfect time. Elsie's over and this thing with Manuel has started up again and fizzled and started up again, and she needs some counsel. You know what I mean. *Girl* talk." Her voice was a little hoarse, maybe from spending the summer arguing tennis calls, or maybe, I thought, she'd been to loud parties while I was gone, college parties where you have to yell over the music, parties with Kermit in his college scene.

I put my head up against the fence, so close I could smell the chemically weather-treated wood, so close my lips almost brushed it. I wondered what Janie smelled like, if she was wearing one of the fruity soaps and lotions from her mother's bathroom basket. "I could help out. Remember you thought my mom was a genius about women's things, and, well, I've memorized a lot of the things she's told me."

"I've got to go."

"Okay," I said. "Okay. I see." And then things were clear to me again. Nothing had changed. I hadn't misunderstood our phone conversation, the tone of her voice. Her mother hadn't been standing nearby, mouthing "Is that Ezra Stocker? Hang up. Hang up this instant." It was over. She didn't love me, had never loved me. I thought that it was possible now even more than before that she thought I was gay, like my father, and out looking for "gay opportunities," whatever they might be.

I bent back down to look through the knothole, but didn't have the stomach to watch her walk away. So I just sat there for a while, my back to the fence. Finally, I decided that Janie Pinkering was no good, that women, in general, weren't worth the trouble they caused. It was almost four o'clock, and I knew that I'd show up at my grandmother's apartment in Dilworth's car just as my mother had asked. I just knew I would, and it made me mad as hell that I couldn't do anything about it. Just then I remembered my grandmother's dead bird in the Nescafé jar. I imagined it now shrunken, puckered, its eyes even poppier, a few feathers having fallen off and now drifting around in the jar. I was pissed. I knew I had to go get it.

I walked to the front yard. There was an old woman hunched down almost hidden under a bush. My replacement. It was then that I noticed that the yard was impeccable, perfectly tidy again, trimmed, the green rows from a wide riding mower striping the lawn, a light green, a darker green, smooth as velvet. I walked down the side yard so the old woman wouldn't see me, and then up the sidewalk. I ignored her, and kicked my shoe around in the patch of pachysandra near the tree where I'd left the jar.

The old woman looked up, squinting under her visor. She was pinch-faced, wearing gardening gloves and slacks. "You looking for something?" she said.

I stared at her and she stared at me. I knew that she'd already found the jar and the dead bird. I could tell by her pruny, pursed face. "No," I said. "Just admiring your healthy leaves."

Just then Dr. and Mrs. Pinkering walked across their porch to the car parked in the driveway. They glanced at me and at each other. Mrs. Pinkering's high heels picked across the gravel driveway like stupid big-beaked birds. I stood my ground, just watched them.

Dr. Pinkering pulled out of the driveway slowly and stopped next to where I was standing, one foot on the sidewalk, one in his pachysandra. "Go home, Ezra," he said. "It's over."

Mrs. Pinkering leaned forward. "Yes, Ezra, it's quite finished. Just go home."

I stood there, not moving.

"I'll call the cops," Dr. Pinkering said. "You hear me?"

I felt sick, flushed, like I might start to cry. I took my foot out of the pachysandra, and he let up on the brakes and rolled out into the street.

I turned to the old lady. "What did you do with it?" I asked. She stood up, a chubby woman. "What did you do with it, huh?"

"I don't know what you're talking about. I've got to go inside to get something." She picked up her spade and hurried nervously across the lawn up to the front door.

I walked home, to the pool bungalow first, pulled the old man's shoe box out from under the bed. I opened the lid and could smell the old leather, a little dry, cracked. I changed out of my shorts to a pair of long pants and then slipped on the shoes, bent over and worked the buckles. I rose up and down on my toes, still thinking that women were just a lot of trouble, that I shouldn't have gone over to Janie Pinkering's house, that Mr. Pichard was right: I should have wondered my whole life, and then I wouldn't have failed and I'd have had this nice little dream tucked away forever, a pillow where I could always rest my head. The shoes were a little tight, my webbed toes shoved together in the tip, but I wore them anyway.

I walked across the yard to the back door of the house,

opening and then slamming it behind me. I heard Dilworth shift in his La-Z-Boy. "That you?" he called out. "Pixie?"

"No," I said. "It's me. I need to borrow your car." I walked into the den.

The chair was upright. Dilworth was sitting up, both feet on the floor. "Oh, I thought it was your mother." He sank back a little into the recliner. He was wearing shorts and the leather squeaked against the backs of his thighs. His shirt had a golden stain still wet from his having just jostled the drink in his hands. "You need the car, you say?"

"Yes."

"Okeydokey," he said. "Fine and dandy, but I might need it back soon. I might need to pick up your mother. She'll be calling for me to pick her up. That's how we left it. Okay? All right? So not too long."

"She's not coming back," I said. "Can't you see that? I mean, she shot you, and she's not coming back. Anybody could tell that much."

Dilworth looked at the TV, a ball game now, a close-up on the pitcher's face, a clockwork of twitches. Dilworth looked back at me over his bad shoulder. "Now, that's just not true, Ezra," he said, his stiff arm bent at the elbow, pressed to his chest in a permanent pledge of allegiance. "It isn't factual. You don't know all the facts here."

He was stupid and pathetic. I felt sorry for him, but feeling sorry for him made me feel powerful all of a sudden. "I know she isn't coming back," I said. "Talk to anyone. It's obvious. You're the only one who can't see it. She never loved you." I almost knew at the time that I was yelling at myself too, because I knew that Janie didn't love me after all, but I only almost knew it, not really.

He didn't move. He didn't say anything. There was just the announcer's muffled voice-over, the knock of a pop-up. He suddenly looked like a little boy, a potbellied kid.

"Aren't you going to come at me? Aren't you coming at me with all that British schoolboy crap?" But he didn't move. "Come on and tell me you think I'm a faggot. Like my dad. She loved him, you know." I couldn't back down. I thought of all the people I should be saving, my mother most of all. Dilworth was the problem.

"You think you know me?" he said. "You think you know everything about me?" He let his scotch glass drop to the floor where it rolled in a circle before it stopped, a semicircular stain from its mouth. His eyes filled up, gleamed. "You don't know a thing." He stood up, started to stagger away from me, but I followed him. "She needs me," he said. "She'd fall apart with-out me."

"I wouldn't be so sure."

He turned around, big then, suddenly right in front of me. A huge-chested man, so close I could see a vein ticking on his temple, another purple vein running up the middle of his fore-head. He slapped me with the back of his left hand, which he kept lifted for a moment, like he might come at me again, his beefy hand stiff and shaking.

My cheek stung at first, and then it was a hot burn. "You want to kill me, Dilworth?" I said. "You want to try to kill me, you one-armed fuck?"

But he didn't say anything. The anger drained from his

face. He looked into my eyes like he might kiss me, he was looking at me that deep. He said, "It isn't good to have a gun in the house. It's too dangerous. I hid it in the punch bowl on top of the china closet. Guns are horrible things." He put his good hand, his left, up to his heart. He said, "She kills me. She's done me in, son." His eyes teared, spilled over onto his cheeks. And he turned then and went back to his chair, his TV. He shoved the chair back to recline, the footrest popping up.

I walked into the kitchen to the key ring and pulled his set off its hook, my body shaking. I said, "I'm not your son." I almost felt as sorry for Dilworth as I felt for myself, but I decided that I was nothing like him. I was nothing like any of them, Mr. Pichard or Mr. Worthington or even my real dad. I slammed out the back door, got in Dilworth's car, revved it, and tore out of the driveway, leaving a trail of rising gravel dust for Dilworth to watch settle from his seat by the window.

I knocked lightly on the door to my grandmother's room, and I could hear her shuffling to stand before she said, "Come in," so that when I opened the door she was upright, barely touching the walker in front of her, a show of her toughness; she's that type of old person. Her hair was tied back tightly. She had on no makeup, and she looked tall again, too tall for her walker.

"Well, Ezra, I've survived it. My brain clicking again. Still too much clicking, an overload, but here I am. A walking short circuit."

"You look healthy," I said, antsy to get out of there.

She leaned forward, whispered, "It's an awful thing, Ezra,

to have to swim in your head, the backed-up blood of your swollen heart." She shook her head. "I sound crazy, but it's only now that I'm making any sense."

I didn't want to understand her. I wanted just to do my job, deliver the old lady home to her crazy daughter. I just wanted for the summer to be over, to seal up my eyes and ears until I got back to school, its stone buildings, perfect playing fields, its sun-swathed classrooms. But I did understand her, the way Miss Abernathy always wants us to understand things: deeply. I knew what she was saying about her swollen heart, about sounding crazy, too, when you were finally making sense.

An orderly wheeled her down to the elevator through the revolving door and helped her into the passenger's side of Dilworth's car. We drove home in near silence, my grandmother still leaking words, *milk,* maybe, *stain,* and *open it, open it,* like she wanted someone to unlock a door. My mother must have been watching for us from the square window in the building's front door. It swung open as soon as we pulled up, and there she was, so much the same that I was shocked by her. She was wearing a sleeveless linen suit, different from the one she wore the last time I saw her. This one was cream-colored. I stepped out of the car. "You look the same," I said.

"What did you expect? A monster?"

I opened my grandmother's door. "No, not at all," I said, but I had expected some change, something to be different. Maybe I'd expected frazzled hair, slippers, and sweat pants, but instead she seemed more herself, an expanded version, more real, like for years she'd been stuck in the film of herself on the reel-to-reel so newly colorized that none of the pinks are quite pink, and only now for the first time was she in real-life color. I'd been thinking of her as ill, but maybe I had it backward, maybe she'd been ill before but was finally all better.

She touched my arm. "I've been sleeping, Ezra, finally after all of these years. Real sleep." She stepped back, looking me up and down. "You seem taller," she said, "but you can't be. It's only been a little while. I must have an image of you as younger, but you're not so young anymore."

"No," I said, "I'm not." I felt old. I thought maybe when I was my grandma's age, I'd feel young because I'd already been old. I'd been Mr. Pichard's drinking buddy, for god's sake.

"You could stay here with us, you know."

"I don't think so," I said. "It's a small place, and I've got all my stuff in the pool bungalow. It's easier to just stay out there."

My grandmother stepped out of the car, one sturdy shoe at a time. I pulled the walker out of the backseat on the other side and set it down in front of her, lifting her up to it under her arm.

"I've got it from here, Ezra," my mother said. "I can take care of her." My grandmother started to walk toward the door with the slow clink and tap of her walker. My mother was at her side and they tilted toward each other, their need like a magnet now between them, as they walked up the cracked and buckling sidewalk.

Pixie

When my mother had just come home from the hospital, she'd stopped talking in that incessant stream of words, for the most part, but sometimes I could still hear her say *coal, consumption*—the two ways her parents had died—and sometimes when a light came on, she'd whisper *Cliff,* in a questioning voice, as if someone had just walked into the room and she'd been expecting it to be her son. There was still a certain strangeness to the way she talked. I could follow along, but she was always saying something just a little off, the way poets never really say what they mean, but seem, sometimes, to be saying things the most clearly you've ever heard them.

That first evening home, she asked me to help her take a bath. I knelt on the fuzzy yellow bath mat in her bathroom to help her, and she said, "I'm a child again, Pixie. They say that happens when you get old. It all comes around, doesn't it?

You're the mother, now." She was sitting in the tub, her knees bent, poking up above the water's edge. I handed her the soap, and she turned it in her thick-knuckled hands.

"I guess so," I said.

"I don't mind going to the coal-crusted honey of my childhood, dipping back into that pot. I loved then the way a child does and I can love again like that now." I assumed she meant that she loved me that way, finally, after all these years. "I could go all the way back, couldn't I? Back to the beginning, a fish, an egg glistening in a sac, the only memory us half fish have of heaven. Remember that we are half fish? I've told you that."

"Yes," I said. "It's one of your famous speeches. That and how Mary should have said no to Gabriel, that she should have refused to have the son of God."

"I was right," she said. "Wasn't I? Mary should have stuck up for us women."

"We've done okay in that department, sticking up for ourselves." We need each other and that need is like water being poured from one cup to another, the two never really becoming even, one always tipping to the next to fill it and then that one pouring some back.

"Yes," she said. "We're allies, aren't we? With our shared secrets?"

I nodded and squeezed a sponge at the base of her neck. She curled forward, letting the water pour down the knots of her bare back. I've come to the conclusion that my mother saved me twice: once when she gave me a lie and once when she gave me the truth. It was what I was thinking at the time, and she must have known it.

She said, "You'd have done it too. You'd have done it."

And I knew that she was talking not only about the bat that she drove down on my father's head and the lie about the man, but also about handing over the whole story to me, finally, the truth. "I guess so," I said. "Yes. I guess I would have."

"You would have." And she looked up at me, her eyes filled with tears, spilling onto her cheeks, one still stiff with its slight sag.

I said, "You know it wasn't your fault. None of it. You know that, don't you? It's almost vain to think that you made the bad things happen just because you were happy once. Can't you see it's a crazy way to go around thinking?"

She sniffed, tightening her chin, wiping her nose with the back of her hand.

"Do you forgive him?" I asked, but I didn't give her a chance to answer. "I forgive him," I said. It was true at that moment that I could forgive my father. But even as I said it, I knew that it wasn't something that I would be able to hold on to, that I would spend the rest of my life forgiving him and then not and then forgiving him again, that for the rest of my life my heart would expand and contract. I only hope that maybe, one day, when I least expect it, my heart will open and stay open and forgiveness will be the only thing left: my father just a kid, the tattooed Hula dancer fresh on his arm, his two free fists raised above his head, my father, shaking water from his hair.

"Look at us," she said. "We're crazy, aren't we? You and me. We'd have to be for having come this far."

"Yes," I said. "We're quite a pair. Crazy, yes, absolutely."

Ezra

When I got home, Mitzie was sitting on the front step. I didn't pull the car all the way in back, just up to the walkway. It was after seven. I remembered it was Tuesday, one of her nights to have dinner with Dilworth. It wasn't dark yet, but the sun was beginning to be pulled from the air, like the dark coming on was a hollowness, the wind kicking up at the tops of the trees. She was sitting there, her back straight, her head to one side.

I said, "Mitz, what are you doing?"

"Ezra? I didn't know you'd come. I didn't know who would come, but I'm happy it's you."

"Come for what?"

"He's dead."

"Who?"

"He's lying in blood. There's a gun on the floor, but I

didn't touch the gun. I didn't touch anything, but I must have stepped in the blood. It's on my shoe." She showed me her shoe, the rubber tip of a white sneaker smeared red, and there was a little footprint trail across the bricks. "He looks like a baby, Ezra. He looks like a little baby, his eyes wide open, like a picture of a baby, frozen like that. His mouth is open, too, like he died singing his favorite song."

I walked past her into the house. Dilworth was slumped on the floor, just as Mitzie had described him, his eyes and mouth open, the pool of blood, the gun. His body was slightly turned on his side, his legs apart, knees bent, like he'd been running, about to jump, and I thought of him skipping along, singing, like Mitzie had put it, but lying down. He'd shot himself, I assumed, in his heart that he'd touched earlier with his good left hand. His shirt was blood-soaked, the floor wet with what seemed like a bucket of blood that had flowed from the curl of his body to the window. The blood was still inching out wider and wider.

I went to the phone, dialed 911. I was calm. My hands were steady, but I could feel something tightening in my chest. I said, "My stepdad shot himself," and my voice sounded like someone else's voice. I called up the Worthingtons. I told Mrs. Worthington to come over and take Mitzie home. I said, "Take her home," because already the Worthingtons' house was her home.

I went back to Dilworth. I sat on the dry floor at his back. His hair still had the fine-tooth-comb lines running through it, but puffed like a bird's feathers when it puffs up for winter. I touched his hair. I pressed it back with my hand, smoothing it. I patted his arm, lightly, his back, like he was just sick, coughing a little. My hand was red with blood. The yard, the house, the walls were stained with red and blue swirling lights. "I didn't kill you," I said, because that was the thing tightening in my chest. I thought of my mother, how she knew that men were fragile. I imagined us walking around, our bones made of glass, my own bones made of glass. I thought about all of the men I knew, my father, Richard, Mr. Pichard, the minister at school, the headmaster. I thought about Mr. Worthington and Dr. Pinkering. I thought about my grandfather who died underwater. I thought of Cliff, his body being blown up in a field. I loved them. I started crying because I loved them all so much. I loved Dilworth. I said it out loud, "I love you." I wiped my bloody hand on my shirt and I said it again and again.

Mrs. Worthington tapped at the screen door. I walked up to the door, and she stepped back. She must have seen the blood on my shirt. The blood on my hand had already started to get sticky, like the juice of a plum. The yard was swimming red and blue. It was raining, a soft solid rain. I stepped out in it.

Mrs. Worthington followed me off the stoop. She had a yellow umbrella, and I wondered how she'd been so prepared. It was as if she'd known that Dilworth was going to shoot himself, and that when he did, it would be raining, and she'd carry a cheery umbrella, something bright and happy, a yellow one. And I imagined how she'd opened it on her front step— not in the house, that would be dangerous—but on the front stoop, how each pleated flap suddenly filled with a snap until the umbrella was tight and rounded. I thought of my heart, how I thought it was just one shape and now it seemed to have opened up like the yellow umbrella, for the first time filling my too-tight chest.

"Mitzie's with us," Mrs. Worthington said. I walked down the steps, and she reached out to steady me, but I ignored her hand. I looked up at the sky, the moon clouded over. I walked out into the middle of the yard, a police car and an ambulance already out front, sirens, far off, still coming. I tried not to think of Dilworth's heart, the bullet that I thought he'd buried deep inside of it. I wanted to know who I was. I wanted to know if I was a murderer. I opened my arms, let the rain wash down on me, let it wet the blood on my hand till my fingers were slick, passing over each other like small fish.

I answered the policemen's questions. I watched Dilworth come out on a stretcher, the blood seeping through the white in small round, widening dots, like red mold, spores growing furiously in the dark. But the sheet wasn't covering his face, and they were working on him, a bunch of white shirts hovering over him, moving quickly. I asked one of the cops what they were doing. "Isn't he dead?"

"No," he said. "If it was his heart he was aiming for, he missed. And by the looks of his other shoulder, he's not the best shot." And so Dilworth failed to kill himself and I was relieved, not completely, but a little. I wondered how I'd thought it possible that he could kill himself, that Dilworth was capable of something so bold and tragic as death. I still felt guilty, but I was relieved that it wasn't as easy as I thought to die, that maybe men weren't as fragile, at least not as physically fragile, as my mother had told me. Stupid, yes, but maybe not always on the verge of breaking. I imagined Dilworth standing on a chair to get the gun out of the punch bowl on top of the china closet where he'd hidden it from my mother. I imagined him thinking almost poetically, as poetically as Dilworth is capable, about his heart, that it was the route of the problem, and how then maybe he tried to use his right hand to cross his chest and take aim. But it was a stupid plan, wasn't it? What with the nerve damage? How could he get it right, and, if he didn't, if he was just enough off, couldn't he blame that on his wife, on his bum arm? And so the gun didn't quite shoot straight. The bullet snagged his other shoulder, and he just fell down and lay there, letting all his red-blooded American blood spill across the floor.

I don't remember everything. One of the cops gave me a pullover, one of my own from the hall closet. Another offered to give me a lift somewhere. "You got some family?" he asked.

He took me to my grandmother's. I remember the cruiser's wide seat, the dull banter over the CB radio. The cop walked me to the door, but I said I was fine from there. The hallway smelled the same, dank and heavy, something frying, piss. I didn't knock at the apartment door. I turned the knob and it opened. It was dark, except I could see my grandmother awake, struggling now to stand up by her chrome walker. Birds flapped around her, birds fluttered across the room, small bodies darting through the light. She was calm. She'd been dozing.

"Ezra?" she said. "What is it? Something wrong?"

I walked back to my mother's bedroom, the one lit from

the crack under the door. I twisted the knob like pulling fruit from a tree, and my grandmother followed. Her mouth was no longer pouring words, but I could still feel the words, the ones that we all had inside of us, each word with its glow, its blueness, rooted and heavy, so many that the room felt like it was swelling with things unsaid, like bread rising and pouring over the sides of its tin.

My mother was in bed, her middle covered by white sheets, her legs bare, her whole body striped in light thrown from the streetlight through the blinds. I sat down on the side of the bed, let it sag beneath my weight. I curled my body next to hers, gently. I didn't want to stir her nightmares, to scare her, but I had to whisper that I didn't kill him, that Dilworth tried to kill himself, but that it had nothing to do with me. She didn't wake up. She pulled me to her chest. She whispered my name, sleepily, like she'd been waiting up for me. I felt something like lovesickness, like hunger, heavy lidded, my whole body stone-heavy. My grandmother stood in the door for a while, light from behind her fanning through her hair. She grew quiet, and then I heard the popping of the rubber stoppers of her walker down the hall. My ear cupped to my mother's chest, I listened to the *shush, shush* of blood, the purr of her breath. She smelled sweet, powdery. She hummed a song I'd heard before, a light song, but I couldn't place the words. She stroked my hair. She rocked me on the bed. I could feel the sway of her breasts against my chest. And then my cheeks grew hot. I was embarrassed. I felt a hard swell. I reared away from her.

"What's wrong, Ezra?"

I must have looked startled. "I don't know," I said. She

leaned toward me, confused. "I don't have many choices," I said.

"What do you mean?"

I was thinking about when I'd stepped out in the yard after I thought maybe I was responsible for Dilworth's death—what turned out to be his botched suicide—that I was a murderer. But now I wondered if I was a faggot, after all, just like my real father, because it suddenly seemed clear that I could only be one of the two, that those were the only two options open for me, for any boy my age, for that matter, Rudy and Pete and all the boys at school, Kermit Willis and Manuel, too. I didn't answer her.

"You're not like other people, Ezra. You're like me. We're a certain kind of person."

"I don't want to be a certain kind of person," I said.

"Do you want to be like them?"

"Like who?"

"Everyone else."

"No, but I couldn't if I wanted to. That's what you're telling me, right?"

She nodded.

"But do I have to be like you?"

"What's so wrong with that?"

"I'd just rather not, if there's another option."

"That's the point, Ezra. That's the kind of person we are, the kind who doesn't get stuck, who can turn things around and go on. We adapt. We can evolve. The answer is yes."

"Yes what?"

"Yes, there's another option, but I don't know what it is. You'll have to invent it."

"I can't save you," I said. "I can't save you. You know that."
And I stood up quickly, my erection gone. "I can't save you."

I was walking to the door. My mother sat up in bed.
"Where are you going?"

"Away," I said, and I walked out of the room and ran to the
door, down the stairs, through the stinking hall, and out into
the night.

My mother had opened her bedroom window screen, and
now she was leaning out of it. She said, "Ezra, Ezra!" And I
looked up at her face lit by the streetlight, her arms long and
straight, her body tilted forward. It had stopped raining. She
said, "Come here." And I walked to the spot under her window
and looked up at her, buttered in light. "Why," she said, "why
would you need to save me?"

"I don't know," I said.

"Don't worry about me, Ezra. We can help each other, but
we can only truly save ourselves, you and me. Isn't that right?"

"I guess so," I said.

"I thought so," she said. "I've always had an escape route,
Ezra, a half-hatched idea of how to get out. I've always needed
one. But it's tiresome. Isn't it better to make a stand? They
need me, Ezra, don't they? Mitzie and my mother and
Dilworth, too, in his way."

And I thought, *You don't know the half of how much he needs
you,* but she would find out soon enough. I couldn't stomach
telling her, not just then. I wanted to get out.

She said, "But you don't need me anymore, not like that,
do you? You're a man now."

"No, I don't need you like that," I said.

"No, you don't," she said. And with that, she gave a little wave. She blew me a kiss. She looked at me sadly, and, for a second, I thought she might jump. I thought she might lift her legs one by one over the sill and jump, her nightgown billowing out like a parachute around her thin legs like Janie's tennis skirt, and I imagined that I would catch her at last. And then I realized that she wanted to save me, that the reason we were so awful together was that we were each always waiting for the other to fall. But, of course, my mother didn't jump. She dipped back into the darkness of her room.

As you know, I didn't go back to school at the end of the summer, to Rudy and Pete and Miss Abernathy, who'd gotten married and changed her name to something plodding and dull like Mrs. Chore or Mrs. Cough, something like Mrs. Clod. I lived in the pool bungalow, staying away from the house and Dilworth as much as possible until school started up, the public one nearby, which isn't as bad as some people would have you think it is. My mother moved back into our house and my grandmother joined us, too. It was unceremonious, just a quiet shuffling one day, the unzip of her suitcase, jingle of clothes hangers, and rustle of birds in cages. As for Dilworth, he's still with us. He doesn't go upstairs. He sleeps in his leather La-Z-Boy recliner, both of his folded arms all bandaged up, hands crossing his chest like he's lying in a casket. But he isn't dead. Far from it. Dilworth sometimes talks about his experience, the tunnel with the light at the end and the voice of someone, maybe God himself, saying, "Go back. It's not your time yet," as if Dilworth's failure at dying had more to do with

God's overall plan than it had to do with Dilworth's inability to
get the job done. He can't do much and so Helga's here more
than ever. She gets him dressed, for example, one foot at a time,
zips up his fly for him. Sometimes he wears his golf pants, the
yellow ones with the turtles. She feeds him her homemade beet
borscht and helps him drink his scotches through a straw.
Sometimes my mother will sit on the sofa next to Dilworth's
recliner, where he likes to listen to talk shows about real people
with real problems. She'll say, "What a shame, huh?" about
some runaway, some cheater, some paternity case.

And he'll say, "Yep, some folks get themselves into a
mess." And there's only a hint of irony in his voice, only the
tiniest recognition.

Once, I asked my mother what was going to happen next.
It was pretty much out of the blue—her hands in rubber
gloves, wrist-deep in a sudsy sink—but it was so out of the
blue that she knew exactly what I meant.

She said, "I can imagine myself packing my things up.
Sometimes when I'm downstairs doing the laundry, I can smell
the cardboard boxes in the basement, the ones stacked in the corner, one inside the other. After a heavy rain, I check to see if
they've gotten wet, if they're still intact. I won't be needed forever." She turned to me, soapy gloved hand on one hip. "It's
funny to me, though, how we all trade places," she said. "My
mother is now my daughter, right? And Dilworth is the needy
one, stripped of his assets like an aging beauty queen," she said.
"I'm finally the mother and the dentist too, I guess. I should take
up golf." And then she went back to her dishes. "I'm taken with
the idea of the future, though, aren't you? It's a new concept for

me." I didn't know what she meant exactly, but I was in love with the future myself, and I could see us both leaning into it.

Mitzie lives across the street at the Worthingtons during the week and with my mother on weekends, as if my mother and the Worthingtons are divorced, and I guess my mother did divorce something like the Worthingtons anyway, something like normalcy, something like the smell of the Pichards' house, mothballs and soup. I haven't seen the Pichards since I left Baltimore, probably won't ever see them again, and I haven't seen my father since his baseball cap flipped off his head on the train. And Janie, no, not her either, except, of course, when I'm fantasizing.

Sometimes there's a happy ending, one that you didn't expect and maybe don't quite believe, but that you can try to hold on to. Imagine us like this, the last weekend of summer, Labor Day. We're huddled around an overturned dirt patch near my mother's rhododendron, the spot where I'd buried Mr. Pichard's boxed-up buckle shoes earlier in the day, and have since told everyone that it is the dead body of my grandmother's bird Cheep-Cheep in the Nescafé jar. I don't know why I chose the buckle shoes to bury except that maybe I've given up on something too, the idea that some things never change, never wear out, the idea that you can have a simple set of rules to live by, and they'll see you through. My mother and grandmother are sitting in lawn chairs in the front yard, Mitzie, cross-legged on the ground in front of the grave, wearing a swimsuit although she hasn't been swimming. Dilworth is inside, watching from his spot by the window. I say a prayer about eternity and all of us being united in heaven. I say it the way I remember

Miss Nebraska does, solemnly, in her Miss Congeniality speech on the reel-to-reel, *And God bless you all.* I'm standing behind my mother and grandmother, almost the man of the house now—even though it's bullshit, it feels right—my hands on the backs of their lawn chairs like I'm steering the two wheels of a ship. And soon we're watching Mitzie dance, an interpretive dance for the long-lost soul of Cheep-Cheep, with sparklers left over from the Fourth of July that none of us remember because it was back before any of this shit happened when we were all kind of blind. She twirls them over her head and spins with her arms wide open around and around until she looks like a carnival ride. We clap for her and this makes her supremely happy because she's making us happy. She's just a kid, the sweetest, so sweet that I could cry, but I don't. Things will change for her, for all of us, because from now on things will always be different. We're all aware of what's around us, like the steam off the street now that dusk is settling in, like the crickets screaming in the thick grass and the lightning bugs rising up, their fragile chests glowing, on and then off and then on again. We clap and clap, and if someone—a neighbor walking a dog, say—passes our house, or Mrs. Worthington pauses in front of her screen door, waiting for Mitzie to be her little girl again, we smile and wave, all four of us together, in unison, our cupped hands swiveling like royalty, Dilworth included, not waving, of course, but nodding from his spot by the window; and it's as if we're in motion, traveling into some future, like we're careening along on a parade float, the perfect American family.

The Miss America Family

Julianna Baggott

A Readers Club Guide

About This Guide

The suggested questions are intended to help your reading group find new and interesting angles and topics for discussion for Julianna Baggott's *The Miss America Family*. We hope that these ideas will enrich your conversation and increase your enjoyment of the book.

Many fine books from Washington Square Press feature Readers Club Guides. For a complete list, or to read the Guides online, visit http://www.BookClubReader.com.

Reading Group Questions and Topics for Discussion

1. In one of the few conversations Ezra has with his father, we hear Russell comment, "I think your mother is unknowable, a beautiful mystery, always." In what ways do you find this to be true about Pixie? Do you think that anyone, even Ezra, truly knows her? Do you think Pixie knows herself? How does this observation from Russell inform our reading of many of the relationships in this story? To what extent do you think the various characters are trying desperately to know themselves, each other, and their families? Are their attempts successful?

2. Julianna Baggott shows the power that sexuality has to change, alter, and shape human relationships. Although all the characters struggle in some capacity with their views of sex and intimacy, Ezra especially is a true-to-life sketch of a boy coming into his own without much guidance from family or role models. Not only is Ezra introduced to his own budding feelings of desire through his interaction with Janie Pickering, but his father's homosexuality is tossed in his lap unexpectedly and without ceremony. What did you think of Ezra's reaction to his father's sexual orientation? Why do you think he questions his own sexuality to the degree that he does?

3. Discuss the ways that Pixie views her beauty as a weapon of sorts, something that gives her power over men and, in her mind, levels the playing field between the sexes. What do you make of the fact that she sees men as "soft"?

4. The concept of motherhood is a complex one in this novel, and, in the case of Ezra and Pixie, it is often difficult to decipher who is acting as the mother and who as the child. To what degree do you think Ezra's development has been affected by his need or desire to act as a mothering influence for Pixie? In what ways do you think his intelligence and his acute ability to grasp the emotional complexity of certain situations is due to this dynamic between him and his mother? Is it because he has, in essence, acted as a mother that he seems so adult in his thinking?

5. At one point Pixie states, "Only a good mother knows how to kill; the baby's born and suddenly there are talons, claws, teeth you never knew were there." But what else, besides protection, does Pixie seem to value about motherhood? Did you find this quote hypocritical, as Pixie often seems to cause Ezra pain rather than protect him from it? Do you think Pixie would consider herself a good mother?

6. Pixie's mother washes away the truth about who attacked her in the same way that Dilworth tells Mitzie that Pixie shot him by accident. How do parents facilitate lies, half-truths, and misconceptions in this novel?

7. How do the "rules" that open the chapters inform your read of the novel itself? As an exercise to better understand what they may represent, write out the chapter titles separately from the chapters on a sheet of paper, separated by character. Do you see these rules as a kind of distillation of the themes that each chapter focuses on? How do Ezra's rules differ in nature from Pixie's chapter titles? How are they similar?

8. Look at the way Ezra interacts with the different men he encounters in the story. The dynamic he shares with them seems so strained, yet there are moments when he connects with them in ways that he can't with women—think of the scene between him and Dilworth after the Janie Pickering incident and after Dilworth's attempted-suicide scene. In what ways do men seem to occupy spaces in this novel that women can never enter? How does the dynamic between males seem to be different than the dynamic between women?

9. We get the sense that Pixie cannot and will not ever let a man, with the exception of Ezra perhaps, into her emotional world. For her, they are utilitarian: people who can provide her with status, goods, and material well-being. Are there instances in this novel where women and men seem to be truly connecting on a deeper level? Does this seem impossible due to the societal restraints placed on male-female relationships?

10. Early on in the novel, Pixie says, "Life, as far as I could tell, was as much about faking things as it was anything else." In what ways does this quote ring true as this story plays out? Do the characters ever free themselves from the roles that they are expected to play?

11. Russell is a somewhat elusive but fascinating character. Do you think that Ezra reaches some kind of peace regarding his father by the end of the novel?

12. Do you think this novel ends on a positive note? What do you envision for the characters ten years down the road? Where do you see Ezra?

A Conversation with Julianna Baggott

Q. You do an amazing job delving into Ezra's thoughts, fears, desires, and emotions in this novel. He grapples with sex, growing up, sexuality, and parental insanity with surprising wit and intelligence. Was it a challenge for you to write from the point of view of a young man? Did you toy with any points of view other than Ezra's and Pixie's?

A. It's a relief to write from a male perspective. I've found it particularly hard, in our society, to write a funny woman—it was one of the greatest challenges of writing *Girl Talk*. A floundering man is perceived as funny, but those same readers would say that a floundering woman is irresponsible; she's putting herself at risk, and that isn't funny. Also, I've found that writing from a male perspective isn't as politically charged as writing from a female perspective. The decisions of a woman somehow take on the weight of a feminist argument, but the decisions of a man in a novel seem to be taken more easily as the decisions of one man, an individual. So Ezra allowed me to write with a lot of humor. That being said, I wanted to explore the pressures on a boy coming of age in our culture, the rigid guidelines of manliness that boys in our society are forced to follow. I pushed Ezra to a point where he felt there were only two options: murderer or faggot. Ezra allowed a balance for

Pixie, who, despite her claims to the contrary, is the most deeply feminist character I've ever written.

Originally, the novel was to have five points of view, but Ezra and Pixie made it clear, early on, that the story really resided with them and was theirs to tell.

Q. The struggle between different age groups (like the Pichards versus Richard in this novel) is central to much of your work. Talk about the tensions that you see between younger and older generations in America. Do you think it is possible for families to find peace in light of generational differences?

A. I think that multigenerational living is one of the greatest advantages I've had in my life. It's the primary reason that I live in Delaware, where my children are being raised by three older generations. It's one of the ways that we know who we are, where we come from, and the great strides that need to be made into the future. I worry about the trend toward long-distance family relationships, all of the history that is being lost. Locally, I've set up memoir-writing workshops for older adults. And my conviction about the importance of preserving oral history has certainly fueled the writing of my third novel, *The Madam,* which is based on family stories.

I love Mr. and Mrs. Pichard, the failed attempt at denying their love of Richard, and how he knows the truth of their love. I was raised in a family where it was a struggle, but ultimately accepted and encouraged, to be openly gay. I adore Richard for not pretending, for being who he is, and for his acceptance of his parents' sad limitations.

Q. Ideas of female beauty, strength, and power dominate this novel, often in contradictory forms. Pixie, someone who may not appear particularly strong from the outside, shows herself to be a commanding presence and an unstoppable force by the end of the story. Even though Pixie does not consider herself a feminist, do you consider her to be one? How do you feel about beauty pageants?

A. Pixie is an ultra-feminist but, like many American women, has felt excluded by the term. Why . . . because she's a housewife, because she's an ex–beauty queen who still puts a lot of effort into her appearance, because she'll feign weakness to get what she wants for herself and her family. Pixie dislikes feminists because she feels misunderstood by them, and yet Pixie is a militant feminist, really, one who believes all women should be armed.

Before I started interviewing beauty-pageant contestants, I wasn't sure what to expect. I was aware of the obvious stereotypes, but instead, again and again, I found these women to be smart, witty, savvy, and ultimately powerful.

Q. What inspired you to write *The Miss America Family?*

A. In doing the research for *Girl Talk,* I came across the first Miss America protests. The clash intrigued me. I also had three short stories, "Ogden Stocker's Back Yard," "Finding

Janie Pinkerton," and "Issie Pitkoff's Moon Women." I found that I wanted to further investigate those characters and situations.

Q. How does your work as a poet influence your fiction writing?

A. I hope the poet in me demands more from each sentence. But I also use my poems in my novels. "The Annunciation: Our Mothers in Church," which is in my collection of poems, *This Country of Mothers,* was hugely influential on the religious themes in *The Miss America Family.*

Q. Was writing this novel different from writing your first novel, *Girl Talk?* What unique challenges did *The Miss America Family* present to you?

A. The alternating points of view was a wonderful challenge. It allowed me to have Pixie and Ezra bounce their narrations off each other. I enjoyed the layer of conflict that their individual slants added to the novel as a whole. I think it also created this rent-apart-and-pieced-together tension that I hadn't planned.

Q. How do you think the publishing industry hurts or helps the work of many young writers today? Is there a difference between writing as a published author and working solely as an artist?

A. As an unpublished novelist, there is the pressure of creating a novel that is undeniable. It has to be so moving and so letter-perfect that an editor won't be able to say no. As a published novelist, there is the pressure that people will actually read this, that it will be in every bookstore, that it will be reviewed in national publications, that people will walk up to you to discuss it, and that finally, therefore, it has to be undeniable. In the end, there's little difference.

Q. Tell us a little bit about your next novel, *The Madam.*

A. *The Madam* is based on the life of my grandmother, who was raised in a house of prostitution in the '20s and '30s in Raleigh, North Carolina. Her mother was the madam of the house. For a number of reasons, I decided to change the location to a town based on Morgantown, West Virginia, where they would survive under the constant rain of ash. This novel is an enormous departure for me. *The Madam* is achingly personal, historical, sweeping, nearly epic in tone. Writing it was wrenching and possibly one of the greatest pleasures of my life.